Secret of the Ossuary

By Steve Parton

© 2014 Steve Parton, Strange Land Books
All rights reserved. No part of this book may be used or reproduced in any manner whatsoever without written permission by the author.

Cover artwork by Mike Trebilcock

"Fogarty's Cove", written by Stan Rogers, SOCAN ©1976 - Used by permission

Please visit:
www.partonbooks.com

Acknowledgments:

For assistance in editing, researching, reading and support, I am extremely grateful to:

Skip Press, Andie Parton, Lynn Johnston, David Tysdale, Isabel Casey, Reverend Rick Spies, Helen Bartley, Rob Bell, Enid Aaron, Greg Stoddart, André van Heerden, Ray Reed, Ariel Rogers, Julia Kollek and Rabbi Bernard Baskin.

~ For Isabel ~

Author's Notes

This book is a work of fiction, based on events as described in the Bible, and as discussed by historians. It is possible this story will propagate some spirited debate, as there are few topics more fascinating than the science of religion. To this I say, bring it on!

Scholars are still debating the language(s) thought to have been spoken by Jesus Christ. Most agree that he spoke Hebrew and some Aramaic, though there is apparently an argument that he spoke Greek as well. In any case, the different languages used in this book are italicized in English.

Jesus of Nazareth had 70 (or 72) disciples. Among these, twelve of the disciples were (later) referred to as his Apostles. Though all of his disciples were followers and students, the twelve men chosen to be his Apostles were specifically charged with the task of spreading Jesus' gospel.

There are a number of images that correspond with the text herein, photos of some of the historical places described in this novel. The photos appear in an appendix at the end of the printed version of this book. For the eBook, you may click on links to the photos as they appear in the body of the text.

Steve Parton
Dundas, Ontario, Canada
February, 2014

MAP OF JUDEA

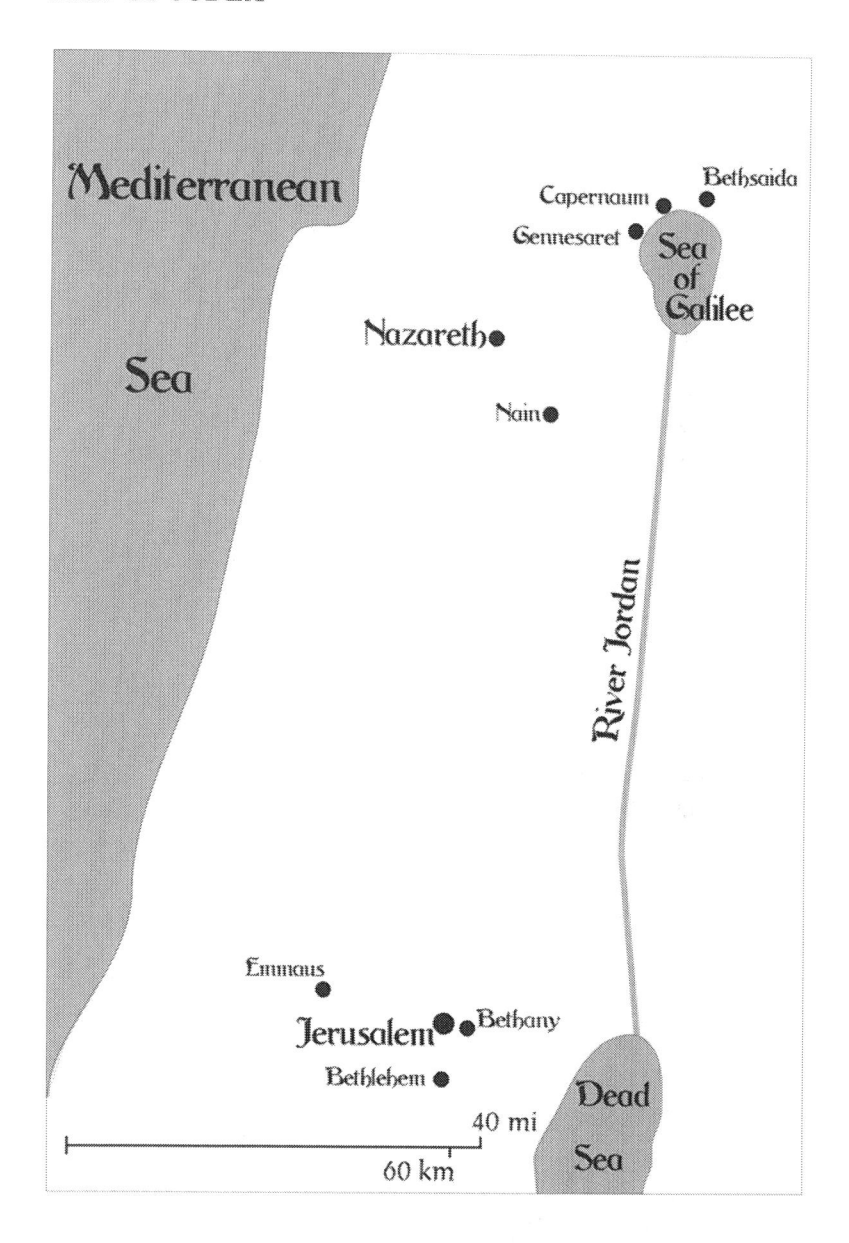

PROLOGUE

November 2, 2015

The cellar was a dark, damp room with a dirt floor, almost cave-like. Two strong men wielded shovels and pickaxes, working dutifully at removing a stone wall, the farthest wall from the rickety steps that led down from the sunlit store above. A wheelbarrow sat nearby, waiting to be filled with stones and debris. A portable light fixture dangled from a ceiling joist, its lone bulb providing the men with all the illumination required for their task. A radio on the ground was blasting out music, despite the dirt caked onto its speaker grill, emitting Arabic melodies sung by a young woman whose very voice made the men less grumpy about their labour. In a surprisingly short amount of time, they were able to break enough of a hole in the wall to confirm their earlier suspicions, that there was indeed another room beyond the one in which they currently stood.

With renewed vigour, and spurred on by the woman's voice on the radio, the two men bashed away at the hole they had made until they had created a crude doorway. One of the men unhooked the portable light and took it with them into the new room. They were excited, but this was solely due to the idea of having more storage space. Their excitement had nothing at all to do with the fact that this was Old Jerusalem, a part of the world that continued to unearth relics, objects that could fatten a man's purse, objects that could contradict long-held beliefs in events that had transpired millennia ago.

The men swung the light back and forth, trying to establish the size of their new room. What they saw before them was a large mound of dirt, something they knew to mean a large amount of work ahead of them.

After the seventh load of dirt was hauled out, one of the men's shovels clanged against an object, the significance of which would bring about the end of their workday—it was a find that would indeed fatten their purses, a find that would in fact contradict long-held beliefs in events that had transpired millennia ago.

PART I

— 1 —

Danny Casey and Ben Strohlberg stood under the expansive glass ceiling of Pearson Airport's Terminal 3. Even at nineteen, they shouldn't have been as impressed with the building as they found themselves to be. Still, they found joy in almost everything their eyes took in that day. Even the short drive from Hamilton was a delight, but only because Toronto wasn't experiencing its normal bout of highway mania.

They found the Air Canada counter and checked their luggage. The boys were close friends, and had been since childhood. Ben had longish curly brown hair and intelligent brown eyes. He wasn't as tall as he thought he needed to be to command respect from his peers, but he more than made up for it in academia. Danny had brown hair, long enough to get tangled, and blue eyes—the kind of eyes that, along with his infectious grin, made more girls return his glance than most young men could claim.

After receiving their boarding passes, they took their carry-on bags, plain brown canvas backpacks, to relax in the waiting lounge of Gate 21. Like the main terminal itself, the lounges were flanked with large glass walls, which welcomed more than enough sunlight to please and assuage its occupants.

A large flat-screen television mounted on a wall was broadcasting the CBC Evening News. Danny looked around the room to see that the other travellers were mostly families and older professionals. "Where are all the girls?" he asked his friend.

Ben rolled his eyes. "We're flying to Jerusalem, not Las Vegas."

"Still, a couple of smokin' researchers like ourselves shouldn't have any trouble. My thesis alone is a guaranteed chick magnet."

"Tracing the footsteps of Jesus Christ?" Ben countered. "Not exactly dance club material."

"Just leave the charm up to me," said Danny. "You make sure your translation is up to snuff."

Ben snorted. "Could you stop referring to yourself, and to me, as researchers? Doing a year of religious studies in Jerusalem does not make us researchers."

Danny laughed. "Nobody outside of Hamilton needs to know that. We're coming from McMaster University, and that automatically makes us smart. I think."

Ben had nothing more to contribute to that useless argument. He looked up at the TV, on which Sienna Wallace, the CBC newscaster, was speaking. Beside her was a picture of an ossuary, an ancient, grey clay box about the size of a small ice cooler.

Ben nudged Danny and nodded to the screen. "Check that out." The boys rose to their feet and walked over to the TV. Ben reached up, felt along the side for the controls, and turned up the volume until Wallace's voice could be heard throughout the lounge: "...has been confirmed to be authentic. It was discovered underneath a shop in Jerusalem. The bones inside date back to the 1st Century A.D. The ossuary also held a small, mysterious container. It's this container that is causing excitement among the archaeologists who are studying the find, though they will not tell the media exactly what it is they have found. In other news, the Toronto Stock Exchange is up— "

Ben turned the TV volume back down, and he and Danny walked back towards their seats. "What could be in that ossuary that they won't show the media?"

~ ~ ~ ~

Shauna Campbell marched purposefully through the doors leading into Pearson Airport's Terminal 3: International Departures. In her thirties, she was an important and respected woman, usually comfortable being the smartest person in the room. Her hair cut, attire and footwear were all business, letting one know what to expect from her even before she started speaking.

She checked her luggage at an Air Canada counter and glanced at the boarding pass the clerk had handed to her.

"This is nonstop?" She didn't make eye contact, not out of rudeness, more due to being distracted by the agenda of the days ahead of her.

"That's right," replied the clerk, clearly used to the preoccupied look. "After you get off in London, the plane continues to Jerusalem."

Shauna reminded herself to glance upward at the pleasant clerk's face and flash an acknowledgement, if not an actual smile, before darting off, attaché case in tow, towards the gate printed on her boarding pass.

Arriving in the waiting area of Gate 21, Shauna sat down across from where two young men were sitting. She quickly surveyed the room, not because she had to be suspicious of anyone, but because it was her job to notice the minutiae of what was going on around her. All the faces she saw were of people dutifully going about their own business—except for that of one of the young men sitting across from her. The blue-eyed one smiled at her, causing her to lock eyes with him longer than she would have liked. She quickly remembered who and what she was, then turned down to her attaché case, inside of which her iPad was waiting to entertain her for a while. She considered changing seats, but she knew the flight would be boarding soon. She did, however, spare a moment to take in the face of the curly-haired fellow sitting next to the would-be charmer.

To the three of them, Danny, Ben and Shauna, exchanging glances was an unremarkable action. Shauna, for her part, registered the boys' faces in her mind, something she was always able to do, even if she didn't think she would ever have the need to recall them.

~ ~ ~ ~

Danny looked out the airplane window at the blackness of the skies over the Atlantic. He saw that Ben was still awake. "So what's Professor Reed like, anyway?" he said.

"Haven't seen her in years, since my family left Nazareth. All I know now is that she has a room for us; she lives near the Via Dolorosa, and she likes Canadians, particularly smart ones."

Danny offered the tiniest of smiles. "You never told me we had to be *smart*."

"That's fine." Ben closed his eyes and turned over on his side in an attempt to sleep. "I'll cover for you."

— 2 —

Professor Agnes Reed was only a few years past her retirement. She was intelligent and spry, and didn't look or act a day over sixty. She maintained a silver ponytail, something that had always irritated some of her female peers at the Hebrew University of Jerusalem, but it still made her feel just a little like Chantilly Lace.

She had relocated from Montreal to Jerusalem in the late 1970's, and decided then never to leave. She spent most of her time alone, and usually liked it that way.

With Benjamin and his friend about to arrive, Agnes tried to remember the circumstances that had brought her together with the Strohlberg family in the first place. After a token effort, she gave up trying to figure out how their first meeting had occurred. What was vivid in her mind was the way the parents, Tim and Kelly, with their shy son, took a shine to her over the years. Sunday afternoon tea-time with the Strohlbergs became a ritual, as they had always seemed happy to drive down from their out-of-the-way home in Nazareth, just to spend time with her. Agnes had watched Benjamin grow up, watched him learn to play the flute, something that pleased his parents. She was sad when Tim and Kelly eventually moved back to Canada, and more than a little upset that she had not been able to fly out for the boy's Bar Mitzvah.

Driving back from the airport with two excited young men in her car, Agnes was actually happy to be having guests in her home for a change. She pulled into her driveway and led the way into her house, a small, cottage-like bungalow. Her bright entranceway barely provided enough space for her to remove her shoes and hat, so with two big clumsy boys in her way, she just waited for them to bounce past her into her living room. They didn't remove their shoes. She frowned, but decided to let that one go for the time being.

Agnes pointed past the reasonably-cluttered one-person kitchen. "The room at the end of the hall has two beds; take your pick."

It took them only a few moments to settle in. They were, after all, boys. After dumping their bags on the floor beside their respective beds, Danny and Ben both marched back through the kitchen, hoping to be fed. Jetlag and fatigue were apparently lost on these two, Agnes noticed. At least she had remembered to fill up on "student food." She opened up her cupboards and started to prepare pasta with pesto. The boys knew enough to step out of a lady's way, so they stationed themselves on the easy chairs in her petite but cozy living room. The small size of the house made it easy to chat with each other, even from room to room.

"Ben, how's your mother?" she called out.

"She's fine, said to send you hugs."

"She's a good woman. Always treated me well. I miss her." Agnes smiled. "And what about your dad?"

"Same and same."

The water in the pot was quick to boil. "Have you kept up your Hebrew?"

Ben rolled his eyes. "Yeah, I've been teaching it every Sunday. I'll be fine communicating around here, if that's what you're driving at."

"Good. When you're settled, I want to go over your itinerary with you."

Danny and Ben, oblivious of local time, and not caring what time of day their body clocks thought it was, were happy to devour the meal they had just been given.

~ ~ ~ ~

Agnes, Danny and Ben gathered around the living room table in Professor Reed's house. The table was littered with maps, books and notes. It was evening, and their mid-day naps had gone a long way towards getting their body clocks adjusted.

"It depends where you start," Agnes was explaining. "You don't have to do Bethlehem first."

"I thought we would stay in Jerusalem," said Danny. "Start with the Via Dolorosa, maybe take the tour, get the perspective of—"

"Don't waste your time with tour guides. You already know what you're looking for; you just have to know some of the rules."

Danny shifted in his seat. "Like what?"

Agnes was happy to get into teaching mode again. "Obviously you want to get yourself to the Lions' Gate. Al-Omariya is still used as a school, so you can't just wander in any time you like."

"That's where Jesus was condemned by Pontius Pilate," Ben put in. "It's the first Station of the Cross."

Danny frowned. "I'm pretty sure I already knew that, but thanks."

Agnes ignored them. "I don't think the archaeologists are out of the area yet."

"What are they doing there?" asked Danny.

"You'll be walking right through the area where they found the ossuary. Did it not make the news in Canada?"

"It did." Danny tightened his lips as he thought about the CBC news broadcast. "There's some strange little container inside the box."

"So they say." Agnes looked doubtful.

With nothing to add, Ben pulled his phone out of his pocket, then dug in his backpack for the charger. "Professor, can I charge my Galaxy?"

Agnes arched an eyebrow. "Come again?"

"My cell phone."

"Sure. There's a plug beside the lamp."

Ben turned to Danny. "Where's yours? I'll charge it for you."

"No need. I brought a trickle-charger; one of those solar-powered things."

Agnes shook her head and smiled at her guests. "You're making me feel old, boys. You just point your phone at the sun to charge it up?"

Danny pulled a small black device out of his own backpack and showed it to Professor Reed. "More or less. It takes about three hours."

Ben plugged his phone into a power converter, then into the wall.

Danny's fatigue was starting to set in. Professor Reed, on the other hand, had not been subjected to a trans-Atlantic flight covering a number of time zones. "So Danny," she began. "Do you consider yourself a scientist or a man of religion?"

Danny would have preferred questions with easy answers, inquiries after his food preferences, for example. But he tried to be polite to his hostess. "Well, I don't believe those two are mutually exclusive."

Agnes leaned forward from her end of the couch. "Continue."

"Well, uh." Danny was starting to become intimidated. Although his thirst for knowledge generally allowed him to be comfortable around the intelligentsia of McMaster University, he felt squeamish at that moment, sitting in an easy chair in the living room of the professor he had just met.

"I was happily indoctrinated at an early age. Our church was very kid-friendly. I even taught Sunday School with my sister for a while, until I realized that I don't really like kids—they kept asking stupid questions."

Ben stepped back into the living room and sat down in the easy chair. Agnes smiled at Danny. "That is a clever side-step to my question," she said.

"Oh. Well, I don't really..."

"Dan," Ben put in. "This is nothing we haven't talked about a bunch of times already. What did—"

"Look, I was always discouraged from asking the questions I had wanted to ask. My mother would have none of that talk around the house. She was on every committee in the church; she even started The Committee to Examine Whether We Have Too Many Frickin' Committees."

Ben stifled a chuckle. "Was that what they called it?"

Danny lost his momentum. "Maybe they didn't use the word, 'frickin' in their title." He looked back up at Professor Reed. "Tomorrow. Or maybe at the end of next semester, I'll give you my detailed answer."

Agnes gave Danny the smile that she had used on her own students, the smile that had made everyone in the lecture hall hang on her every word. "You already did. Let me know if that changes."

~ ~ ~ ~

Lying in their beds, Ben thought about what it must have been like to have a brother to share a bedroom with. Danny, on the other hand, was quite used to having someone in the same bedroom to annoy. That evening, though, their late-night chatter was all about their coming adventure.

Danny started it off. "So how do we know for certain that the Via Dolorosa was where Jesus walked with his Cross?"

Ben turned over in his bed. "I don't know, it's just generally accepted as fact."

Danny snickered. "Spoken like a genuine researcher, always in search of the truth."

"I walked it once or twice as a kid, but it never had the same connotation for me as it does for Christians. I never really thought about it."

"But they can't even agree on where the crucifixion took place."

Ben frowned. "That's the same issue that historians have with the gospels, because they were written decades, or centuries after the events supposedly took place."

"Ah, and that brings things back to us, the intrepid explorers."

"Dan, do you really think we're going to unearth new information here?"

"Not necessarily. But it will be good to experience things in the actual places where the events occurred." He thought about it. "Or, where we think they probably occurred."

— 3 —

Ben felt like a short-order cook, but he was happy, as they were closer to being able to get out the door. He called out from the kitchen to Agnes, sitting in the living room with her coffee and the morning paper. "Professor Reed, do you have any more sandwich-size Tupperware containers?"

Agnes thought about it. "No, just the one. Take a sandwich bag if you need more. Bottom drawer."

Ben used the plastic container for Danny's sandwich, not worrying about the possibility of his own sandwich getting crushed inside a baggie. It's time to live dangerously, he thought. In the next room, Danny was going over their checklist of supplies, adding things to their ever-growing backpacks. "Man, what do we need all this stuff for?" he said.

"Don't you remember Boy Scouts?" Ben called out to him. "Being prepared, and all that?"

Danny grimaced. "You know we'll be back here for supper, right?"

Ben emerged from the kitchen. "Stop whining, Princess; I'll carry the heavy stuff." He handed his friend his sandwich, along with an apple. Danny held up the two backpacks, deciding that they were both made of molten lead.

Agnes looked up at the plain canvas bags. "Those are pretty boring. I thought you'd have Star Wars knapsacks or something."

Ben smiled at her. "Hmph. Having pictures on our bags stopped being important around the time that having a Scooby-Doo lunch box went out of style."

"Besides, our bags aren't completely without style—note the Canadian flags we sewed on them back home."

Ben turned on Danny. "Wait—WHO sewed those on our bags?"

"Sorry. Ben here did a spectacular job of sewing a Canadian flag on each of our bags. Now, nothing bad can possibly happen to us. You'da man."

"That's right."

Agnes grabbed her car keys and the boys followed her outside. In the driveway, she glanced down at their feet. "You're going to spend the day walking in those?"

Ben looked at the sandals on his feet. He and Danny had spent a small fortune on their footwear. "Professor," he said. "One of these days, you will learn about the genius of Birkenstocks."

Agnes smiled. "Don't forget who you're talking to, sweetie. My generation *invented* Birkenstocks."

~ ~ ~ ~

Professor Reed's car pulled away from the curb, and Danny and Ben were left standing not far from the entrance to the first of many street markets that seemed to be located all over the place. It was fascinating to them, the juxtaposition of the slick, modern shopping malls, built within sight of Old Jerusalem, with its traditional style of markets and vendors. After a few steps, they found themselves in the narrow corridor, engulfed in the colours and aromas of the merchants' wares. Authentic silk scarves, potted vases, beads and jewellery were displayed from floor to ceiling, alongside cheap luggage and imitation designer handbags.

<<Photo01>>

As they walked, Danny offered his first quip of the day. "So why are we going shopping?"

Ben looked at his friend. "We're just getting a feel for the area. We're pretty close to the first Station of the Cross, anyway."

"Well, at least we'll get our souvenir shopping out of the way. My brother's always wanted a, a—what the hell is this, anyway?" Danny had stopped in front of a stall and picked up a garment that looked like something you would either wear to a rave or else use to change your motor oil.

"Put that back. Am I going to have to start looking after you already?"

"Sorry, mom."

The two continued on.

Danny had to admit he was intrigued by all the new sights, but he was feeling a bit anxious to get to the Lions' Gate and start their planned walk. As they passed a stall selling smart-phone paraphernalia, Danny noticed an odd-looking medallion necklace displayed beside a rack of iPod cases. The medallion was Egyptian in style, fashioned from wood-coloured plastic. It had hieroglyphics inscribed on the face of it. Right in the middle of the disk was a small black circle that, upon closer inspection, was revealed to be a miniature camera lens.

Danny examined the medallion closely, seeing that it had a slot in the bottom that appeared to be made for a memory card. He caught the merchant's attention and gestured towards the necklace, communicating with a shrug of his shoulders. The goateed merchant was far less aggressive than the salesmen in the other stalls they had passed. He simply showed Danny the small box that came with the necklace, which stated that the device had a hidden camera and microphone built in.

Danny was thrilled. "This. Is. Awesome." He turned to Ben. "It's a POV camera."

Ben didn't care. He thought the necklace was ugly, and he felt that any person with a modicum of good taste would readily agree with him. "Hmm." He turned away, but Danny would not be ignored.

"POV: a Point-Of-View camera. Check it out." Danny found that there was a whole stack of the boxed necklaces. He took a still-wrapped one from the pile, and paid the merchant for it. They examined a few more trinkets, then moved on.

In the distance, they could see the huge yellow-domed shrine that made Jerusalem recognizable in any photo in which it appears. Danny was fascinated. "Man, that thing's huge!" he said.

Ben looked up and followed Danny's eyes. "The Dome of the Rock?"

"Yeah. How old is that thing?"

Ben thought about it. "I think it was built around 600 or 700 A.D. Don't you remember Dr. Louis' lecture? He called it the most contested piece of real estate on Earth. Christians, Jews and Muslims all have some sort of claim to it."

<<Photo02>>

The boys continued walking until, at last, they arrived at the Lions' Gate, the entrance to the Via Dolorosa. The impressive, castle-like wall received its name from the large jungle cats carved into the façade, above the passageway. Danny pointed up at it. "Are those really lions?"

"They're leopards, actually," Ben replied. "My dad once told me that someone a long time ago thought they were lions, and the name stuck."

From where they stood in front of the entrance, they could not see very far on either side, but they were aware that the ancient wall before them, with its turrets and its slit openings, stretched around the Old Quarter for more than four kilometres.

<<Photo03>>

The two boys passed under the archway and walked the short distance to the school, Al-Omaria, taking a route that passed through dozens of market stalls. The building was the site of the former Antonia Fortress, but was best known as the first of fourteen Stations of the Cross. At first glance, only the basketball court painted onto the pavement outside the building gave it any indication of being a school. It otherwise resembled the former fortress, with its uninviting walls and darkened windows.

Danny and Ben were planning to walk the fourteen stations, photographing, marking and studying each one. Even though this pilgrimage had been heavily documented already, the details of which had appeared on their exams back at McMaster, the boys felt it would be good to experience the walk for themselves. They were going to try to imagine what it would have been like to be present amid the mayhem at the time when Jesus, flanked by his followers and his foes, walked from the site of his conviction to the site of the Crucifixion. Standing in front of Al-Omaria, Danny looked up at the small circular plate mounted on the faded brick wall, on which the Roman numeral "I" had been engraved. He felt that he needed no tour guide, even though he had never been here before. "This was the location of Jesus' trial," he told Ben as he pointed to the Church of the Condemnation.

They took off their backpacks. Danny removed a notepad and a pen; Ben took out a video camera he had brought from home, a small, silver consumer-grade Sony camcorder made for home movies and tourists. He shot some rather unremarkable footage, and Danny scrawled notes. There was not too much to write about; he mostly dictated how he felt while looking around.

At every turn, he was introduced to new sensations. The air he took in was quite different from that of his home on the other side of the planet. Danny was also struck by the lack of any comfortably discerning language around him. He could understand a surprising amount of Hebrew, but only if he focused on one person at a time. And that was hard to do, when everyone within earshot talked over top of one another.

Right across the street from where Danny and Ben stood was the Franciscan Monastery, the second Station of the Cross, its towering walls stretching along the alley. On the building's exterior wall, another circular plate, this one marked with a "II", was mounted beside a plaque explaining that this was where Jesus was flogged and given his thorny crown.

"This was also where they gave him his Cross to carry," said Danny, looking up from his notepad. They walked on.

The third Station of the Cross was a Polish church at the intersection of the Via Dolorosa and El Wad Street. A tablet carved into the wall above the church's door depicted Jesus, falling under the weight of the cross he had been carrying. Danny pointed it out to Ben. "The first fall," he said.

After some photographs, after the notes and scribbles, Danny and Ben looked down El Wad Street, one direction, then the other.

"I think this is where the route turns off," said Danny, turning right.

"No, I think it's one more street up, said Ben. "Remember that I've been here before."

"Right, but you were a kid at the time." Danny pointed to a vendor down the street selling hats, T-shirts and robes. "Let's ask that guy."

Ben didn't move. "He probably gets bugged about this all day long."

Danny nodded. "And so he'll know where to send us. Besides, maybe I'll buy a T-shirt from him for his troubles." They jogged over to the vendor, further off their path, but still within site of the third Station of the Cross. As they reached the man and his display, Danny feigned interest in the cheap clothing and wares for sale, while Ben dug through his backpack for his street map. The vendor was just finishing a transaction with a group of three muscular blond men in their late twenties. It sounded to Ben that they were speaking Dutch. They had each bought robes from a display rack, and were taking photos of themselves. They handed a camera to Ben and motioned for him to take their picture. One of the fellows had a cigarette dangling from his lower lip, the middle one had his robe open to reveal a T-shirt bearing the logo for the band AC/DC, and the last fellow held his hands up in a heavy-metal symbol, the first and fourth fingers pointed up like devil's horns. Ben grinned and took a few snapshots for them, remarking to himself how ridiculous the three of them looked.

He returned their camera and turned back to Danny, who had indeed made a purchase. Ben opened up his mouth to chastise his friend's impulse buying, but instead turned to the vendor, asking him to orientate them. After a brief exchange, Ben looked around for Danny, who had already started wandering away. Ben caught up to him, and they started walking back the way they had come.

"I was right," Ben said. "It's one more street up before the route turns off." It was only then that he noticed what Danny was holding under his arm. "What's that?" he asked, though he knew the answer.

Danny held up two robes, not unlike the garments that the three Dutch tourists had been wearing. "They're awesome, right?" he exclaimed.

Ben frowned as they walked. "I'm not going to wear that," he stated.

"Oh, come on. We're in Old Jerusalem."

"You can go ahead and look like a fool if you want to."

Danny pushed one of the robes at Ben. "Just for a photo," he said. "I already paid for the things." He took the robe from Ben, unfolded it, and draped it around his shoulders. Ben looked down at himself and shook his head at the "authentic robes from ancient Jerusalem". Danny pulled out his Galaxy, put his arm around Ben, and photographed a selfie of the two of them. He turned the device around and looked at the picture. "Perfect," he said. At the bottom of the image was an icon inviting him to post the photo to his Facebook page. Danny tapped it without hesitation, typing the following explanatory text: "Me and the Nerd in Old Jerusalem."

— 4 —

Ten minutes later, it was Danny's turn to frown at Ben. "Remember the part where you said you had been here before?" he said. "How's that working out for us so far?"

They stopped walking, and Ben looked up and down the Via Dolorosa. "This can't be right," he muttered as he consulted his map. There were enough tourists around them that they knew they couldn't be that far off their route. But they were unable to find the fourth Station of the Cross, an understandable conundrum, considering that the old sandy-yellow brick buildings were all starting to look alike, as were the street vendors' wares in front of them.

After a few more steps, the boys came upon another small storefront that displayed T-shirts bearing images of Sponge Bob, Hard Rock Cafe, Coca-Cola, and so on.

<<Photo04>>

There was no vendor out front, so they ventured inside. The small room in which they found themselves was so cluttered with garments that Danny and Ben could not decide if it was a display room or a storage area.

"Maybe the owner got lost in the pile of clothes," suggested Danny, gesturing to the mountains of colour on either side of them. "We should try to find his next of kin."

Ben shouted out in Hebrew, "*Hello!*" His sense of smell and hearing brought him further into the store, as there was an aroma of baked goods and Arabic techno music both emanating from a doorway, an egress that the boys had not seen initially. He followed the sound and the smell through the door to a back room, windowless and poorly lit. With a small shrug of his shoulders, Danny stepped in behind him. Looking around the room, the boys saw the source of the music: a small television, sitting on a counter against the wall amidst baking utensils and mixing bowls. Other than some shelves, the room, with its pale green walls, was fairly sparse. Danny shouted "*Hello!*" in Hebrew.

Standing in the middle of the small room, Ben noticed how the floor boards creaked, as if their body weight was straining the wood. "I think this floor is weak," he said, looking down.

Danny shook his head. "Nah, it's fine—look." He jumped up in the air to demonstrate. When he landed, the floor crashed in on itself, and he and Ben went hurtling downward.

Before they could even consider what was happening, they crash-landed into a chamber below. The new room in which they now found themselves was dark, damp and barren—and was located about eight feet below the ground floor above. The boys were still winded from their fall as they lay on the dirt, moaning. Their landing had stirred many years' worth of dust up into the dry air. When they stopped groaning, they cocked their heads and listened. All they could hear was the faint sounds of the television in the room above them.

They took a few moments to gather themselves and recover from their shock. Ben spoke first. "Way to go, moron."

Danny rubbed his shoulder. "The floor looked strong from up there." He glanced apologetically at Ben. "Are you hurt?"

"Besides my butt? No."

When they looked up, pieces of broken floorboard could be seen hanging from the ceiling, but they could see nothing that would allow them to haul themselves back out. The small amount of light that came down from the room above did not afford the boys an opportunity to look at their surroundings, as their eyes had not yet adjusted to the darkness. They could not see the walls, and so they could not even gauge the size of the room they were in.

Ben got to his feet, held out his hand and helped Danny up. Both boys instinctively pulled out their smart phones and turned on the flashlight app. The devices produced only enough light to show them that they were alone, and that there was nothing they could use to climb out of that room. The walls seemed to be made of dirt; the floor was layered with dirt as well.

"Time to play acrobat," Danny said. "Can you get on my shoulders?"

But Ben was feeling his way along the walls. "Hold on," he said. He continued examining the room, making his way along each wall. Almost immediately, he encountered what appeared to be an opening. He stepped back and shone his light at the area. "Look at this."

Danny walked over and stood beside Ben. Sure enough, they found themselves before a crude opening leading into darkness. Abandoning the idea of climbing onto each other's shoulders back into the room above, they stepped purposefully into the passageway.

To Ben's relief, the tunnel in which they found themselves was more than just a crawlspace, and they discovered that they were able to walk erect. After about ten steps forward, the space started to widen a little. Ben shone his light up ahead, but the feeble beam was not strong enough to illuminate the path. He turned his light around and made the same discovery behind him. They continued on.

The sound of their footsteps in the narrow passageway was the only thing breaking the silence, until another sound made its way to their ears. Danny stopped walking, and held up his hand for Ben to do the same. They both cocked their heads and tried to identify the new sound.

"Water," said Ben, after a moment. Danny closed his eyes—not that it made any difference in the lightless tunnel. And indeed, the distinct sound of falling water could be heard coming from an indeterminate distance ahead of them.

The two young men marched forward, holding their lights ahead of them. After less than a minute, the sheen of a wall blocking their passage could be seen up ahead. Although it shimmered like a glossy curtain of silver, it was clearly the source of the sound. The wall of cascading water blocked their passage. Both boys turned around to consider the idea of returning from whence they came. Once again, they were met only with a penetrating darkness.

Turning back to their new quandary, Danny reached into the waterfall to feel the wall behind it. To his shock, he was met with no resistance. His arm passed through the water to his shoulder, and he almost fell in.

"Let's figure out what options we have," Ben started, as Danny pulled himself back.

"Good idea. You first." Danny pushed his friend into the waterfall. Ben yelled as he tumbled through. He gasped for breath, coughing as he fought a fear of drowning by the mysterious water into which he just been pushed.

Then Danny jumped after him. He found himself standing beside his friend in a curious grotto. The room was not large, perhaps ten feet across, but there was a large pool of water in the middle of the floor, and the ceiling was not much higher than their heads. They did not think to seek out the source of the water, owing to the pressing need to escape their predicament. Instead, and with no other choices presenting themselves, Danny and Ben trudged into the ankle-deep water, through to the other side, where the entrance to the tunnel awaited them. They continued their way.

Ben thought about the grotto. "That was a crazy thing to find underneath a store. In Old Jerusalem."

A few steps ahead, Danny stopped moving. The tunnel had ended. At first glance, it appeared to be a dead end, but the wall ahead of him turned out to be flat and smooth. He shone his light at it, and found he was facing an old wooden door. He pushed, and it opened into a room not unlike the one they had recently fallen into. But this was clearly a storage room of sorts, cluttered with pottery and wooden boxes. One of the closest boxes appeared to Ben to be a clay ossuary box.

As much as Danny wanted to stop and explore the items, his desire to see daylight won him over. Ben had already walked beyond the clutter and discovered a set of shallow stone stairs leading upwards. He looked at Danny. "That tunnel probably led us down the street from where we started."

Danny stepped forward and mounted the stairs. They were uneven and narrow; the stone walls on either side almost seemed to close in on them. "This sure beats trying to balance myself on your boney shoulders back there," he remarked.

At the top of the stairs, they came upon another door. It opened easily, into a large room full of activity. Strong incense, an aroma resembling sandalwood, pervaded the air. Eight women, wearing light robes, headscarves and sandals, each sat at a loom, weaving grand sheets of cloth, their feet on treadles, their hands working the spinning distaffs. Thick spools of thread and long bolts of fabric were stacked along one beige wall. A brown-robed man with short black hair and a long bushy beard walked between the women and their looms. He looked up at Ben and Danny with surprise and suspicion as the two boys attempted to walk nonchalantly through the room. There was only one other door, and they presumed it would lead to a way out, back to the street. They walked past the man, whose face had just morphed into anger. Ben decided against asking him where the fourth Station of the Cross was located. Some of the women glanced furtively up, but quickly turned back to their work. The man shouted something incomprehensible as the boys passed swiftly through the door.

In the next room, Danny and Ben found themselves behind the counter of a textile storefront. Samples of different coloured fabric hung on the opposite wall. A large, robed middle-aged man, apparently the proprietor, looked shocked at their arrival. Ben tried to smile at him, but the shopkeeper, without so much as a how-do-you-do, screamed and grabbed a large, thick wooden stick similar to a baseball bat and swung it at the boys. The shop was small, and there was little room to manoeuvre. The man continued to scream as Danny and Ben tried to dodge the stick. Danny headed towards the exit, but Ben was still within swinging range of the merchant's arm. The bearded man from the back room emerged, and saw Ben dashing around the large wooden counter in an effort to avoid the stick. The man produced a large knife and raised it as he rushed at Ben. Danny turned back around to see the knife being raised, ready to be thrust into Ben's back. Danny kicked the legs out from under the man, who crashed to his feet as Ben weaved his way around towards the front door. Danny screamed out, "Sorry!"

  The scuffle made its way out onto the street. Danny and Ben burst through the doorway of the store and ran straight into a passerby, nearly knocking him over. The man, clothed in a simple dark green robe with a woollen sash over his shoulder, was in his 30s; his red hair and beard were both cropped short. The two merchants piled immediately out of the store after the boys, brandishing their weapons. The passerby looked up and surveyed the scene. He put himself in harm's way and held up his hands to the merchants. He spoke to them in Hebrew: *"Peace, friends."*

  Danny and Ben stood behind their new guardian, while the merchants screamed, *"They are thieves!"*

  The man smiled, and calmly replied, *"They don't look like thieves. What have they taken from you?"*

  Danny and Ben didn't pause to consider who this man was, and why he had spoken for them. Instead, they took this opportunity to flee down the street. Without slowing, they turned back and saw the merchants wave them off and return to their shop. They stopped running, and the red-haired passerby continued his walk up the street, in the direction where the boys stood catching their breath. As the man approached them, Ben said to him in Hebrew, "*Thank you very much.*"

The man had an intelligent, intense look about him. He smiled, and said "*Peace. Strangers, you should watch your step.*"

The boys nodded and smiled at the man, who then took his leave.

— 5 —

With the sudden departure of their rescuer, Danny and Ben took in their surroundings for the first time. At a glance, they knew something was wrong, but it took an entire pirouette right there in the street before any judgement could be made. The first thing they noticed was that there were no streetlights. The road, no longer put upon by vehicles or even bicycles, was adorned by pedestrians, flanked with donkeys pulling carts. The stores had no illuminated signs, but instead had hand-painted storefronts. Merchants lined the street, customers were buying their wares. Everyone in sight wore period costumes, robes and sashes. Even the architecture was noticeably different, as if a well-intentioned crew had just ducked in to patch up the façades of all the buildings in the district.

Looking up the street, Danny and Ben saw a commotion, a group of people approaching them. It was clear that the people were not intent on the two of them, but would surely run them over unless they changed their course. Ben pulled Danny out of the way of the crowd, which grew larger as the neighbouring pedestrians joined in the march. He climbed up onto a ledge of the building behind them, affording himself a glance further down the street, before he lost his balance and returned clumsily to the ground.

Danny asked Ben what he saw.

"They're carrying a post, or some sort of wooden beam, I think."

Things were revealed a few moments later as the crowd continued its path, for the wooden beam espied by Ben was in fact a large cross, borne by a swarthy man who was naked except for a loin cloth around his waist. The man's thin body was covered with visibly fresh wounds from being whipped and beaten. His long, sweaty hair hung in his face as he staggered along. Ben noted the absence of a thorny crown. As the man passed Danny and Ben, he called out to them in Aramaic.

"*I didn't do it; it was not my fault!*"

Danny looked questioningly at Ben. "Did you get that?"

Ben shook his head.

The man with the cross continued past, followed by more people. Some started shouting a name: "*Florian! Florian!*" Danny and Ben watched everything with surprise, intrigue, and more than a little rising fear. After a few moments, the crowd moved on and the boys were left alone. They looked at the backs of the people walking away from them, the wooden cross sticking out above their heads. Danny was the first to venture a suggestion.

"Is this a movie set?"

Ben frowned. "Where's the camera crew?"

"Maybe it's one of those passion plays."

Danny hopped deftly onto a short wall and easily gained access to the roof of one of the buildings. He called down to his friend.

"Ben—get up here."

Ben climbed onto the roof with Danny. They were not very high up, but they could see around them for quite a distance. They saw the same ancient-style buildings they had seen before they had walked through the tunnel, but there was no modernization, no cars, no lamp-posts. Highway 417, which should normally run to the east of them, was no longer there.

The boys stood there on the rooftop and tried, without success, to comprehend what was happening.

Ben's cool started to slip away from him. "Where the hell *are* we?" He stomped across the roof, looking out at the other side, not actually expecting an acceptable reply from his companion.

"Uh, Ben?" Danny's focus was on the horizon to the west. "Ben. That big yellow dome—"

Ben stopped moving. "The Dome of the Rock. What of it?"

"Where did it go?"

Ben grimaced and followed Danny's outstretched arm to the place where Jerusalem's most iconic building should have been.

It was not there.

They both climbed back down to the street. The people around them all looked, smelled and acted differently than anyone else they had seen in Israel. There were beggars everywhere, on both sides of the streets, largely being ignored by the mosaic of people who marched by, either on foot, or in roaring chariots. Livestock seemed to appear out of nowhere, a sheep and two goats wandered around as if lost. Posts with brass street lamps appeared after every third or fourth building.

Danny was having an increasingly difficult time keeping his panic at bay, but he did manage to control himself. Ben had no such luck. He grabbed a passerby, a man with a trimmed beard, garbed in a robe like everyone else around them, and addressed him in English. "'Scuse me: Do you know where we are?"

The man looked at him with puzzlement and suspicion, but Ben carried on. "Where's the Lions' Gate?"

Danny grabbed Ben's sleeve. "Hey—in Hebrew, man."

The passerby quickened his pace. Ben got hold of his senses enough to address the man properly—in Hebrew. He ran after him. *"I'm sorry. Can you please tell me where we are right now? We seem to be lost."*

The passerby stopped and gave a curt smile. When he spoke Hebrew, he had a peculiar accent, one that Ben had not heard before. *"You are in Aelia Capitolina."*

Danny caught up to Ben and frowned. "Well, that doesn't help us. Ask him where the bus stop is." He pulled out his cell phone, only to see that he had no signal. He held it up to the sky and wandered around in a circle.

Ben tried again. *"Sir, could you please direct us to a bus stop? Or a policeman?"*

The passerby was visibly shocked at the request. *"Why would you be so foolish as to bring the Roman Guard upon yourselves?"*

Danny's Hebrew was not nearly as proficient as Ben's but he tried to join in on the conversation anyway. *"Who is the president?"* He stopped himself. "No, wait. Shit. I mean..." He tried again. *"Who is your...ruler?"*

The passerby was becoming amused at the boys' display and their discomfort. He said, simply, *"Pontius Pilate, Governor of Rome."*

Ben wheeled on Danny. "Man, don't you dare ask this guy what year it is."

"I won't, because I think you know what year it is now."

"Sure it is; it's the year twenty-frickin'-fifteen!"

Danny grabbed Ben's arms. "Calm down."

Ben pushed him away. "Why don't you ask him if the Earth is round? Ask him if he thinks Brazil is going to take the World Cup. Where is The Dome of the Rock, Danny? Where is the damn traffic?!"

By this time, the passerby had become tired of the boys' ranting. He turned and continued on his way up the street. Danny grabbed Ben and physically hauled him towards an alleyway.

Nobody took notice of the two young men and their struggle. Ben did not enjoy being carted off like an errant school boy, but was not able to do much about the iron grip that Danny had on his upper arm. In the alleyway, Ben started to scream. He screamed because he was being man-handled, but he knew, even consciously, that he needed to scream—at anyone, about anything, anything except for the glaring problem of their world having been turned upside-down. After a few moments, Danny had had enough of the noise. He slapped Ben across the top of his head. It didn't hurt him, but it shocked him into silence.

Ben finished his meltdown. It was to be the first of several such reactions to the events that would unfold over the next little while, as Ben started to consider that he might not be sleeping in his own bed that night.

There in the alleyway, Danny was only slightly more successful in keeping himself together. "I don't know... I don't know what's going on," he said.

Ben looked up at his friend like a child hoping for reassurance. "Where *are* we?"

Danny's reply was far from soothing. "I don't know, dammit!"

They both slid to the ground and sat against the wall. Danny thought about what his mother would have said to him, were she here to provide counsel. She would have put the entire problem directly back onto his shoulders, where it apparently belonged. This was no different than any childhood problem he had brought to his mother. When fellow Grade 6 student Doug Saunders had stolen his homework and handed it in as his own, Danny told his mother, so she could march on down to the school and give the teacher a stern talking-to. Maybe she could call Doug's parents and arrange for him to be grounded as well. But when he presented the problem to his mother, she had replied with only, "What are you going to do about it?" Danny was a bit confused by the question. What he had been planning to do about it was to stand by and let The Wrath of Mom make Doug Saunders cry. He learned, then, at age 11, that whatever he was going to do about his problems, he would have to do it by himself. In the end, he had confronted Doug Saunders, made him confess and made him cry. Danny got his homework back—and got suspended for bullying. His mother had not said anything about the bullying, only reaffirmed that he had handled it himself. This was a pattern that was to follow Danny always. It took years before he stopped expecting a different reply from his mother. Even serious problems were put back onto him, almost as if his mother didn't care, or was uninterested in getting involved in the trifling problems of a 17 year-old. When Danny had hit a pole while trying to parallel-park his friend's family car, he was shocked as always to hear his mother ask him what he was going to do about it.

Sitting on the ground in a Jerusalem alleyway like a street urchin, Danny pictured the conversation he would have with his mother if he could get her on the telephone: "Mom, I think I'm lost, probably for good. I don't know how to get home, I don't think I'll ever see you or dad again. I'm scared." He could hear her voice as clearly as if she were standing in front of him. "And what are you going to do about it, Daniel?"

Danny stood up. Ben, still on the ground, looked up at him. "What are you doing?"

"I'm gonna look around some more; gonna do something about our problem."

"What's that?"

Danny shrugged. "I don't know. But I'm not going to just sit here."

They picked up their backpacks and walked back into the street.

"Let's find something to eat," Danny suggested.

Ben decided this was a fantastic idea. He managed a smile, then grinned the way he did when he wanted his father to laugh. "Sure. Hopefully these people take MasterCard." His father wouldn't have laughed now, but Danny afforded him a weak smile. Not far away, they found a turbaned food vendor with a rickety wooden cart laden with pastries, situated on a street corner passed by shoppers and people on the move. Ben pointed to something square and delicious-looking, and handed the vendor a five-shekel bill. The man's reaction to the currency showed that he would have been equally enthusiastic to receive a dead rodent as payment. He took the money from Ben's outstretched hand, looked at the photograph of the bespectacled man on the face of it, and let it drop to the ground.

"*Roman coin only*," he said, dismissively.

Ben reached down and retrieved his apparently useless currency. Empty-handed, he and Danny walked off to find a place to sit down. They decided to eat the sandwiches they had packed that morning.

That morning.

The same day as today.

The things Danny and Ben had done after getting out of bed, eating breakfast at Professor Reed's house, seemed inconsequential and distant.

Ben felt a headache coming on. He looked into his brown canvas backpack, wondering if he had indeed had enough foresight to pack some aspirin. No such luck. He had his travel guide, his notepad with extra pens, and their camcorder—but nothing for a headache.

He knew Danny would have packed things he deemed essential: his smartphone, the solar-powered trickle-charger, his earbuds, the Guy Gavriel Kay paperback, probably a couple of his Walking Dead graphic novels and some Kit Kat bars. And that stupid POV camcorder necklace. Yup, ready for anything.

Ben took his sandwich out of his backpack, removed it from the baggie and threw the plastic away, not giving a darn about littering. Danny watched it float about, dancing on the ground at their feet. He looked at his friend incredulously, his friend whose list of past punishable crimes included jaywalking and now littering. Danny stood up to retrieve the baggie. Ben spoke with his mouth full of jam and bread. "You going to give that to someone to recycle?" he said.

Without replying, Danny took his own sandwich out of its Tupperware container. He stuffed the reclaimed baggie inside the plastic box and placed it into his backpack. "You never know what will come in handy."

— 6 —

After they finished eating, the boys set out walking again. Without putting a great deal of thought into their direction, the streets they chose to traverse brought them east, towards the Mount of Olives. They came upon a stone wall, right where the highway should have been. The wall ultimately barred their way to the mountain, though it was not clear if the builders wanted to keep people in or out of the city. The wall was about ten or twelve feet high, so scaling it was not possible. Both boys started to feel the onset of acute claustrophobia, but it was short-lived. Continuing south along the edge of the wall, it didn't take long for them to come upon a small arched opening. They stepped through, and had their nostrils assaulted. Their sense of smell took precedence over all other senses at that moment. They wanted to run, but they were not able to see. Blinded by the tears that quickly welled up in their eyes, Danny and Ben pulled up the tops of their robes to cover their mouths and noses. The coughing fits came next. Ben fell to the ground and leaned against a wooden pole. He pried his eyes open, and was met with the sight of a bony foot, dangling in front of his nose. With shock, he leapt to his feet, to find that the foot was attached to the naked body of a dead man. Ben gasped and stepped backwards. He looked up, and saw that the man was nailed to a wooden cross, his arms outstretched. The crucifixion had probably taken place more than a couple of weeks ago, judging by the way the corpse had been rotting.

    Ben realized that Danny was no longer by his side. Unable to take his eyes off the horrible sight before him, he called out, "Danny?"

    He only then turned away from the dead man, and saw Danny, a few steps away, looking down the length of the exterior city wall. Ben followed his gaze, which fell upon about twenty other crosses, all along the way, each about four or five meters from the stone wall. Every cross they could see bore a victim, each body in a different stage of decomposition. The smell of death pervaded the air all around them.

At the third attempt to find their bearings, the boys started to run, heading up towards the Mount of Olives. They found a lonely footpath, and knew it would likely take them away from this scene of horror. The path immediately started to rise, and they began to follow it up towards the top of the hill, as the sun, with its still unforgiving heat, began to set.

The stench of decaying flesh began to abate, as the boys put a fair amount of distance between themselves and the horrid sight of the crosses below. As they walked further, they saw a clearing not too far ahead of them. It appeared that they would be afforded a lookout back towards Jerusalem, and that this would be a good place to rest. As the two of them arrived at the clearing, they discovered four more wooden crosses, each adorned with long-dead bodies. And the pungent stench was back.

Danny was the first to shout. "What the hell is wrong with these people?!"

With a sound like the crackling of twigs, one of the bodies chose that exact moment to fall off its cross and go crashing to the ground at Danny's feet. The impact caused the body's bones, some of which had little to no skin attached, to crack apart and dislodge themselves from the rest of the body.

Like a pair of young boys fleeing an amusement park haunted house, Danny and Ben tore away, continuing the path up the hill. They screamed until they had no voices left, and they ran, suffused with panic, until their legs nearly gave out. When they eventually stopped to catch their breath, they found themselves at the top of the mountain.

<<Photo05>>

The mighty Mount of Olives appeared considerably less than mighty when Danny and Ben finally sat down atop the peak. The view of the city of Jerusalem was considerably less than spectacular as they gazed down upon it. It was now full dark, but the waning moon stared down at them with enough diffused illumination that they could make their way around the small patch of the hill they were to call home for the night. And there was just enough moonlight to illuminate a few of the buildings below. A smattering of small lights dotted the landscape of the city, but it was clear that they were not electric devices; lanterns burning in the windows flickered and danced.

Wanting to discuss anything other than the sights they had witnessed on their way up the hill, Danny spoke absentmindedly to his friend. "The Dome of the Rock is still missing."

Ben looked at him, then swept his hand over the cityscape. "This should all be lit up with lights."

"Face the facts, man. Obviously that tunnel brought us—"

Ben snapped at Danny. "Don't talk to me about time travel."

They sat in silence. After a few minutes Danny checked his phone again for a signal.

Nothing. Zero bars.

"You're wasting the battery," Ben remarked.

Danny shook his head. "There was lots of sun today. And I'm pretty sure there'll be lots of sun again tomorrow; my solar charger can power the phone in about half a day."

Ben, looking dejected, said, "Let's get some rest. Maybe tomorrow will be better."

They both placed their backpacks under their heads for pillows and stretched out on the ground. Danny looked up at the constellations. The sky above him was almost as spectacular as the starry sky he gazed at last summer from the shores of Manitoulin Island on Lake Huron, with nothing to obstruct the view of the heavens. It was certainly not the same night sky he had looked at more recently from Hamilton, where the stars have to compete with the city lights.

"Maybe," said Danny, "we're on a reality show."

Ben remained staring ahead. "Are you an idiot?"

"No. I've just run out of ideas."

"OK, but a reality show?"

"That explanation is only slightly less crazy than the idea that we travelled through time. Think about it—this is all a big hoax." Danny pointed out towards the dark city. "There are probably video cameras everywhere, filming us as we stumble around Jerusalem looking stupid. They probably even have POV cameras like the one I bought yesterday. They're planted on the people we interact with."

Ben considered buying into Danny's theory. "Alright. This is a hoax?"

"Yes. Everyone here is in on it. All those people are actors on the payroll of a TV company."

Ben thought some more. "What about The Dome of the Rock? Thousand year-old temple, and they tore it down for us. For a reality show."

"No, they didn't tear it down, they—they made it look like it's not there from up on the mount."

"Fine. Let's check it out in the morning."

Danny had run out of arguments and so remained silent. Lying there, he tried to focus on something other than the rocks digging into his back and the hunger pangs in his belly.

Ben was also far from comfortable, but he specifically lamented the absence of a bedside lamp. He had always read before sleeping. The ritual had started with his first copy of the book *Encyclopaedia Brown: Boy Detective*, and continued to this day.

Before long, the two boys succumbed to sleep.

— 7 —

The morning was serene, bringing a promise of a welcoming new day, though one look over the cityscape told Danny and Ben that this day was not going to be much different from the one they had left behind. They looked down at the spot where they remembered the Dome of the Rock to be. But what caught their eyes from this height was an enormous temple, walled in with battlements around a magnificent courtyard, which was replete with fountains and statues.

With empty stomachs, and with no better ideas, they decided to head down the easy slope of the mountain and walk back to the Via Dolorosa. Not wanting to encounter any more crosses, they wound their way around the hill, with the intent of entering the city from the north.

It was not long before Ben finally led the two of them through the streets to the exact area where one would normally have passed through the wall near the Dome of the Rock. They continued to walk until they arrived at the Wailing Wall, constructed in 20 BC by King Herod the Great. Ben had vivid memories of his visit to the Wailing Wall as a child with his parents. His mother had not taken any issue with the fact that the women's area of the wall was so much smaller than the men's area.

Standing there now with Danny, Ben noticed three palpable differences in the wall. For starters, there were no small folded papers with handwritten prayers stuffed in the cracks between the enormous limestone rocks. Secondly, there was no longer a partition dividing women's access to the wall; everybody was permitted to worship at the wall as he/she saw fit. "Gee, maybe we actually travelled to the future," Danny quipped to himself.

The third problem was that the wall itself appeared to be much taller than Ben had remembered. He shifted his gaze to the top of the wall, expecting to see extra-high ramparts. Instead, the top appeared to be just as he had remembered it. He looked down at his feet, and saw that he was standing on a dirt ground, unlike the smooth paved stones that made up the floor from his twentieth-century memories. Ben felt it possible that, if the wall had not become taller, the ground indeed had become lower. "Let's walk some more," he told Danny.

They left the Wailing Wall and Ben took them both around to the walkway that should have brought them to the outer wall of the Dome of the Rock. But the temple simply was not there. Ben ran his fingers along the sand-coloured walls of a modest temple that stood precisely where the famous Jerusalem landmark should be. The temple was still under construction; a line-up of workmen hacked at stones in a pile pickaxes. The men were not clothed in any sort of appropriate construction attire, but wore short skirt-pants, with bare chests and bare feet. A second glance saw that the men's ankles were all chained together. A centurion appeared on the scene with a menacing long brown whip, which he cracked upon the backs of the men nearest him.

Shocked and frightened, Danny and Ben turned quickly away from the horrible scene. They found the Via Dolorosa, but the street signs they remembered from the day before were not there. After another half hour of exploring the area, the boys were mentally and physically exhausted. Then they found themselves standing on a street corner which they recognized as the exact spot where they had stood twenty-four hours earlier, discussing their route to the next Station of the Cross. Today, however, there were no tourists photographing the buildings or each other. There were no merchants selling maps, there were no market stands hawking Hard Rock Cafe T-shirts. Ben looked at the street corner. Yesterday morning, just down the street from this very spot, there had been a vendor's stand selling those ridiculous robes. Period costumes, the man had called them. It had seemed to him like such a silly idea at the time. Now, they were happy to be able to blend in. They *did* blend in, at least until they opened their mouths and revealed their ignorance with every word they uttered. *Excuse me, could you tell me what year this is?* Ben could not get over how absurd that sounded. But the two of them could no longer argue that they were not in a different time, or dimension, or that they were not in an episode of The Twilight Zone.

Danny was looking at his surroundings with suspicion. He knew he was not on a reality TV show. He didn't seriously expect to find any hidden video cameras, but he was compelled to look anyway. He tried to get passersby to reveal themselves as television actors. He stepped abruptly in front of one young man and grabbed the fellow's arm. "We're on to you, man! Tell the producers their money has been wasted!"

The young man was shocked. He quickly became fearful, then aggressive. He pushed Danny's arms off his shoulders, side-stepped him, and continued down the street.

Ben stood in front of Danny and grabbed his shoulders. "Hey! You've got to stop that! If nothing else, we know that we are in a situation that's messed up. Right now, we've got to try hard to not mess it up even more. And one way to ensure that is by not accosting people on the street."

Danny stared down at the dusty street. "Alright," he muttered.

But Ben wasn't finished. "Now. You got that shit out of your system?"

"No," replied Danny. "Not even a little bit. But I'll be good. Let's move on."

They continued to walk, retracing their steps from yesterday. There was only a handful of people walking around, but there were no vendors looking after their stores. Anything that appeared to be there for commerce was boarded up with what appeared to be wooden shutters. After some consideration, Ben decided it was probably the Sabbath.

Presently, they found themselves standing in front of the textile store in which they had nearly received a beating the day before. With wonder, they looked at the building, the store through which they had transcended time. The solution to their predicament suddenly became clear to the both of them.

Danny put the idea forth. "I don't mean to suggest that this was not a wonderful time," he started. "But let's go home. It only makes sense that the tunnel will bring us back."

"Sure," said Ben. "Let's just hope there isn't another gladiator-type guy waiting for us on the other side this time."

Danny knocked on the rough wooden front door. "Hello!" he shouted through the door. "Avon calling!" He tried the iron latch, but the door was fastened shut, probably from the inside. There was no alley to the side of the store, as all the storefronts in this part of the street were part of a long row of low buildings.

Ben considered how they were going to gain entry. "If we go to the end of the block, there might be an alleyway leading to the rear of all these places. Sort of what they do in Toronto with all those row houses."

But Danny had a different plan. "Up and over, man."

With surprising ease, the two boys hoisted themselves up to the thatched roof of the building. The surface on which they walked did not feel particularly solid, so they walked slowly and carefully. In no time, they were on the other side, and they lowered themselves skilfully down to the ground.

They were in a tiny backyard, with little vegetation. Some tools resembling, among other things, a rake and a hoe were leaning up against a wooden table.

Looking at the back wall of the building they had just conquered, they were presented with a rear door and another shuttered window. The door was locked, but the shutter swung open easily, giving them access to the inside. As they climbed in, Ben remarked, "Why do they even lock the doors if they won't lock the windows?"

"I guess it's to keep the stupid criminals out," said Danny. "But their security system is obviously no match for skilled thieves like us."

"I guess there's not a lot of break-and-entering here."

The sunlight shone through the window onto the floor, affording them enough illumination to look around the room. But even in the slight darkness, Danny and Ben knew there would be two rows of looms here—and a door to the basement.

They were clearly alone, so they crossed the room, swung the door open and started down the narrow stone stairs. By the third step, it became pitch dark, so Ben turned on his smartphone's flash light. They reached the bottom of the stairs and stood in the storage room, with its pottery and boxes.

Danny activated his own phone's flashlight and surveyed the room. "Where was the door?"

Ben headed straight past the wooden shelves to where he remembered the door to be, but he was met with only a stone wall. "Yesterday when we arrived in this room from the tunnel, the first thing we saw was those shelves, right?" He stood against the wall, trying to recreate their entry into this room. He pointed over to the clutter, then wondered aloud. "We came in right through here. So where the hell is the stupid door?" Ben tried to figure out what was wrong with the situation.

Danny carried the thought. "Are we even in the right basement?"

Ben swept the room again with his Galaxy's light. "No, this is the one," he replied. "There's that ossuary with some poor guy's bones in it."

"Well, didn't everyone have those things lying around back in those days? Back in *these* days?"

"I don't know, Dan. I think so."

Danny took charge. "Let's cover the entire perimeter. You start that way, I'll do the opposite. Run your hands and your light across the stones until you find the door."

It only took a few minutes for the boys to conclude definitively that there was no door down there, nothing to lead them to a tunnel back to home.

Once again, the whole concept sounded ridiculous to them. Even the reality show theory started to make more sense.

Danny's light shut itself off. He hit the Home button on his phone, looking for a signal. "Nothing," he said. "Let's get the hell out of here."

Following Ben's light, they both ascended the steps to the textile store. When they reached the top, Ben turned his phone off, noting that he still had enough of a charge for a few more hours at least. The boys marched through the shop to the storefront. They decided not to use the front door as their egress, because they would be unable to lock it again from the outside. Danny pushed out the shutter on the window, allowing them to just climb out, as if that was what they were supposed to do.

There were not enough people around to take notice of the two young men emerging from the textile shop window. As Danny and Ben stood on the street in front of the store, Danny wondered aloud what time it was. Ben checked his phone, but it would not display the time, as there were apparently no satellites for it to access. He looked up at the sun, still rather close to the horizon, and less than halfway to the top of the sky. "No wonder I'm so hungry; it must be well after 9 AM."

Danny looked up and down the street, stopping his gaze at each building. "One of these has to be the T-shirt store from yesterday," he stated. Let's try to go backwards.

Ben was less than convinced. "It could be any of these places," he said, looking up and down the way.

But Danny started walking, diagonally across the street. "We walked in that tunnel for about twenty seconds. That should bring us," he looked up ahead of him. "...right about here."

Ben started to get frustrated. "This isn't it," he said.

"But picture the T-shirts out front," cried Danny. He didn't even bother with the door handle, but instead grabbed the window shutter, flung it open, and climbed inside. Ben did the same thing, only he took care to glance up and down the street for a policeman, or a guard, or whoever the heck would take notice of their second break-and-enter.

Inside the shop, Ben had to agree with Danny that this was probably the building they had been inside the day before. They trotted through to the door at the opposite end, and found themselves again in the room with the creaky old floor. Only this time, the floor wasn't old, nor was it creaky. Danny went so far as to jump up and down on the floor in an attempt to recreate the events of yesterday, but it would not give.

Ben suggested they look around for a staircase, anything to lead them down to the basement, but there was nothing at all in either of the two rooms. The only door in the rear led to a small backyard, similar to that of the textile shop down the street.

At this point, Danny started to lose his cool. He stamped his way out to the backyard, found a long tool that looked like a primitive shovel, and brought it back inside.

"What are you doing?" asked Ben.

"Get out of the way," growled Danny, as he lifted the shovel over his head. Ben leapt aside as Danny brought the tool crashing down onto the wood floor. But the floorboards held fast, and the resistance caused the shovel to send shivers of pain up his arm. He dropped it to the ground, and Ben picked it up, noticing that Danny's efforts had caused enough of a dent in one of the floorboards that the shovel could be used to pry it up.

And Ben did just that. He poked the tip of the shovel into the edge of the wood and, with some grunting, managed to lift up the eight-inch-wide piece. Danny then used his leverage to remove the whole length of the wood. But instead of peering down to a basement, all they saw was a dirt ground, directly underneath where the floor had been laid down.

Ben handed the shovel to Danny, who threw it across the room, denting the wall. They looked down at the floor with the upended piece of wood, and turned on their heels. They burst through the front door and stepped out onto the street once again. With nowhere to go, they both just plopped themselves down onto the ground, leaned their backs against the front of the building, and sulked.

— 8 —

"How are my friends with the funny tongues?"

Danny and Ben looked up at the sound of a familiar Hebrew voice, and came face-to-face with the red-haired man from yesterday, walking purposefully down the street they know as the Via Dolorosa. It took only a moment for Ben to see the opportunity in attaching themselves to a local. *"We're lost. Can you help us?"*

The man smiled warmly, in contrast to a face that seemed to default to a stern expression. Ben continued, in Hebrew. *"Is there a soup kitchen around here? We need some food. We are willing to work for it."*

The man reached out and hooked his hand around the Velcro strap of Ben's backpack. *"That is a peculiar bag,"* he remarked. *"From where did it come?"* His tone was one of curiosity, rather than accusation.

Ben thought about their backpacks, and how he and Danny had bought them back when they were starting university. They liked the fact that they were made of plain brown canvas—they didn't want to be walking advertisements for any corporation. But with this stranger inquiring after the bags' origins, Ben then became conscious of the weave of the fabric and the knit used to hold it together—and the little red-and-white Canadian flag sewn on it.

The man seemed particularly interested in the Canadian flags. He looked at the boys for a reply to his not-unreasonable question.

"We bought them from a vendor in a land far from here," began Ben. *"Even farther than the sea."* He thought some more. *"We do a great deal of travelling."*

The man paused, and looked the boys up and down thoughtfully. He seemed to accept their reply. *"Come with me,"* he decided. *"I can introduce you to the teacher, Yeshua. He will help you find your way, and we will fill your bellies."*

Danny looked at him with apprehension, but Ben moved forward to shake the man's hand. *"Thank you for your kindness. My name is Ben; this is Danny."*

"I am Yehudah."

The sound of this name slapped Ben in the face: Judas.

Danny, in his turn, may have acknowledged that the name Yehudah had graced one of the textbooks in Theology 301, but he didn't care. His decision to blindly follow their new friend was inspired by his hunger, and the boys followed him without another word. They turned around to walk north, heading out of the area they knew as Old Jerusalem. It seemed foolish thinking of it that way: the entire city, as it now stood before them, was Old Jerusalem. Ben told himself that he should be the one taking control of the situation, but the fruitlessness of seeking familiarity in this world he thought he knew depressed him all the more.

As they walked, Danny had nothing to say to this man. His Hebrew was elementary at best, and he couldn't think of anything to talk about. This was a new concept for him. Normally, small talk came easily to Danny—and not just with pretty young women. Danny could make friends in elevators. He used to charm the cafeteria ladies at high school, as well as the school bus drivers. Nobody would be in the same breathing space as Danny and not hear an interesting sentiment, observation or story. But walking beside the man who called himself Yehudah, Danny was quiet. He of course had a couple of hundred questions, but he felt it best to wait things out, at least until after they were fed.

Yehudah marched on, occasionally greeting people they passed in the street. In most cases, he introduced these people to Danny and Ben. Some people nodded a greeting to the boys, others hugged them affectionately. Each new person looked quizzically up and down at the strange robes the boys wore. Nevertheless, being associated with Yehudah started to give Ben a feeling of belonging. Of course, he would rather have had the feeling of digesting an omelette instead.

Eventually, the three of them arrived in front of a house, as plain as any of the small, square yellow houses they had passed in the last half-hour of walking, with its dirt-coloured walls and dusty walkway. A young girl sat in the doorway, playing with a wooden toy. She smiled when she saw Yehudah, then stood up and dashed into the house. Moments later, eight people came out, men and women. Yehudah embraced them all in turn, then gestured towards Ben and Danny. A simple-robed woman wearing a spicy fragrant about her person produced some dry bread, yellow cheese and water, and a man sat the boys down so they could break their fast. A friendly affair—it was clear to the boys that there was a great deal of love and respect in that group, with a discernable amount of deference towards Yehudah.

Shortly, everyone prepared to take leave. Two of the women were apparently staying behind with the children, while the others were to join Yehudah to—to what? Ben looked at Danny, who shrugged his shoulders. "I guess we're going with them. It's not as if we have pressing business to look after."

"Right," remarked Ben. "Except for the need to get home, wherever that may be, and to get our lives back."

"Well, other than that, it seems like our only course of action is to follow our new friends."

Ben agreed. They would need food, and eventually lodgings, and these people appeared to be able to provide for them—at least for the time being.

~ ~ ~ ~

The whole group started walking, nine of them now. Soon, they reached what appeared to be the edge of Jerusalem. It was clear how much smaller the city was now, with none of the sprawl, such as it was, that had taken place over the past two millennia. They started on a dirt road heading north. Ben looked around at the landscape, and leaned into Danny. "This is so weird. There used to be highways here. Route 404 headed towards—"

"You mean, there WILL be highways here someday."

"Hmm. What?" Ben pulled himself out of his reverie and looked at Danny. "Oh. Well, whatever. There aren't any bloody highways here now, are there?"

The boys increased their pace a little, and soon walked alongside their guardian.

"*Yehudah?*" Ben called out, switching to Hebrew. "*How much farther until we arrive?*"

Yehuda smiled and turned around. "*Have patience, friend. It takes time to get to Nazareth.*"

Without thinking, Danny blurted out, in English, "Wait: Nazareth?! That's like an hour's drive from here!"

Ben clarified to Danny, "It's about 150 kilometres, if I remember right."

Yehudah squinted at hearing an unfamiliar language, but he gave the boys his warm smile again. "*It is only a five-day walk. There will be food along the way.*" He fell out of step and engaged one of the other men in the group.

Ben frowned at his friend. "Maybe yelling at him in English isn't the smartest thing to do. We don't want them to think we're crazy."

"Right now it's hard for me to argue that we're NOT crazy."

Ben considered this. "These people embrace superstition more readily than they do reason or logic." He rubbed the back of his neck. "Just, maybe try to work on your Hebrew while we're here."

Danny glanced up at the still cloudless sky. "I understand it better than I speak it."

"Me too."

"You? I thought you were fluent!" Danny started to get agitated.

"I can speak present-day Hebrew. But the dialect of all these people here is two thousand years older than mine."

Danny had a hard time letting that sink in. "Two thousand years, eh?"

Ben nodded. "Yeah. This isn't reality TV. It's not The Truman Show." He looked at his friend, thankful that he was not in this mess alone. He couldn't think of anyone else he trusted to be as calm and cool in a crazy situation like this. He needed to be brave, and it was easier to be brave when standing beside Danny—Danny, who could have any friend he wanted. Even some of the professors (female *and* male) had looked at him like they wanted to bed him or date him or just hang out with him, were it not for such complications as the teacher-student dating rules—and the occasional spouse. If Danny didn't know the answer to a problem put forward by the textbook, he could worm his way into an acceptable response with enough finesse to impress the prof, even if his answer was wrong. And Danny was brave enough (or perhaps stupid enough) to not back down in an altercation at the campus pub, even when he stood a fantastic chance of getting his ass handed to him. Theology students usually don't get into fisticuffs with football students. Actually, theology students usually don't get into fisticuffs with anybody. Ben couldn't remember Danny ever really getting into a fight, but his friend seemed to have such confidence that nobody messed with him.

So Ben needed to be brave, and he was happy to have Danny with him. Of course it was Danny and his stupidity, jumping on that old wooden floor, that had led them into this whole situation to begin with.

Ben looked at his friend. "So Hebrew only, ok?"
"Sure, that's fine."

As they walked, the smell of rotting corpses suddenly drifted through the air. Although it was not as fierce as yesterday's odours coming off the corpses at the base of the Mount of Olives, Danny and Ben knew what was next. The group had only been walking for a few minutes when the road bent slightly to the west. When it straightened, they saw the crosses, six of them, lined up along the side of the road, all with bodies nailed up on them. Nobody took notice of them except the two Canadians. Danny remarked to himself that their new friends, all of them, appeared indifferent to the tortured bodies suspended on either side of the road. All of a sudden those pesky Highway 401 billboards that annoyed his father back home didn't seem like that big a deal.

Danny tried not to look up at the victims as they passed by them. Then he heard a voice, in Aramaic. *"Help me!"*

He stopped in his tracks, while the others continued on. The voice came from one of the bodies on the cross beside him. The man speaking to him looked dead, all the bodies did. But this poor guy was able to move his lips. His chest heaved slowly in and out, but his shoulders did not move much at all. Danny put his mind into gear, trying to recall some of the Aramaic phrases that he had picked up in his studies. He tried to find some words, any words would do, but his voice was devoid of eloquence as he stammered, "*Why... how...can I...*"

A strong hand suddenly grabbed Danny's arm and yanked him away. It was Yehudah, dragging him ahead, towards the rest of the group. "*What are you doing?*" he said, in Hebrew. "*You know not to talk to them!*"

It was only then that Danny noticed that the others were many steps ahead of him. Even Ben had not realized that Danny had stopped walking. As he hurried to catch up with the others, Danny thought to himself, *Alright, NOW I know not to talk to them. Sheesh.*

— 9 —

It was early the same afternoon, and Ben and Danny, with Yehudah and all his travelling companions, marched along a road heading north through the desert. There were surprising numbers of houses, small, flat-roof buildings the same colour as the yellow sand that stretched for miles in every direction. The villagers who took notice of the group passing by were intrigued by their numbers.

The sun was high overhead and the day was sure to become hot and dry, much more so than they were used to back home. Southern Ontario had an incredibly wide range of temperatures, but the heat they felt as they walked through the desert was approaching the point of being unbearable. Despite that, the mood among the group was jovial, almost celebratory. Danny and Ben fell back a little, away from the others, so they could speak English in private.

Ben spoke up first. "The person we are supposed to be on our way to see, our guide called him Yeshua. Do you know what that name is in English?"

Danny had to think for a moment. "It's Jesus, but that's a pretty common name."

"Fairly. Only he also called him 'The Teacher.'"

Danny looked up at the people walking ahead of them. Their number had increased to a couple of dozen. There was now a donkey, and one of the newcomers had a baby bundled to her chest. "And all these people are crossing the desert to meet him—in Nazareth, no less." He looked at Ben. "I think we are going to see Jesus Christ."

Ben didn't reply. He had nothing to say, as his hunger won out. "I thought that guy was going to feed us."

Danny was feeling the hunger as well. "Yeah, I pictured more restaurants and less sand."

Ben had had enough of walking, and he wheeled on Danny. "I only agreed to come to Israel with you because Professor Reed said we could stay with her. I've never been without a bed, man."

"What's the big deal? You survived last night."

"That's fine, but I'm hungry."

"Let's face it," replied Danny. "Wherever we are, we're not seeing any drive-thrus."

"You might like camping, but I don't. Where are we going to sleep?"

Danny shrugged his shoulders. "I don't know. I'm open to suggestions outside of following these guys, if you've got any."

"You came here to study Jesus and his history. The plan was not to chase the actual guy across the desert."

"It appears like we're going to meet him. Maybe I can interview him for my paper."

"Danny, for gawdsake, can you please be serious? We are totally screwed! I want to go home."

"I *am* serious. If we meet him, he might know how we can get back home."

Ben snorted. "Sure, we'll just let him know we're from the 21st century. Do you know what they do to crazy people here?"

He looked up to see that everyone, led by Yehudah, had quickened their steps. A hamlet was visible ahead of them, with not more than a couple dozen single-storey dwellings. From one of the larger outer houses, its walls matching the hue of the surrounding dirt, a group of people could be seen emerging, carrying baskets. An elderly lady sat spinning at a loom out front. A young barefooted boy with a dirty but happy face followed the others; he carried a tiny marmoset monkey on his shoulder.

When the travellers arrived in front of the house, there were greetings all around. Everyone hugged everyone and, after a few moments, food was passed around. Cheeses, bread and skewered fowl, as well as some leafy greens with sweet-smelling oils—Danny and Ben ate their meals with alacrity, despite being unable to recognize much of what they put into their mouths. The marmoset climbed down from the boy's shoulders and inspected the new arrivals, occasionally climbing a leg in search of a snack.

Shortly, with bellies full and spirits replenished, Danny and Ben rose with the group and continued northward, on the road to Nazareth. By the time darkness started to show signs of falling, a site was picked out for a rest, and everyone spread out under the canopy of the night sky. The moon did not grace the group with its presence, but nobody concerned themselves with the need for illumination; sleep came quickly for most of them.

By the third day of travelling, Danny and Ben began to fit in a little with the rest of the group, which by this time had grown to over thirty people. As they walked, Danny rubbed his hand over the pathetic excuse for a beard that four days' growth afforded him. He was dying for a shave, a hot shower and a change of clothes. He looked at the costume robes he and Ben were still wearing. When they had first seen the robes displayed by the street vendor, they thought they looked silly and novel. Here, amidst people wearing similar garments, it became clear that the robes they had purchased were cheap and flimsy—made for a photograph to send home, rather than for walking through the desert for days on end.

"Gee, if I had known we'd be living out here," Danny said to Ben. "I'd have asked you to buy me the deluxe version of this costume."

"And some sunscreen," Ben put in.

Danny continued the complaining. "My sunglasses are back at Professor Reed's place."

"I'm tired of walking. And I miss air conditioning."

"Me too."

Ben looked down at the $110-dollar sandals on his feet. "At least we're wearing quality footwear, thank goodness for that. How are your feet?"

"Surprisingly good." Danny grinned. "I could use some more dirt between my toes, though."

They continued to walk, but Ben had one last gripe in him. He looked at his friend. "Damn it, Danny, if we had to go back in time, why couldn't we have gone to 1964 to chase The Beatles? Plus they had toilets then. And toilet paper."

~ ~ ~ ~

Sitting under a tree, leaning on its trunk, Danny reached up to accept two large pieces of thick, coarse bread and a small chunk of cheese that Ben held out to him. He sniffed the cheese and wrinkled his nose at it. Ben turned away to get drinks from the woman who was pouring a yellowish liquid from a pottery decanter. Ben didn't know what it was, but it looked delicious. He considered the unlikelihood of it being citrus Kool-Aid.

Danny called after him. "Ahem. Garçon?" Ben turned back around and raised an eyebrow at Danny, who held up his food. "Please send this back to the kitchen. I distinctly remember asking for my stale bread and cheese to be melted in the microwave."

Ben smiled broadly and gave his best French waiter imitation. "Would monsieur prefer to select another meal? Perhaps zee bowl of sand with, how you say, a side of rocks?"

Danny frowned. "I did not choose to dine here so you could insult me. Get me the manager."

Ben laughed and turned away. Shortly, Yehudah stood up and motioned that it was time to move on. Everyone rose, grabbed their belongings, and the whole group started walking again. Ben and Danny fell back as usual. Making sure there was a bit of distance between them and the last person in the caravan, Danny pulled out his solar-powered trickle charger.

"Let me charge your Galaxy," he said to Ben.

Yup, Ben thought. There is definitely enough sun out here to power all their electronics. He handed his phone to Danny, who plugged it into his charger. The phone stayed in the folds of his robe, but the solar cell was placed over his shoulder. Nobody would be able to see what they were doing unless they came quite close. As it was, nobody paid any attention to the two Canadian theology students trailing along at the back of the group.

Towards the end of the afternoon on Day Five, it was clear that they were getting close to Nazareth. The group had become larger still, and there was a buzz in the air. Eventually, the modest city could be seen in the distance. Ben had no idea what to expect. At the very least, they would probably stop walking for a while.

The city sprawled outwards, as if to meet the travellers. Yehudah brought the group to a halt outside a small cluster of dwellings. The modest buildings were close together, row houses in which many families all lived together.

Ben was amazed at how much his memories of Nazareth, and all of Israel, did not have any relevance to the sights before him. The landscape was completely different after two thousand years. When he had been here as a boy, he saw how tourists often had to descend into deeper layers to visit buildings of historical significance. Even the location of the house where Jesus Christ apparently grew up had been built upon by other structures. But here in the first century, the houses could be visited by walking straight in from the street level.

The city's cobblestone roads gave the promise of less dust to be kicked up by feet, whether cloven or shod. The entire group stopped in front of one of the larger abodes. Children, playing outside the front door with small wooden toys, ran in to announce the new arrivals to the adults within. Soon, four men emerged. No women, no food. Ben could tell immediately that these were men of consequence. Yehudah, at the front of the group, hugged all four of them, and they all rejoiced like long-lost brothers. One of the men called out, and women came out of the surrounding houses bearing wooden trays with bread and bowls of hearty soup. The four men moved among the newcomers. Everywhere they went, people kissed their cheeks or their hands; some bowed to them. Everyone was joyful as they all started to sit themselves on the ground.

Danny and Ben were exhausted, and relieved to be off their feet. They looked around them, and noticed a lack of hotels and restaurants. Danny whispered, "I wonder what our accommodations will be like."

"I could sure use a shower," Ben replied. "And I'm way overdue for a shave."

Danny looked around at all the bearded men, then rubbed the stubble on his own face. "Somehow, I don't think that's going to happen."

Bread and some mystery meat soaked in brine were passed around. Danny sniffed at the meat but ate it without complaint. Ben, on the other hand, was delighted with the meal. "This food reminds me of dinner at my grandmother's house," he said.

The four important men who had greeted Yehudah sat together to eat. They all had hair slightly longer than the others; their beards were trimmed. One of them had bejewelled hands; another was taller than the rest and seemed to take on a fatherly attitude towards everyone there.

Ben wondered what made them special. He decided to take a chance in revealing his ignorance to a young man who had sat by himself nearby. *"Brother,"* he said in Hebrew. *"Who are those four men?"*

The young man didn't take issue with the question, and was in fact happy to answer. *"They are The Teacher's students."* Seeing from the look of confusion on Ben's face that he had not fully answered the question, he clarified. *"They are Ya'aqov, Cephas, Mattithyahu and Phillip. The others should be here soon, I believe."*

Ben smiled in thanks, and turned back to Danny, who was absorbed in his own thoughts.

"Danny, do you know who those men are?"

"Our new buddy there said the name Philip. And Mattithyahu is obviously Matthew. I think Cephas is Hebrew for Peter. I don't know about the other guy, though."

"Ya'aqov," Ben said. "It's either James or John. I think it's James."

"Ben? I just figured out who our tour guide is. Yehudah is Judas; it's the same name—as in Judas Iscariot, the one who betrays Jesus. I wasn't sure before, but I am now."

Ben contemplated what Danny said. "Do you think he—wait: what's going on?"

There was a small commotion in one area of the group. Everyone stopped talking. Danny looked over and saw that three more men had arrived. Slowly, all the people present rose to their feet, whether for deference or simply to get a better view of the newcomers, Danny couldn't tell.

The man in the middle was a little shorter than the two men flanking him. He had long dark hair and a neatly-cropped beard. His face was warm and friendly, despite the fact that his eyes looked as if he was carrying the weight of the world on his shoulders. Like most of the men there, his robe and sash looked to be designed more for comfort and practicality than fashion, and his sandals were made of leather and rope. The men on either side of him appeared important, and were clearly proud to be standing where they were. Cries of *"Yeshua!"* rung out. A few people shouted the name *"Jésu!"*

Danny and Ben, overwhelmed with humility, watched Jesus Christ greet his disciples. The two of them, by virtue of their presence, were also considered to be disciples. Danny's hand covered his open mouth; he had trouble standing. Ben was awestruck and motionless. The young man next to them saw their faces and smiled at them. *"Many people react that way when seeing Jésu for the first time."*

Danny couldn't even reply to him. He just whispered towards Ben, "Dude, you have no idea."

— 10 —

The meal ended, and the entire group sat and gathered under the welcome shade of a copse of trees to listen to Jesus speak. Some of the Apostles joined in on the discussion, but Danny and Ben listened silently with the other disciples and followers. The message was not entirely clear to Ben, and it was completely lost on Danny. Occasionally, someone spoke up in Aramaic. Danny recognized it as such, but could not fully translate what was being said. Despite the difficulty with the languages, Danny and Ben were both content to sit and listen, to take it all in.

Soon, the Apostles fell quiet, leaving only Jesus to speak. And while he spoke, he looked over the group of people seated before him. Twice, his virtuous eyes stopped on Danny and Ben, making them shift uncomfortably where they sat. But there was a feeling of euphoria throughout the gathering, the source of which was recognized by all as emanating from the man who sat cross-legged on the dirt, preaching to those who would listen. Jesus' dialect was that of a small town, but he spoke with kindness and authority.

Ben heard Danny whispering to him, but didn't reply.

"I said, pass me my bag."

Ben surfaced from his trance and soundlessly passed the backpack over to his friend. Danny reached in, dug around and pulled out his smartphone. Ben frowned at him. "I'm pretty sure you're not supposed to text in church."

"I'm not texting." Danny held up his phone, loaded the camera app—and took a photograph of Jesus Christ.

Ben had to hold himself back from swatting his friend across the head. "Are you nuts?" he exclaimed. "You don't think the people here will get curious, and then accusatory, if they see that thing?"

Danny put his phone away. "Relax, man," he said. "You're probably not wrong, but everyone here is pretty fixated on our guest speaker right now."

Ben was aghast at his friend's apparent lack of humility in the presence of the person who was supposed to be his saviour. "We just need to be a little less reckless with our 21st-Century gadgets, is all," he said.

"Fair enough."

The sermon continued for a little over an hour. After Jesus finished, people in the group stood up, and most of them dispersed to settle themselves in for the evening under the twilight sky. Danny and Ben hadn't realized that they were still looking at Jesus with incredulity. As they stood there frozen, Jesus crossed through the people milling about and walked directly to them. Under a bright starry sky, in the warm night air, two Canadians, Daniel Casey and Benjamin Strohlberg, received the hand of Jesus Christ. Danny's eyes were wet. Ben lost control of his lower lip as he considered the significance of standing before history's most famous Jew.

Jesus spoke to them as he held on to each of their hands. He spoke quietly, that only they could hear. He spoke slowly and expressively, enunciating his words carefully, in Hebrew. *"You two are not native to this land. I think you have travelled farther than any man here."*

Danny and Ben just stared at Jesus, who smiled back. He then gave the boys a knowing look and turned away to speak with the Apostle Peter.

~ ~ ~ ~

The group settled in for the night. Danny and Ben found a spot of land, reasonably flat and comfortable, away from the others. They lay down with their heads on their backpacks, looking up at the stars. The belt of Orion showed itself, midway above the horizon.

Danny broke the silence. "I guess seeing Jesus Christ in person is shaking your faith as a Jew."

Ben wrinkled his brow. "We never doubted Jesus' existence; we just don't believe he is the Messiah; we don't think those miracles ever occurred."

"Oh."

They listened to the sounds of the other men talking quietly in their own groups, spread out among the patches of ground nearby. In the distance, the lowing of cattle could be heard. The sound was just comforting enough to give Ben a reason to smile. "Dan?" he said in the dark

"Yeah?"

Ben turned over on his side. "When this adventure is over, think we could go visit Moses?"

Danny continued staring up at the stars. "Sounds good to me."

PART II

— 11 —

For Danny and Ben, morning came earlier than they had expected; they were shocked out of their sleep by shouting and pleading. Before he even opened his eyes, Ben's first instinct was to leap out of bed, grab his slippers, dash through his bedroom door and run downstairs to see what the commotion was all about. But the hard ground on which he had been sleeping started to register in his lower back, reminding him that he was not in Hamilton anymore. He squinted, focusing on the movement around him, until he saw that a group of about ten people had descended upon their camp. Two of the newcomers were carrying a gurney on which a lay a young man, motionless except for his heaving chest.

In short order, most of the disciples were huddling near the gurney, surrounding its occupant. The boys picked up their backpacks and made their way closer to the action, inasmuch as the gathering crowd would allow.

Everyone there seemed to have an idea of what was going to happen; only the Canadians watched with curiosity and wonder. A woman, clearly the mother of the man on the gurney, leaned over her son, clinging to his chest. Opposite her, Jesus stood, smiling at the prone body.

The noise of the crowd rose to a discernible crescendo, and then stopped abruptly. A few quiet words were spoken by Jesus, and the man, unbelievably, stepped off the gurney, found his footing, and did a little dance. With a small roar of applause, the man's mother and friends celebrated the miracle of the healing. Danny and Ben witnessed all of this from the back of the group. They watched as the formerly-crippled man continued to dance, this time with his mother, swinging her around in his arms. The gurney was taken away, and most of the people in the crowd of well-wishers and witnesses dropped to their knees to pray, before eventually moving on. Presently, the disciples were alone again. It seemed then to everyone to be a good time to eat. Food was produced and passed around—goat cheese with vinegar and some ripe yellow fruits.

As they sat and ate, cross-legged on the ground under a tree, Ben looked confused. Danny, wearing an expression of doubt on his face, said, "I thought I would be more excited, witnessing a miracle." He spoke quietly, so no one could hear their English.

"What were you expecting?" Ben replied, with a mouthful of food.

"I don't know, I just..." Danny tried to mull it over. "Look, we don't even know that the dude was actually crippled."

Ben was incredulous, and he didn't mind showing it. "Wow," he said. "I'm supposed to be the doubter here. Both of our religions preach that we have to have faith. And you may have actually witnessed an act of your messiah."

Danny thought for a while before replying, before putting words aloud to a thought that had begun forming in his mind the moment he saw that man leap off the gurney and pronounce himself healed. "I think my faith was stronger before I saw this."

Ben couldn't hide the indignation in his voice and, in actuality, he didn't care. "So what the hell are you saying? For chrissake, man, you—"

Astonished at his gaffe, Ben cut himself off and looked straight over to where Jesus was sitting, and was mortified to find himself locking eyes with the man. He slowed down his breath and turned away, looking sheepishly back at Danny. "You going to just let that hang there?" he said.

"Yup," said Danny. "You just took the Lord's name in vain. And he was within earshot. Nice going."

They looked around the camp to see people still looking over at the two of them. They continued eating in silence. After everyone there had finished his meal, nobody showed any signs of leaving. Instead, people just milled around in small groups, as if this was an informal garden party. Jesus had left, but most of the Apostles were still there.

Danny and Ben were still included in the important aspects of being one of the followers—meal times, for example—but they were able to stand apart from the gatherings if they wished. They seemed to still be successful in their attempts at becoming unobtrusive. They walked over to an area apart from the trees, and continued their discussion.

Ben still felt he needed an explanation from his friend. "Didn't your mom bring you to church with your brother and sister?"

Danny was more than ready to continue his stance. "Yes she did," he said. "But that's not why I enrolled myself in Religious Studies at McMaster. I never wanted to become a preacher; it was because I can't get my head around the science of it all."

Ben was still defensive. "Man, don't start on me about the need for blind faith. I hear enough of it myself, and I teach it to kids at synagogue."

Danny started to lose his temper. "But faith is no longer needed. Look around you, Ben! All we have to do is hang out here, keep our mouths shut and our eyes open, and we'll see what we need to see."

"Or we'll see what we *want* to see."

"Look, the main problem with the canonical gospels is that—"

"The what...?" Ben cut in.

Danny lost his stride. "Canonical, New Testament stuff, the four books written by John, Luke, Matthew and Mark. They're the first-person accounts of what happened."

Ben was happy to not be a Christian as he attacked Danny's words. "And do all four of their stories corroborate each other?"

Danny shook his head and frowned. "Well, no. As a matter of fact, there are a bunch of contradictions among them—which is weird, because they were supposed to have been written by men who were all in this together."

The two of them calmed down a little. Ben started to show some empathy for Danny's plight, having had a great deal of experience in this arena. "It's even harder for me," he began. "Abraham, Isaac and David didn't exactly keep diaries of their days. Their accounts were written by other people, long after the events took place—hence our need for faith."

"Here's the thing," put in Danny. "Historians have all sorts of reasons to doubt things—stuff like Jesus' birthplace. I think the story-weavers made the birth happen in Bethlehem for political reasons. Why would people actually have to travel to the town where they were born for a census?"

"What's your point?"

"Man, my point is that, although you can shoot down so many of the facts around Jesus, nobody seems to be able to dispute the miracles he apparently performed."

Ben laughed out loud. "I know a few atheists who might disagree with you there."

Danny held onto his patience. "I'm talking history, not science. There are so many written accounts of the miracles, things that did not make it into the Bible, but which managed to stick around until the invention of the printing press. The irony of us being here is too bloody much."

"No it's not, man," said Ben. "You came over here to study Jesus, and now, we are officially part of his entourage."

That fact was capable of blowing Danny's mind. Atheist, agnostic, Christian or Jew, nobody could dispute the miracle that put the two of them right in the middle of Christianity-Central.

And then Ben laid it all out for them. "You know all the details of the fantastical things this guy supposedly does. We'll film him. Just keep our camcorder charged up with your solar thingy. How many memory cards do we have?"

"What?" Danny focused back on Ben. "Uh, lots. Seven or eight. But how are we going to—"

He cut himself off as a man walked over to them. The fellow looked to be about the same age as the two of them. He had bright eyes and wore a smile that showed genuine friendliness. His face was clean-shaven. Ben made a note to himself to ask this guy where he managed to get his hands on shaving supplies.

The newcomer spoke first, in Hebrew. He revealed himself at once to be an Apostle. "*Be of good cheer. I am Andrew, brother to Peter, son of Kaleb.*"

Danny couldn't help but grin as he put his hand to his chest. "*I am Daniel, uh, son of John.*" Hebrew was starting to become a little more comfortable for him.

Ben took this rite more seriously. "*I am Benjamin, son of Timothy.*"

Andrew shook each of their hands. "*Peace be with you. We are leaving shortly.*"

At that, Ben's decorum disappeared. "Wait—what?" Andrew didn't reply to Ben's English reaction, but instead gave a parting nod, and walked back to be with the others. Ben turned to Danny to continue his rant. "AGAIN? We just got here!"

— 12 —

After a long day of walking, the group finally stopped to rest, on the outskirts of a small town north of Nazareth. And like most other habitats they had passed through, this town's roads were dirt-covered, and the air was arid. Dust made its way into everyone's nostrils once again. Most of the dwellings were small, but many of them had gardens nearby, the greenery of which broke up the eternally pale-yellow landscape. One house in particular stood out among the others for its white Greek architecture and gaudy fountains. The others were the standard yellow-sand colour with flat roofs.

Two newcomers to the group had recently brought along four camels to add to the processional, so everyone's burden had become a little lighter. Ben was sitting on a fallen tree trunk, rubbing the backs of his calves. "And I used to complain about the bus ride between Toronto and Hamilton," he said aloud, to himself.

Danny was showing interest in one of the merchants near the entrance to the town, a sandy-haired woman selling garments. She was dressed in a rich cotton dress, and an ivory pendant hung around her neck. She was displaying a collection of robes she had apparently made herself. Danny sifted through them, trying to decide which one he wanted to buy. Ben stood up from his seat and walked over to join him. "How are you going to pay for that?" he whispered. Austerity was a way of life for them now, as it was for their companions. They often wondered how everyone paid their keep while on the road.

"Just pick one," replied Danny, pointing at his friend's outfit. "Unless you would prefer to wear that thing forever."

Ben looked down at the robe he had bought back in 2015. It was already getting old and wind-worn, and a tear had begun to form along the bottom. Clearly, the company that made this robe was thinking more about a costume party than a life walking in the dessert. Even the merchant looked askance at the boys' attire. But they had become quite used to being stared at like that, as almost everyone they had encountered had looked at them with curiosity or reproval.

Danny picked out a pale green shirt. It had no laces or buttons, just two sleeves and a hole for his head. It was way too large for him, but that seemed to be the preferred fashion of those around him. He then chose a dusty grey robe from the rack and placed it around his shoulders. It felt comfortable, but he had to admit to himself that he missed wearing T-shirts and jeans.

Ben still wanted to know what currency Danny had in mind to use, but he knew enough to trust that his friend had a plan. So he also picked out a shirt that looked like it came out of the wardrobe department backstage at a production of The Pirates of Penzance. *If my dad could only see me now*, he thought. Ben grabbed a dark blue robe for himself, and two small lengths of rope, tying one around his waist and passing the other one to Danny.

The vendor stepped forward to assess the boys' purchases, and made a calculation in her head. She produced a number out loud, but it meant nothing to them. Anticipating this, Danny removed a gold chain from around his neck and showed it to her. She examined it, smiled in agreement, then waved the boys on their way.

As they walked off, Ben said, "Who do you think got the better part of that deal?"

"I don't know," said Danny. "It's possible she gives a discount to all the guys who walk through town looking like they're wearing brown garbage bags."

They continued walking until they arrived at the hillside where Ben had been sitting on the tree trunk a few moments earlier. Being in a reflective mood, a small problem occurred once again to Ben. "Who pays for all of this?" he asked out loud, gesturing to their camp. "The food, our supplies. Not every town we've been to has people bringing food out to us, but we always seem to have stores for everyone."

Danny thought about it. "I remember Professor Raynor discussing it once. It was actually a point of contention among scholars that Jesus marched all over Judea without a source of income. The guy didn't exactly ask for handouts, and he didn't charge a fee for healing someone. And here, people are still bringing out food for all of us, and letting us sleep on their lands."

Ben was unconvinced. "Yeah, but those things aren't enough, I'm sure."

~ ~ ~ ~

It was supper time. Danny and Ben, eating beans with garlic and olives brought over by somebody from the town, sat apart from the rest of the group, under a clearing of trees, wearing their new outfits. When they finished their meal, Ben looked around to make sure no one was watching them. "So how are we going to do this?" he asked Danny.

Danny reached into his backpack and pulled out the box he had purchased from the vendor selling electronics outside the Lions' Gate. He split the cellophane wrapping, removed the medallion necklace with the built-in point-of-view camera, and put the empty box back into his backpack. This was the first time Danny had been able to examine his impulse purchase. He had been planning to send it back home to his brother in Canada when he bought it, but that seemed unlikely to happen now.

He set his sad thoughts aside and turned his attention to the camera. It was a pretty simple one; the face had no settings and no controls, other than one button in the centre of the medallion. This was apparently the Record/Stop button. The medallion was made in China, but the ornamental design on the face of it clearly appeared to be inspired by the Egyptians.

There was a tiny hole at the top, inside of which was a miniature microphone. On the underside of the medallion, there was a slot for a memory card. It appeared to be the same format as the cards that had been included with the camcorder he had brought from home. Upon closer inspection of the design on the face of the medallion, Danny noticed several small-sized solar panels, ensuring the camera kept its charge as long as it received regular exposure to sunlight. The tiny brown plates hadn't been visible at first, due to the way they had been camouflaged into the medallion's design.

Turning it over, Danny saw a tiny LED display on the back, illuminating the numbers 06-11-15. "November 6, 2015," he said to himself. There were also three pinhole buttons for adjusting the date.

Danny was pleased with his purchase. At a glance, it still looked like an ancient Egyptian artefact. In any case, he was sure that nobody around here would suspect that his necklace was anything other than jewellery, and certainly not a video camera.

He whispered to Ben. "I need to pull out the other camcorder. Keep six for me, okay?"

Ben grimaced. It annoyed him when Danny used expressions that nobody understood except him, his grandfather, and perhaps Ian Fleming. "Keep *what*?"

Danny rolled his eyes. "Keep six, as in six o'clock. It means, watch out behind us."

"That's delightful. You couldn't have just said, 'keep a lookout?'"

"No," said Danny. "'Keep six' is faster."

"Of course. You get the spy equipment together, and I'll keep six for you."

Ignoring the quip, Danny pulled the Sony camcorder case out of his backpack. He found several tiny plastic containers in one of the side pockets, opened one and removed a fresh memory card. It fit perfectly into the slot at the bottom of the medallion camera. He placed the Sony case back into his backpack.

Holding the POV camera in his hand, Danny pressed the button in the centre of the medallion. A small red LED light flickered on and off for an instant, indicating that the camera was in record mode. He put the vinyl cord around his neck and turned towards Ben, who posed and smiled in front of the lens.

"Check-one-two, can you hear me?"

Danny looked around at the rest of the group, a large but quiet gathering. He saw Jesus, seated in a conversation with Judas and the Apostle Philip. He turned to Ben. "I'll be right back."

Ben watched as Danny strolled nonchalantly over to Jesus, as if that was the most normal thing in the world to do. As Danny passed near them, Judas smiled up at him and Philip nodded an acknowledgement, then turned back to Jesus, who was still speaking to them.

Danny circled around and doubled back to where he had been seated with Ben. He reached up to his necklace, felt for the button in the middle, and pressed it, stopping the recording. As he sat back down beside Ben, he thought of a small complication. "How are we going to play the video back? This thing doesn't have a screen."

"You are supposed to put the memory card in a computer. But we can probably play it back on the Sony camera. Can you pass me my bag?"

All of that made sense. Ben grabbed the other camera while Danny removed the card from the medallion and passed it to him. The SD slot in the Sony was occupied, so Ben removed it and inserted the new card. He flipped open the three-inch

LCD screen and hit the 'Play' button—and there he was, posing and smiling on the screen. The picture quality was surprisingly sharp, and the sound was clear: 'Check-one-two, can you hear me?'

The two of them watched the small screen, cheek-by-jowl. The picture was a bit bumpy during the next few moments, as Danny had been walking away. But the jittering stopped when he had stopped walking. Jesus, Judas and Philip filled the small video frame. Jesus could be heard speaking to the others.

Ben turned the Sony off and closed the LCD screen. He removed the card and gave it back to Danny, who replaced it back into his POV camera. The two of them looked at each other incredulously. "Jesus Christ," Danny said. "We just captured Jesus Christ on video." Both of them pondered the implications of that for a moment, and then he continued. "I think this pretty-much guarantees top marks on my thesis."

Ben looked at him doubtfully. "Do you think so?" he said. "I can't wait to see how you present the video to Professor Raynor. He'll just say that Jesus is actually Travis McLeod in a flannel toga and sandals."

— 13 —

The group was on the move again. The landscape had thankfully offered up alternatives to sand, by way of yellow mountains and brown valleys. They even passed the occasional farmer, with a field full of crops. Danny and Ben had stopped complaining about the travelling. At this point, the two of them had accepted that their lot in life was to walk, sleep on the ground, then get up and do it all again. Sometimes, a townsperson would provide actual indoor accommodations, but there were usually just enough beds or cots for the thirteen important people—Jesus and the twelve Apostles. The rest of them, disciples and followers, usually fended for themselves. On occasion, Ben and Danny were given cots to sleep on—and they were glorious—though Danny had remarked that the cots were too small to allow him to invite one of the local young ladies to join him. This comment had been made on the road north of Nazareth. Hearing this made Ben grumpy. "Are you actually complaining about your bed?" he asked. "We'll probably be sleeping on the ground again tomorrow."

Danny wasn't thinking that far ahead. "Yeah, but have you ever tried to be with a girl while in a cot? It's probably worse than trying to get it on in a hammock or a waterbed."

Ben reflected on his own unadventurous past attempts at romance. "You've tried both of those places, I assume?"

"Yeah, the waterbed was ok; the hammock, not so much."

They continued to walk, and Ben wanted a change of topic. He pointed to the medallion camera Danny was still wearing around his neck. "I don't know if that thing is going to do us much good," he remarked. "We're not exactly part of Jesus' inner group."

"Well," said Danny. "We could give it to someone else to wear."

Ben looked around at the people walking along with them, spread out in bunches all over the dirt road. "Who?"

Danny also glanced behind them. "Someone like—" The Apostle Andrew was walking up behind them. "Like this guy," finished Danny.

They fell in step with Andrew, who smiled at them with his clean-shaven face. He put his hand on Ben's shoulder. *"We are happy you both could be with us. These days, we need as many allies as possible."*

Danny didn't catch the meaning for the Hebrew word "allies," but he had a pretty good idea what Andrew's point was. Ben took the lead: *"What do you mean?"*

The road began to ascend slightly, as Andrew explained himself. *"Some people are angry with the Master's words. But he does nothing to put them at ease."* For the first time since meeting each other, Andrew took a good, long look at the faces of the Canadians. He was curious but not accusatory when he asked them, *"Where are you both from?"*

Happy to be treated on such friendly terms, Ben dropped his guard. *"I grew up in Nazareth, but I moved to Canada when—"*

Danny belted Ben open-handed on his shoulder. "Hey!"

Ben slapped his own forehead, but Andrew turned his attention to Danny, looking at the necklace he was wearing. *"That is a very interesting—what is that?"*

Danny didn't know the Hebrew word for "necklace" but he knew what he had to do. He looked at Ben, who nodded. Then he geared himself up for Salesman Mode, palming the medallion and caressing it. *"THIS, my friend,"* Danny began. *"This is my favourite, um—"* He leaned into Ben's ear. "How do you say, 'accessory?'"

"I don't know. Try, *'jewellery.'*"

Danny tried again. *"This is my favourite...jewellery."*

Andrew looked fascinated, or at least suitably impressed. Danny removed the medallion and put it around Andrew's neck. *"Here: I want you to have it."*

Andrew was delighted. *"This is beautiful,"* he said. *"Where did you get it?"*

Danny looked over at Ben, as if he really didn't know where the necklace came from. Ben faced Andrew. *"It came from a merchant we met in our travels, far away from here."*

Andrew seemed to accept the explanation and, more importantly, he accepted the "gift". He embraced both boys and walked away.

As Andrew walked off, Ben gave Danny his furrowed brow and tight-lipped frown. "Hey, Stupid: you forgot to hit record on that thing."

Danny watched Andrew move among the other disciples. "The real problem," he said, "is how to get it back from him when it's time to watch the videos."

~ ~ ~ ~

Four weeks had passed since Danny and Ben had first walked through the tunnel, and they were still adjusting to things. Every time they thought they had become comfortable with their new way of life, something would come along to let them know they were still strangers in this strange land.

The group was eating a meal, resting in a field by the Jordan River. It was not a lush meadow, rather, it was another expanse of dirt, with occasional green or brown vegetation cropping up. Jesus and all twelve of the Apostles were present, as well as a couple dozen disciples.

Danny and Ben were seated together with Andrew and Matthew, enjoying each other's company. They were all laughing except Danny, who was focused on three women, eating their own meals in a nearby area within the troupe. At first glance, they looked not unlike any of the other females encountered in the towns, Mediterranean beauties with ornate robes, bejewelled hands and light headscarves. But Danny could see that something was different about these three women. They possessed an inordinate amount of grandeur in the way they carried themselves. He had first seen them with their group a couple of weeks ago, and had noticed that they did not carry supplies or do any chores. They also appeared to command a near equal amount of reverence as that received by the Apostles.

One of the women, the shortest and prettiest of the three, had long brown hair that flowed down from under her headscarf. The woman beside her possessed a certain air of royalty, which made her look out of place among this lot, though she did not appear uncomfortable with her station. The third was fairly tall, a kind-faced graceful woman whose years of hardship made her look a little older than she probably was. Her two companions appeared to defer to her.

As the meal ended, Andrew and Matthew rose up and walked away, leaving Danny and Ben alone. Danny looked over at the women again. He caught the attention of the shortest one, and received a smile from her. But he didn't know what to make of it. The smile could either mean, "I'm just being polite—don't bother me," or else, "Come on over here and say hello to me." For the first time since he had started university, Danny was unable to interpret a girl's smile, nor was he able to discern her age.

Fighting back mild panic, he turned to Ben, sitting beside him. Ben, his best friend in the world (this one and the last one), was not going to be any help. Ben was usually uncomfortable speaking to any woman who did not possess the moniker "Mrs." or "Professor". Or Mom.

Knowing that he was about to wade into unfamiliar territory, Danny ran his fingers through his hair and stood up. He put on his most charming smile, and turned around, walking towards the three women.

But they had already walked away. Apparently, the object of Danny's affections did not in fact wish him to go over there and say hello.

Ben was sympathetic. "Rejected, even without a cool opening line."

Danny sat back down. "My Hebrew is still clumsy," he said.

"Well, it's coming along fairly well, all things considered," replied Ben.

"I can understand it pretty well now, but I still feel like an idiot stumbling over my words."

"Past tense is brutal," Ben conceded. "Worse than French."

Danny was still looking over towards where the three women had been sitting. They had not actually walked that far away; all he had to do was walk over to where they now stood and introduce himself to the shorter one with the "come hither" look. But not yet. He turned to his friend.

"Ben, you know when someone comes over from Quebec, and they speak English with a thick French accent?"

"You mean like Jean-François?"

"Yeah, and every time he opens his mouth, the girls want to throw themselves at his feet."

Ben knew exactly what he was talking about. He hated that about Jean-François, despite the fact that he was a great guy. "What's your point?"

Danny thought about his question. "When I speak Hebrew with my Canadian accent, do I sound charming like Jean-François?"

Ben laughed out loud. "You mean, will girls throw themselves at your feet because of your accent?"

"Yeah, kind of." Now Danny felt ridiculous.

Ben, still laughing, said, "No. Your dumb, clumsy accent isn't going to help you at all."

Danny frowned. "Now you're being mean."

"Dan, you're better off keeping your mouth shut. Nobody here but you has blue eyes, and some of the girls have been looking at you like, well, I can't tell if they're freaked out or horny. Maybe both."

"I think I need some help translating my flirting."

"I think you need some help learning how to flirt with women who don't care that you can play Bon Jovi on the guitar."

Danny saw that the three women walked back over to where they had been standing earlier. They were looking at him again, or at least in his direction, with intrigue, or perhaps curiosity. He got to his feet, his mind made up. He swaggered on over to the ladies, who giggled as he approached. Ben watched as Danny put his normally infallible charm on the woman who appeared to be the closest to his own age, then watched as she laughed at him. Danny tried to engage her in conversation, no doubt asking where she was from. With no success, he turned around and headed back over to Ben. The women chuckled again as Danny walked away.

"That was embarrassing," he said.

"What?" said Ben. "Doesn't she want to go back to your place and hang out, listen to music?"

Danny shook his head. "She's Mary. From Magdala."

"So?" Ben missed it.

"Mary Magdalene," said Danny. "She's pretty-much already spoken for, as Jesus' concubine. And that makes her quite a bit older than she looks."

Ben decided to take on a new tactic. With no responsible adults around to control Danny, the job fell to him. "You know you can't sleep with anyone here, right? Or do we need to discuss the Butterfly Effect?"

Danny grimaced. "What?"

Ben was getting impatient. "That's where you step on a butterfly in the past, and next thing you know, you've changed the course of—"

"I know what the Butterfly Effect is. I just don't think it's—well, it shouldn't prevent me from getting lucky."

Ben smiled. "Don't worry; your personality will look after that."

— 14 —

The entire group was once again on the move, this time heading west on yet another dirty road, kicking up dust as they marched. A modest-looking city could be seen up ahead, surrounded by a slightly fortified wall barring entry to undesirables. Spires and pillars protruded from behind the wall, displaying the wealth that the city once possessed. The entrance gate was not large and elaborate like those in Jerusalem; there would be only one sentry. Danny and Ben knew they would be welcomed into the city, what with the company they were keeping. As usual, the two of them made up the rear of the ensemble. Just ahead of them, the Apostle Matthew turned around and acknowledged them. They caught up to him and fell into step. Ben addressed him in Hebrew. "*What city is that?*" he asked.

Matthew was not known for his verbosity. "*Nain,*" he said. He quickened his pace, and the Canadians were alone again.

"I know what happens in Nain," Danny began. "This is where Jesus raises some guy from the dead. I think we're going to see a miracle today."

Ben looked at him doubtfully. "But that assumes Jesus only made one visit to that city. I'm quite sure they toured all up and down the countryside several times. That event could have happened during another visit."

Danny shrugged his shoulders. "Let's plan for the best-case scenario."

They still had a little way to go before reaching the town gates. Out of view of the others, Ben took the camcorder out of his backpack and turned it on. He directed it towards Danny, who held up an imaginary microphone below his chin, like a newscaster. "Thanks, Jimmy. We're here, about a half-kilometre from the front gate of the city of Nain. Our sources tell us that Jesus will be performing a miracle today. We'll just have to wait and see. Back to you, Jimmy."

Ben stopped recording, and chuckled just enough to not encourage his friend any further. He kept the camcorder in his hand, but held it within the folds of his robe. As they got closer to the town entrance, they could see that a small delegation was coming out, walking down the road to meet them. Ben and Danny elbowed their way close enough to the front of their group to see what was going to happen. Of the people that emerged from the town, one man—the prefect—looked stately in his dress, a thin crimson velvet cloak. After a few words from him, Peter and Judas began to discuss the group's entry into the city. It appeared that there were conditions to be met before the group would be permitted to enter and seek out food and lodging.

The taller of the two women who had been accompanying Mary Magdalene stepped forward and approached Judas. She had a majesty about her as she reached into her satchel and produced a small leather bag, which she handed over to him. He received it, and looked at Jesus, who nodded. Judas recorded the transaction on a papyrus ledger, and passed the small bag onto Peter.

Peter turned and handed the bag to the guardian of the gate, who emptied the contents into the palm of his hand. Coins poured out, clinking onto each other. After a moment's assessment, the man pocketed the money, then stood aside for the group to continue the rest of the way into the city. As everybody started to pick up their belongings, Ben saw Andrew nearby, wearing the medallion POV camera around his neck. Ben walked over and put his hand on Andrew's back to get his attention, then pointed to Mary's friend. *"Who is that woman? The one with the purse."* he asked.

"She is a woman of considerable influence. Her name is Joanna," replied Andrew. As they watched, Jesus stepped

forward and kissed the woman's forehead in thanks. *"She is the wife of Chuza, who manages King Herod's household."*

"What is she doing with us?" Ben found it peculiar, hearing himself speak in the first person regarding Jesus' disciples. Danny noticed it as well, but chose not to address it just yet.

Andrew smiled at the memory of meeting Joanna for the first time. *"About a year ago, she witnessed The Teacher perform a miracle outside Jerusalem. She eventually came down from the palace to meet Jesus and inquire after his ministry. She spent most of that day with us, listening to Jesus preach."*

"And she is now one of the disciples?" Ben asked.

"These days, she spends a bit of time with us, more so when Chuza is away. King Herod would not be happy knowing his steward's wife supports Jesus."

"She supports him?" put in Danny.

"Yes she does," continued Andrew. *"She is a very wealthy woman, and Chuza does not ask where her money goes—where HIS money goes."* Andrew pointed to the other woman who was usually seen with Mary and Joanna, now wearing a dull green gemstone around her neck. *"And that's Suzanna. She is the wife of one of the most successful merchants in Galilee. She also believes in our cause. She and Joanna are glad to pay for our expenses as we travel the land, spreading the word of Jesus. Her money just ensured that we will be given food and beds while we are here."*

At that, the group started to move, continuing the rest of the way down the road to the gate of Nain. Danny moved himself close to Andrew, abruptly changing the subject. *"That looks good on you,"* he remarked. He reached out to fondle the necklace, hitting the record button in the middle of the medallion, then watched as the tiny red LED flickered, indicating that it was now recording. Andrew smiled at his jewellery and marched forward to the front of the processional with Jesus, where he belonged.

Danny fell back to walk with Ben, who still had the camcorder on 'record-ready'. Up ahead, Jesus, with the Apostles Judas, Peter and John, arrived at the town gate. The gate-keeper, having been sufficiently bribed, escorted them to the entrance and stepped aside to let them all pass through, but the gate was abruptly flung open from the inside. The Apostles stepped quickly out of the way as a small crowd of townsfolk burst through, carrying a stretcher on which a wretched young man lay still.

Four men bore the stretcher. An older woman, likely the man's mother, walked behind them, sobbing to herself. As they passed through, followed by the other townsfolk, it was clear that this was a funeral procession; a dead body was being carried away for burial. In this case, the courteous thing for the newcomers to do was to step aside and respectfully let the processional pass. Dead bodies were thought to be unclean and, according to the Law of Moses, still adopted here, anyone who came into contact with a corpse was to be thought of as adulterated, dirty, for a period of two days and nights.

Everyone outside the gate stepped dutifully aside to let the funeral procession pass—except Jesus. He stepped in front of the stretcher, blocking the bearers' path. At first, the townsfolk were stunned, then shocked, as Jesus put his hand, his bare hand, on the dead man's chest.

The crowd closed in towards the stretcher, disciples and townsfolk both. Danny pushed his way through, and managed to secure himself a ringside spot, right behind one of the stretcher-bearers. His elbow brushed against Jesus' arm.

Ben remained about ten feet back, trying to surreptitiously capture the event on video. Looking down through the viewfinder, he could see Danny next to Jesus. On the other side of the stretcher, beside the weeping mother, stood

Andrew, unknowingly recording everything with his necklace camcorder.

Danny took in the scene. The young man sure enough appeared to be dead. Feeling brazen, Danny leaned forward slightly, reached out and touched the man's neck, feeling for a pulse. He was immediately pushed aside by one of the bearers, just as Jesus touched the dead man's forehead.

Jesus spoke words in Aramaic, words that could be heard throughout the entire crowd of people. *"Young man, I say to you, rise up."*

Without hesitating, the man on the stretcher obeyed Jesus' words, as if he had simply been waiting to be told to do so. He sat straight up, and the crowd gasped, one collective sound. The young man looked around with bewilderment. He felt the back of his head for a moment, then stepped to the ground with understandable trepidation. The crowd applauded and gave praise for Jesus' miracle, and shouted out happiness for the young man. In all the commotion, Danny managed to walk forward and reach over to Andrew. He then hit the center of the medallion, turning the recording off. In short order, the whole group was welcomed through the gates into the city, and everyone was soon led through the streets to a garden-laden courtyard within a large opulent temple, grapevines twisting their way up its walls. Two large statues of intimidating-looking Greek gods overlooked the visitors, as if daring them to misbehave.

After a few minutes, platters of food were brought out and everyone feasted, surrounded by vegetation.

Danny and Ben received their food and drink, cold, pickled sausages filled with garlic, then found a corner to themselves. Danny didn't start eating just yet. He looked squarely at Ben. "He's not dead," he said.

"I can see that," Ben replied, looking over at the former dead man laughing and eating with the others.

"No," said Danny. "He wasn't dead to begin with. The guy had a pulse."

Ben stopped chewing his bread. "So what just happened out there?"

"I don't know. I saw it, but..." Danny shook his head in disbelief. "I don't think Jesus raised the dead. What the hell is going on?"

Ben thought about it for a moment. "That guy's mother seems to think her son got brought back from death."

"I don't know," said Danny. "At best, the dude was sick, or in a coma or something."

— 15 —

Growing up in Hamilton, Ben was not a jock by any means, but he certainly was not a nerd. He did not try out for sports teams at school because he knew he would not get picked for anything. Even in Phys-Ed, his classmates knew that no team would benefit from his participation. This knowledge did not usually weigh too heavily on Ben, but sometimes he thought about how good it might have been to be on the football team—or at least to have the opportunity to speak with the kind of girls who would fawn over the guys on the football team.

Ben's outlook changed one day as he stood nearly naked in the Jordan River, with its large willow tree branches extending over the water. Many of the disciples would come down to the river to bathe, and he and Danny would look after each other's belongings. As Ben rinsed himself off in the knee-deep water, he caught Danny looking over his body, a peculiar expression on his face.

For the first time in a long while, Ben felt embarrassed to be without his clothes. "What the hell, man," he started. "Why are you looking at me like that?"

Danny just laughed, and said, "Hold on. Don't move."

"Dude, just pass me the old robe so I can dry off."

"No. Wait there." Danny pulled out his smartphone, looked around to see that the others were sufficiently distracted, and took a snapshot of his friend, standing in the river with a scowl on his bearded face. "Wonderful. Thank you; you look lovely." He dug into Ben's backpack. "Here's your robe."

Ben took the robe from Danny. It was one of the original robes they had bought from the merchant in 2015. These days, it came in handy as a towel and a pillow.

After he dried off, Ben took the phone that Danny held out to him. He looked at the photograph of himself, and his jaw dropped. The young man in the picture had his face and his ever-growing brown beard, but the body was not one that he recognized. "I have muscles," he exclaimed.

"Yes you do," said Danny, laughing some more. Ben looked at his photo again. He now saw the effects of walking all day, every day for the past few weeks, with the weight of all his worldly possessions on his back. His arms and shoulders were muscular, his belly had abs that he had only seen on the cover of men's fitness magazines. Now, he felt ready to join a football team—if only he could figure out how to throw the stupid oblong ball.

"Think about our diet," Danny said, as he undressed to bathe. Ben looked his friend's body over for physical changes, but Dan had always been fit and trim. If nothing else, he had a better tan.

"Yeah," said Ben, considering their current lifestyle. "No fast food, no steaks, no donuts."

Soon, the group was called back to the road, and they moved on, heading to another town. As they walked, Ben had all the time in the world to get lost in his thoughts. "So this is my life now," was a notion that made its way to the front of his mind.

~ ~ ~ ~

At the back of the group, allowing themselves a cautious distance behind the others, Ben and Danny hopped and skipped as they walked. In a way, they were almost dancing. Each had his smart phone in hand.

"I've got one. Here," said Ben. He passed his earbuds to Danny, who put them in his ears. Ben hit play on his phone.

Danny heard a recognizable voice, over distorted electric guitars: "...*my word, it didn't come, it doesn't maaaatter...*" His face lit up. "That's easy—Tragically Hip, Courage." He returned the earbuds to Ben and replaced them with his own, dialling up a song. "OK, gimme a sec."

Name That Tune: Rock Band Edition was on.

After a moment, Danny passed his earbuds to Ben. He hit 'Play', and Ben could hear a white man rap over top of a quick-paced funky-ska sound: "...*hold it now and watch the hoodwink, as I make you stop think...*"

It took until the chorus before Ben was able to shout out, "Barenaked Ladies! One Week—great tune."

Danny stopped the song. "I never thought I'd actually need a Desert Island collection," he mused.

"I always thought that was a stupid analogy," said Ben. "If I'm on a deserted island with my ten favourite CDs, what the heck am I going to play them on?" He tucked his smartphone away.

"I guess that concept came out before MP3s and playlists. Alright, my turn." Danny gave Ben one earbud and kept the other for himself. They walked shoulder to shoulder so they could listen to the next song together. The opening guitar riff from "The Spirit of Radio" by Rush, blasted through their earphones. Ben held up his arms to air-guitar it, while Danny played air-drums with his fists waving invisible drumsticks in relative time to Neil Peart's intricate drum fills.

Right there, at the back of the caravan of people, Ben decided for the first time since arriving in this world, that perhaps his life wasn't all that bad. He felt his muscular left bicep as he played his imaginary Fender Stratocaster, and pictured himself standing up to a bully in a bar. "Hey, let her go, man; she doesn't want you to bother her." The jock would see Ben's muscles outlined in his too-small T-shirt and walk away, knowing what was good for him. The girl would be thankful for being rescued, and run her hand along his chest, looking up at—

A hand slapped Ben hard, across the top of his head, sending the earbuds and his thoughts flying off into the dirt. The Apostles Philip and James had come up from behind the boys. Philip grabbed the phone out of Danny's hand. The earbuds popped out of the headphone jack and the music stopped abruptly. Philip held the device in his hand and examined it. He immediately started shouting at them, in Hebrew. "*What is this?*"

Danny made a poor attempt at nonchalance: "*Hello, Philip; hello, James. Peace.*"

Philip looked at the device in his hand as if it might explode. "*How did you come by this thing?*" He was still shouting.

"*It's mine.*" Danny spoke calmly, hoping to encourage Philip to do the same. But Philip's anger only increased in the face of such pestilence.

Ben stepped in front of Danny and put his palm gently on Philip's chest. "*Peace, brother,*" he said. "*We bought that from a merchant we met before we came to Jerusalem. I don't know where it came from.*"

Philip's shouting started to attract the notice of the others up ahead. Some of them stopped walking and turned around, watching the spectacle.

"*Lies!*" Philip pointed an index finger at Ben, pushing it hard into his chest. Ben no longer felt like the tough-guy in his daydream of a few seconds earlier, and so was thoroughly relieved when Judas appeared on the scene and stood between him and Philip.

Judas spoke quietly, and with authority, as if his suggestion was in fact a directive to his fellow Apostles: "*Let them be, friends.*"

In the tableau that followed, Danny, seeing the wisdom in holding his tongue, reached over and gently slipped the smartphone out of Philip's hand. Unhappy with Judas' attempt to mollify him, Philip spun around, but Danny had already tucked the device away into his backpack.

James faced Judas gravely, waving a hand at the Canadians. *"These two will bring the Roman Guard down on us with that evil thing."*

Judas started walking ahead, an indication that the others were to do the same. *"We must be careful, yes, but fighting amongst ourselves will not help things."*

James would not back down. He scowled at the boys. *"We do not know these men with their strange ways and their strange tongues."*

"They have been followers since Nazareth," said Judas. *"Here for the same reason as you and me—and the Master accepts them."*

Philip shook his head. *"It's foolish of him to do so. They are spies or demons."*

"They are neither," said Jesus.

Nobody had noticed Jesus' arrival, Mary Magdalene at his side. Philip looked at him with shock, upset that his words had been overheard.

"These boys are messengers." Jesus touched Danny's shoulder. *"When they are ready, they will give me their message."*

Jesus smiled and walked off ahead with Mary. When they saw that he was out of sight, Philip and James turned on Danny and Ben.

"What message?" Philip growled. *"What is he talking about?"*

Danny began nervously with, *"I don't actually know..."*

"Of course you do!" yelled James. *"Are you saying Jesus is lying or that he is mistaken?"*

Danny stared down at the dirt road and sighed. *"I don't have any message for anyone."*

James looked accusingly at Judas.

— 16 —

Jesus of Nazareth continued to travel around the holy lands with the Apostles and his disciples, two of whom had come from far away and who spoke with mysteriously indiscernible accents. Some of the Apostles were tolerant of the two strangers; others, like Judas, Matthew and Andrew, went so far as to regard them as friends. This made some of the others uneasy, and therefore sceptical towards the strangers.

Ben and Danny, for their part, knew where they stood with everyone. They knew not to trust anyone; they knew they could confide in nobody except each other, as it was far too easy to inadvertently reveal their ignorance to those around them. It seemed that the people of this time would crucify anyone for any fraction of an offence, for displaying behaviour deemed unacceptable or bizarre by the authorities.

Yet, despite all of this, Ben and Danny were accepted by Jesus, and were therefore of the stature of disciples. Ben had a hard time with this position; he had difficulty accepting this incredibly significant change in his life. It was easier for him to acknowledge the physical changes in himself and in Danny—their hair was longer, their beards were fuller.

Ben had never set out to follow anyone. He had no plans to modify his beliefs, no plans to renounce his Jewish upbringing. He liked who he was, and he embraced his religion. But if he acknowledged the possibility of Jesus being the Messiah, would that jeopardize his Jewish identity? He wished Rabbi Katzen were here to help him figure that out. Rabbi Katzen was so knowledgeable that other churches in Hamilton, *Christian assemblies*, often invited him to speak for their congregations.

Ben played out an imaginary conversation in his mind. He wasn't even sure exactly what his question would be, but he was quite certain Rabbi Katzen would reply to his query by saying, "This changes nothing, son. Keep your mind open. You are still Jewish, and you're surrounded by Jews. Jesus' teachings are based on Jewish principles—so what's all the fuss about?"

It was the middle of the afternoon, and the group had recently passed through the town of Bethsaida, near the Sea of Galilee. The air was hot and humid, almost a welcome change from being hot and dry. They had situated themselves on the crest of a large hill. Jesus sat at the top, above everyone, while the disciples spread out on the ground devoid of grass, making themselves comfortable while listening to the sermon.

Danny took notes. Since becoming a disciple, he had been able to discreetly use his notepad and pencil, and jot down thoughts, reactions and ideas, while Jesus spoke. Ben found it best to pull out his phone and just record the sermons. He could keep the smartphone in his hand and still capture the video, with nobody the wiser.

Listening to Jesus preach, Ben was amazed at how easily he found he could relate to Jesus as a fellow Jew. He couldn't help thinking that Rabbi Katzen would appreciate meeting Jesus, Messiah or not.

The Apostle Matthew passed Danny a flask of red wine. He drank from it and gave it to Ben who, at Matthew's urging, passed it on to the two men sitting beside him. Life was good.

Danny pulled out his smartphone out of habit. With a smile, he noted that nobody had emailed him lately, and he also saw his battery was low. "Ben, do you have the solar charger?" he asked. Ben nodded and took his friend's phone to charge it up. He looked around at the other disciples gathered with him, and remarked to himself that the crowd appeared to be growing. Their numbers of course changed from town to town as more people joined and others left, but this afternoon's sermon attracted a larger-than-usual lot.

Over the other side of the hill, an immense group of people started to make its way up to the area near where Jesus sat. Ben turned around and looked at the bottom of the hill, only to see another horde headed towards them. There were so many people, it looked as if they were gathering for an open-air rock concert, like one he had attended in Toronto the previous summer.

Where they sat on the hill, they were close enough to the Sea of Galilee that they could see boats drifting towards them. Within an hour, the boats had all docked, and the occupants, many hundreds of them, climbed up the hill to join the party.

As hundreds more people arrived on foot, on camel-back, and by sea, somebody designated himself the resident scribe, and stood up to take a census of the gathering. The boys knew the number five thousand would make it into the history books, into the Bible, regardless of the actual number of people present. Nonetheless, the hillside was covered with faces where, two hours earlier, there had only been Jesus and his companions.

Danny and Ben knew what was going to happen, and they knew what they had to do. Danny stood up to go find Andrew. Ben opened his backpack and pulled out the camcorder. He checked the memory card, and saw that it still had plenty of space on it; the amount of recording they had done had barely put a dent in that card's capacity. As for the camera itself, it still looked brand new.

~ ~ ~ ~

As Danny navigated his way around the hillside, he wondered how he was ever going to be able to activate the medallion camera around Andrew's neck without revealing what he was up to. He saw then how their great idea was starting to have some complications. Danny thought perhaps he could switch on the camera if he hugged Andrew. These guys were always hugging each other—when they part ways, reunite, or when somebody suggests a good song for all to sing. But the hugs were usually a manly embrace, not so much chest-to-chest. That was probably a good thing, or else their medallion camera would likely be turning itself on and off with each hug Andrew gave or received.

    The density of the crowd thickened as Danny approached the summit. People pushed him back when he tried to pass through. Presently, he spotted Andrew. The Apostle was trying to direct traffic, and looked ready to give up as more newcomers attempted to get up the hill. Danny walked towards Andrew and waved at him, but at the last moment, he decided against the hug ploy. Pretending to trip, he threw himself at Andrew and bumped into his chest. Andrew braced himself from falling back, and Danny saw the LED flash as he hit the medallion's button. After an apology and a shared laugh, Andrew headed back up to be with Jesus. Danny attempted to follow him, wondering then how many more times he was going to be able to pull off that trick. The Apostle Peter saw him and grabbed his forearm. *"Go down the hill with Thomas and Simon. Help them arrange the people in groups of fifty."*

    Danny, pleased as he was by the speed with which he had been able to pick up Hebrew, did not know the Hebrew word for "fifty." But, once again, his knowledge of scripture assisted him in filling in the blanks—he remembered that the people on the hill had been split up into groups of fifty.

    At the top of the hill, Jesus held court under the pleasant afternoon sun. The other Apostles stayed near him. Before Danny turned to descend the hill, he saw James holding two baskets, each looking worn and dusty. He knew that one likely contained a couple of fish, and the other a loaf of bread—as a child, he had been told the parable of Jesus feeding the multitudes with just that. Simon saw Danny coming, and directed him towards the other side of the hill, away from the sea.

Danny did his best to control his area of the crowd, but the people around him ignored his directives, deciding instead to roam where they chose to roam. Danny heard a shout go up from the top of the hill, and a basket teeming with fish was passed down. Exclaims of delight and surprise were heard throughout the hillside. Empty baskets were produced by the people on the hill, and were sent up to be replenished with fish. Then came the bread. Someone put eight loaves in Danny's hand, and he passed them to the people below him.

I guess I'm a waiter now, Danny thought. He unloaded another armful of bread, then headed back up towards where Jesus was situated. As he walked, he looked around for Ben, who was supposed to be filming this event, this miracle. But all he could see were hundreds or, quite possibly, thousands of people distributing the feast that came from on high. In short time, he saw Ben farther down the hill, waving his arms. There were probably four or five hundred people between them. Danny felt himself becoming annoyed; Ben was supposed to be the one filming this miracle up close, but he was nowhere near the action. Danny reached into the side pocket of his knapsack to record the video from his phone, but remembered that he had given it to Ben to charge for him. Ben clearly came to the same observation; Danny saw him farther away down the hill, waving the camcorder in the air, the crowds too focused on the free food to notice the strange object. Looking around the hillside, the two of them saw how much food had already been passed around. It occurred to them that the miracle might be over in the next few seconds. Ben, seeing that Danny was much closer to the action, motioned to his friend to get ready to make a catch. He held his arm back to throw the camera over the heads of the crowd. Before Danny even had a chance to consider what a crazy idea it was, Ben hurled the device into the air, with all the skill of a drunken gorilla. Danny followed the arc of the object with his eyes, caught the sun full-on in his face, then braced for impact, knowing the camera was sure to clock him on the head.

It didn't hit him at all. A moment after Danny lost sight of the flying object, he heard a clunking sound near him, followed by an expletive that was sure to be Aramaic. He spun around and saw a person in a simple robe holding onto the top of his own head. The man appeared to be in pain, and was not happy about it. Danny tried to make himself invisible while the fellow looked around for his attacker. He crouched down on his knees to search for the camera. As it was silver, he knew it would be fairly easy to spot—by him or by anyone else. He found it resting between somebody's feet, a few steps away. Danny kept to the ground and slithered his way over to his quarry. He picked up the camera, slipped it under his robe, then dashed away from the commotion.

Danny pushed his way as close as he could to where Jesus and the Apostles were stationed. Praying that the fancy camcorder could indeed sustain a tumble, he flipped it open and was relieved to see the 'record-ready' icon illuminated. He started filming again, camouflaging the camera in the folds of his robe while he shot. Through the three-inch LCD screen, and with his own eyes, Danny saw Jesus, with the help of Peter and John, reaching into large baskets in front of him and passing out scoopfuls of fish and armloads of bread. It appeared as if the food had been there all along. Danny did not witness a miraculous duplication of foods; he did not see fish and bread multiplying themselves.

After a minute or two, he turned his camera off, put it in his backpack, and made his way over to find Andrew, who was still near the top of the hill. As Danny reached over and hit the button on Andrew's chest, he decided that he didn't care if his movements were questioned. But Andrew said nothing, probably chalking up the strange actions to a custom of his homeland.

Danny headed back down to find Ben. Someone passed him a chunk of bread, and he chewed on it as he walked. He could see small fires dotting the entire hillside. By the time he located his companion, who was settled in with a friendly-looking group of people, the sun was starting to set. Ben's new acquaintances were gathered around a fire on which a dozen fish were frying. Quietly, Danny sat down beside his friend. Everyone ate with gusto, but Danny was not in the mood to celebrate with the others. There was enough noise that nobody paid attention when he and Ben started to quietly speak English to each other.

"So what did you see up there? Did he grow extra fish? Did you see a little easy-bake oven or something?"

Danny shook his head. "There was no miracle here today. I don't know where all the food came from; I think he just had some big baskets sitting behind him or something, I don't know." The smell of fried fish was all around him. "I'm not hungry, but I should probably eat. Load me up, ok?"

He ate his fill, then the two of them found a nearby area of ground to stretch out on for the evening. The beauty of the constellations was lost upon him that night.

— 17 —

A spectacular golden-red sunrise greeted the morning on the hill. Most of the fires on the hillside had burned themselves out. Music could be heard from two different areas nearby, singing and some hand percussion from the hangers-on who had celebrated throughout the night.

The Canadians were still amazed at how they could sleep outside nearly all year round in this climate. It was a luxury for both of them, though Danny felt he would probably get depressed when the hockey season came and went without him. He wasn't sure if he would be more upset about not hitting the ice with his pals, or about watching the Toronto Maple Leafs take another beating.

All around them, people started to rise up and ready themselves for their journeys back to wherever they had come from. The disciples, spread out throughout the crowd, all started to regroup at the top, where the Apostles directed the gathering of their supplies.

When Danny and Ben arrived, Peter gave them each a chore, and they busied themselves with the others. Andrew approached them to talk about the incredible events of the day before. He had witnessed firsthand how Jesus had been able to feed all those thousands of people with only five loaves of bread and two fish.

Danny was quick to question him. *"But how did he do it?"* he asked.

Andrew looked at him excitedly. *"Nobody knows how the Teacher works his wonders."* He smiled, then turned and went about his business.

Although it had been interesting meeting new people around their campfire the night before, Danny and Ben were glad to be on the move again. Life was easier with a group of fifty or sixty, much easier than with five thousand.

Their new destination proved to be an easy stroll; they arrived by the middle of the afternoon. All through the day's walk, the scenery had been beautiful, as the road had taken them along the rolling-hill shoreline of the Sea of Galilee. Having grown up on the shore of the enormous Lake Ontario, Danny found it peculiar how the small body of water before him could be considered a sea.

<<Photo06>>

Peter had sent someone ahead to make arrangements. The plan was to sail to Capernaum, on the west side of the water. Three wooden boats were docked and waiting. Ben had expected them to be primitive and rickety. Each had only one mast, but the hull could easily accommodate twelve people or so. As the nearest boat unfurled its sail, it became clear that the crafts were actually strong, capable sea-worthy vessels.

The blue, dulcet water was a welcome sight for the Canadians, especially this close up—in their travels here, baths were sometimes hard to come by. Everybody dropped their belongings on the ground off the roadside, and those without immediate duties headed straight for the water. Danny and Ben waded in up to their hips. They bent over, brought water up to their heads and scrubbed their faces. It was chilly, but invigorating. Danny looked around him and noticed that the group of bathers was made up only of men. On the shore, the women were working. In their travels, the men and women seemed to share the chores, but it was always the men who received their meals and necessities first.

A large fire had already been started. Not everyone would be going on to the boats, so some were preparing to settle in for the evening, to wait for the others' return. Other than the Twelve, it was not known who else would be sailing. In any case, a large meal was prepared for everybody.

The men dried off and came ashore to eat. Danny and Ben sat down, ready to devour whatever food was put before them. Somebody passed around a basket. The boys each reached in to help themselves to a portion of cheese, bread and olives, then they passed the basket on to the next person. Danny opened his mouth to eat, then put his foot back down. He noticed the women waiting for their meals. There were four of them, including Mary Magdalene. Joanna and Susanna were not with the group that night, having been sent ahead to make arrangements in Capernaum. There were three food baskets circulating around. Two of them quickly emptied, and were not replenished. The third and apparently final basket was nowhere near the women.

"Give me your food," Danny said to his friend.

"What? You've got your own."

Danny grabbed Ben's bread away from him and stood up. Along with his own untouched meal, he walked over to the women. The ladies seemed resolved to the fact that they might not receive the same meal as the men, if anything at all, that evening.

Danny approached them and smiled. He held out his food offerings to the women. For a moment, they didn't move, just returned his gaze. As he stood there proffering the food, a sharp kick to the back off his calf sent him straight to the ground. He bounced his head on the dirt as the bread and cheese tumbled out of his hands. Too stunned to move, Danny opened his eyes to see a skinny hairy leg stamping on the ground in front of his nose, squishing the fallen food. He pushed himself up onto his hands and knees and brushed the dirt out of his face. As he rose to his feet, Danny knew there was a chance he would get knocked down again. When he came upright, he faced his aggressor, a Canaanite man who had only joined the group that very morning, a recent follower from the hill at Bethsaida.

What Danny found peculiar was the fact that the fellow, for all his manly facial hair and thin pale lips, was a fraction of Danny's own sinewy height and build. Despite this, the man stood poised to fight him. But before Danny could even think about defending himself, or teaching this guy a lesson, the man stepped back. He pointed at the women and shouted at Danny in Aramaic. *"You do NOT serve them! They serve us!"* When he yelled, he opened his mouth and, although they were used to the people of this time having less-than wonderful oral hygiene, this fellow had particularly horrible teeth, brown and staggered.

The man stepped again on the food Danny had been offering, then took a seat in the crowd. By that time, Peter and Judas were on their feet. The two of them calmly walked over to the man and calmly beckoned him to follow them outside the circle of disciples where nobody could see them.

Then they beat him. Calmly. It only took a minute. Leaving the man on the ground alone with his blood, Peter and Judas returned and walked over to where Danny still stood by the women. Peter reached down, picked up the remnants of the bread and cheese, and handed them to Danny, motioning for him to sit back down.

As Danny returned to Ben's side, he looked back at Mary and the other women who, by that time, had been given food of their own. He was unable to decide if Peter and Judas' actions were motivated by empathy for the women, or a need to defend Danny–or neither. He sat down and looked at the ruined food, thinking about how much he still had to learn about the volatile societies of first-century A.D.

~ ~ ~ ~

Thirty minutes later, Peter stood up and announced that it was time for the Apostles to depart. He started loading his belongings onto one of the boats, as Judas and the others milled about preparing the supplies. For the first time since being welcomed into the entourage, Danny and Ben felt left out. They were not worried about being left behind, as they could just continue on foot around the lake with all the other remaining disciples. But they had grown accustomed to being accepted near the reach of the Apostles. Nevertheless, the two of them made sure their things were packed and ready to go, should someone allow them passage on one of the boats. They stood in the fray with their backpacks and tried to make themselves appear ship-worthy.

Ben looked at his friend, happy to have someone to talk to. "I wonder if this is where Jesus will walk on the water."

Danny was also glad for small talk. "Well, this is the Sea of Galilee, where that all happened—walking on water, calming the storm." People continued to weave around them.

Ben grinned "You know you're talking about Jesus in the past tense, right?"

"Oh," said Danny, looking out at the water. "I still have trouble wrapping my head around that."

"*What are you waiting for?!*" John's voice rang out. Danny and Ben looked around, and saw that they were the ones being addressed. John waved them towards the dock. "*Get on the boat!*"

"Uh, *which boat?*" Ben asked, but John had already boarded the nearest boat, along with Jesus, Philip, Andrew, Mary Magdalene and seven other disciples.

Judas appeared out of nowhere to help the boys. "*I'm sailing on the second boat with James and Bartholomew,*" he said. "*There is room for you both.*" He turned on his heel and headed straight for the dock. The boys hustled behind him. Ben considered how remarkable it was that Judas still had a habit of coming to their aid.

"Do you know how to step onto a boat?" Danny asked as they arrived on the dock.

"Sure, I guess."

"I'm not talking about yachts or cruise ships. You have to step into the middle of the hull."

Danny demonstrated his boat-boarding expertise by stepping into the middle of the boat, at which point he lost his balance and fell into James' arms. Ben, watching this, placed his feet over the side of the boat and rolled himself in like a travelling puddle of spilled milk. He felt as ridiculous as he knew he looked, but at least he didn't have to force a hug upon an unwilling shipmate like Danny had done.

— 18 —

John Casey's favourite Crosby, Stills & Nash song was "Southern Cross". The romanticism of being on a boat had made for great singing when the aunts and uncles came to the Casey house, guitars in tow. As a boy, Danny and his sister loved hearing their father sing this song, even though they didn't know that the lyrics were more a metaphor for lost love than about sailing: *I have my ship, and all my flags are a-flyin...*

On the Sea of Galilee, sitting beneath the boat's unpainted awning, Danny thought about his father and his acoustic guitar, and he smiled. His dad would have loved it out here on the water. The green and brown mountains rose up all around, providing a beautiful landscape no matter which direction you were facing.

All three boats sailed quite near to each other, with very little wake. They were close enough to the shoreline that those passengers with the ability to swim could easily make their way to land, should a boat capsize. It was for this reason alone that Ben was okay with being on such a small craft. Despite Danny's earlier teasing, Ben did indeed prefer to travel on boats that came with a buffet and a mini-putt golf range. The boat he was on now had a single mast, with one big triangle-shaped sail. He had probably drawn this exact boat with crayons when he was a preschooler—a banana-shaped hull and a pie-slice for a sail.

Turning his thoughts elsewhere, Ben considered whether Andrew was still wearing the medallion camera they had given him. He looked at Danny. There was enough loud chatter on their boat that it was probably safe to speak English quietly to each other. "Did you manage to hit the record button on Andrew's necklace before he got onto his boat?" he asked.

"Oh no, I didn't," Danny replied "Too bad they didn't have a remote control for that thing."

They stopped and looked straight at each other.

"Did you keep the box?" said Ben.

"Stupid..." Danny muttered to himself. He dug around the bottom of his backpack and wrapped his hands around the small box that had held the medallion camera. Keeping it inside the canvas bag, he felt around the plastic inner packaging. He grasped a thin instruction booklet, a warrantee registration card, and then a small plastic piece that could only be a remote control. He pulled it out of his backpack, and palmed it. Looking up at the other ten passengers, he happily saw that nobody was paying him any mind whatsoever. He had no desire to get caught again with any one of their modern mystery devices, lest Philip (or anyone else) snatch it away and toss it overboard.

Danny opened up his hand and saw his prize. The little black device looked as if it could start up a car, or at least cause the doors to unlock or the engine to honk. He turned it over, slid open the back panel, and checked that there was a disc battery inside.

The three boats were sailing rather closely to each other. Danny and Ben looked at the boat just in front of them. The wind shifted slightly, and they found themselves nearly side by side with the other vessel. Andrew looked over at their boat and waved. Danny waved back. He held up the remote, pointed it at Andrew and pressed the button. He was close enough to see that Andrew was smiling, but not close enough to see the red LED light blink. He had to just assume he made contact. Modern electronics, especially junk from a market stall, was not always reliable.

Danny noted that they were not able to see Jesus on the boat with Andrew. At first, the boys thought they had been mistaken, that Jesus must have boarded the third boat. But a dip in the waves altered the varying depths between the two boats, only for a moment, and Ben saw that Jesus had lain down for a nap in the stern of his boat.

Ben elbowed Danny, and said quietly, "Is Jesus asleep? It doesn't look like he's about to leap up and walk on the water for us."

~ ~ ~ ~

First came the rain. The air was still warm enough that precipitation did not automatically bring frigid air, but the rain was a nuisance enough. Before long, the winds built up into gales, and a storm gathered strength. Squalls started to spill water over the sides of the boats, and the passengers were tossed around.

Ben was extremely unhappy with the situation, sitting there in the hull of the boat with no life jacket. He was a strong swimmer, but he wasn't sure he'd be able to keep his head above the surface, should the boat tip over. Considering the ferocity of the storm, he wasn't sure that Johnny Weissmuller, the original Tarzan himself, would be any more successful at not drowning.

Danny was no better at displaying bravery. "This would be a fantastic time for Jesus to show the storm who's boss," he shouted through the noise of the wind and waves. He did have a firm grip on the side of the boat with his left hand, such that he felt confident enough to use his other hand to reprise his role of videographer and newscaster. He managed to get out the Sony camcorder and turn it on. With the storm rocking the boat, nobody noticed his actions. Danny focused the camera on the next boat, but Jesus was still asleep in the hull. As he watched, he could see John reaching down to Jesus, trying to shake him awake. His memory of the scripture told him that John would be shouting at Jesus right now: *"Teacher! Don't you care if we drown?"*

As Danny continued to record, he saw Jesus stand up and look around at the storm. Another squall hit the boats and

Andrew went tumbling down, landing on his back. Although everyone else regained their balance, Andrew remained lying down. Danny couldn't tell if he was unconscious, or if he had chosen to stay at the bottom of the boat for fear of being knocked over again.

Jesus then got to his feet and waved his arms at the sky. His shouting could clearly be heard by the passengers of all three boats. *"Quiet! Be still!"*

It took an entire minute to notice any change in the weather. But the waves did settle down and the water became still, so much so that the boats no longer moved forward, or at all.

The thirty-six people were silent on their boats. After a moment, Jesus looked around at everyone and said, *"Why are you so afraid? Have you no faith?"*

Danny and Ben looked over to see Andrew being helped to his feet by Matthew. They were glad to see that he was apparently unhurt.

Just then, the wind picked up. Those nearest the masts remembered their duties, and the boats were steered into the wind, veering toward the town of Capernaum.

John's voice could be heard clearly from his boat. *"Even the wind and the waves obey him!"*

At his words, it was as if the others now had permission to react to the miracle that had been witnessed by all. Smiles of relief, laughter all around, and even cheers were heard. Danny shut off the Sony and put it away. He dug out the medallion camera's remote and pointed it at Andrew, having no idea if it would turn it off, or if he had even been successful in turning it on before the storm had begun.

~ ~ ~ ~

From out on the water, the entire town of Capernaum could be seen. The city was once prosperous, as evidenced by the architecture of the storied buildings. Danny and Ben were quite looking forward to being on land again.

By the time the three boats had moored, it was evening. Everyone gathered their belongings and the supplies, and stepped onto the shore. Joanna, along with several of her handmaidens, had arrived from the town to greet Jesus. They came bearing food for all, steaming pots of soup.

A large but intimate camp was set up. It was temporary, just for the purpose of the evening's meal. The remaining disciples, those travelling on foot around the lake, were expected to arrive before too long.

Danny and Ben took their usual spot on the fringe. Dinner that night was a dish that resembled pasta, served in ornate wooden bowls. Ben believed he had eaten it once or twice as a child, but could not remember what it was called. In any case, it was delicious. One thing they had come to appreciate was that, in these days of sporadic meals, almost everything they ate was delicious, especially considering the alternative, that of going without food.

Danny finished eating first. "That was a lot less remarkable than what I had expected." He pointed out to the Sea of Galilee with his forehead. "I witnessed a miracle, and it wasn't all that miraculous."

Ben spoke through a mouthful of his supper. "It's possible the storm was small enough that it simply passed us by."

"I don't know, I—I don't know that Jesus' hand-waving had anything to do with the storm disappearing."

Ben swallowed in time for a rebuttal. "It's possible all these people know something we don't. I'm not sure how we are expected to act when confronted with a miracle."

Danny stood up. "What the hell are we doing here, Ben? That guy will be dead in a couple of months, and then what are we going to do—wander around the desert until we're old?"

"When you say 'that guy', I assume you're referring to Jesus?" Ben stared up at his friend.

"Look, I thought we had a purpose here. It justified walking all over hell's half-acre, sleeping on rocky hills and eating stale bread."

Ben put down his bowl. "I think you need to see things in—"

"I think I need some night life. Don't wait up." Danny marched with a purpose towards a group of three young women. He put his Canadian charm into full gear and, within moments, he had them laughing and blushing. Finally, Danny had learned how to make a first-century girl smile.

— 19 —

The group spent three days in Capernaum. The town was a bustling hub of culture and activity, and Ben enjoyed exploring the streets and walkways. He passed mosaic walls and well-tended gardens. Most of his chosen paths afforded him a view of the sea. On an exquisite spring morning, translucent and warm, it was hard to not have a skip in one's step. Ben sang quietly to himself as he stopped to look at the wares being sold in one of the markets. On one occasion, he happened upon an interesting piece of pottery from a vendor's cart. He picked it up, thinking he should buy it for his mother. Feeling foolish, he remembered his lot, and returned the item to its place.

Ben had been observing the people of this time period for several months now, and one thing that struck him was a distinct lack of patriotism among most everyone here. The majority of his own countrymen had always found ways to show their pride in being Canadian. And their American neighbours knew better than probably anyone in the world how to be proud of their country. But here, today, the people were divided into many types of classes and sects, and were more apt to identify themselves by how and to whom they prayed, rather than by their country of origin.

Continuing his stroll about the town, it was peculiar being without Danny at his side, but a bit of space was probably not a bad thing. Danny had gone off with one of the entourage girls on his arm. If past experience was any guide, the lass would be in tears before long, and Ben would have someone to hang out with again while Danny tried to figure out what the heck he had done wrong.

Looking up at the cloudless sky, Ben knew it was time for lunch—and not just because of the sun's position, but also because of his belly's warnings. Andrew had mentioned that

Jesus was to be preaching again this afternoon, and Ben didn't want to miss it.

Since their arrival in Capernaum three nights ago, Joanna had arranged for everyone to relocate in a central area of the town. A wealthy vendor owned a building that contained a large courtyard with stone monuments and a fountain surrounded by a colonnade, its white plaster pillars topped with gingerbread. This was where everyone set up camp. A corner was set aside for Jesus to sit while he preached; everyone could gather around to listen.

Ben found a place to sit with Andrew, Matthew and Simon. Lunch was a soup that would have been called Italian Wedding, had it been served in a 21st-century restaurant in Toronto.

As he finished the bowl, Ben knew not to ask for more, as there was not always enough for everyone to have first servings, let alone seconds. But what the soup lacked in quantity, it made up for in taste.

"Strohlberg, my man!"

Ben cringed. Hearing English shouted at his back ruled out the possibility of it being anyone on Planet Earth except Dan Casey. He turned around and saw his friend, accompanied by one of the female disciples. She was one of the more attractive of the ladies, young enough to be impressed by a foreigner, but old enough to be out on her own, if only just. She had a shapely figure, wrapped tightly in an elegant robe, her hair beneath her headscarf billowing on her back.

Danny swaggered over. "Hello, Benjamin. My usual table, please. I hope Maurice is cooking tonight. Let him know I'm here, would ya? There's a good lad."

Ben tried to escort Danny away from the others. "You've got to knock off the English, man."

Danny held up an index finger to the girl. "Be right back, Sweetcakes." He walked a few steps with Ben. "Hmm," he started. "Remember what an awesome wingman you used to be back home?"

"How could I forget?" said Ben. "I was pretty good at making sure YOU got laid."

"Yeah, it's harder here—not as many girls around us."

Ben sniffed. "You're drunk." It was not a question.

Danny turned around and winked at the girl. "Bubbles did it. We found someone offering apple cider, but I don't think it had any apples in it. She told me I'd love it."

"And her name is Bubbles, is it?"

"I think so. I did my own translation." Danny snickered again. "And now I forget what her Hebrew name is."

"Just lay off the English, ok? Seriously, man."

"Alright. Sorry." Danny walked back to retrieve his date. He had to switch gears in his brain to start speaking Hebrew. "*Are you hairy?*" Then in English: "Shit. Wait. Ben, what's the word for—"

"*Hungry,*" Ben said, in Hebrew.

"Right. Thanks. Well, Sweetcakes, are you—"

For the second time that month, Danny was knocked to the ground. This time, he was sucker-punched from behind. This time, he was hit hard enough that he didn't immediately get up from the dirt. He looked up and saw who had attacked him, and decided the ground may be the best place for him, lest he get knocked down again. A bearded hulk of a man with bushy eyebrows and unkempt hair screamed at Danny and pointed to the girl. He spoke with an accent that showed him to be Galilean, from north of Nazareth.

Danny rolled his eyes and shouted at him in English. "Cripes, not again! I never gave her any food, ok?"

The man grabbed "Bubbles" by the arm and escorted her away. She turned around and looked back with regret as Ben bent down to help Danny to his feet.

"Do you think that was her husband or father?" Danny wiped the dirt off his robe.

"I don't know," said Ben. "It doesn't matter. But try to find a woman who is not already spoken for."

Danny started to sober up. "Little flaw in your plan. How do I know who is—"

"That's easy," snapped Ben. "Every female you meet in this land and in this time is betrothed, married or otherwise spoken for."

"Alright." Danny looked at his friend earnestly. "Thanks for helping me out."

"I didn't actually do anything."

"Well, you know what I mean. Is there any food left?" Danny spied the large serving pot.

"I'm not sure. Jesus is supposed to be preaching again soon. Let's take a seat."

"Oh. OK. I guess so." Danny went over to pour some soup.

Ben looked around for Andrew, Matthew and Simon. They had saved his seat. Jesus had just finished his own meal. He walked over to Ben and greeted him warmly, putting his hand on his shoulder. "*Peace, Ben*." Jesus smiled to him and walked over to his place in front of the moderate crowd. He knows me by name, Ben thought, as a huge smile made its way across his face. Right then and there, Ben felt accepted, more so than he had ever experienced in his life.

— 20 —

After the evening meal, Peter announced that everyone was to move on, that the boats were being readied again. Without complaint, all the disciples packed up the supplies and picked up their belongings. Ben was fascinated at what a well-oiled machine they had all become. Danny, for his part, had pulled himself out of his stupor enough to contribute his share of the chores.

Down at the shore, Danny and Ben did not wait around for an invitation to board a boat this time. They paused just long enough to see Judas select one of the crafts, then they marched after him. On the dock, Andrew approached the two of them to wish them safe passage.

Danny smiled in thanks, and asked, *"Where are we going now?"* Ben was happy to hear that Danny could once again align his brain to make his tongue default to Hebrew. He looked around and saw that Jesus was not there with them. Guessing his thoughts, Andrew clarified. *"The Master has gone out alone to pray. He has instructed Peter to lead us all on to Gennesaret without him, and that he will join us after."*

It took only a short time for everyone, or at least the privileged three dozen, to board the boats. The rest of the disciples loaded the remaining supplies onto the camels and mules, and headed west on foot. Jesus was nowhere to be seen.

As soon as they were pushed back out into the sea, a gentle breeze took hold of the boats' sails. There seemed to be just enough wind to press them on to Gennesaret, and Danny figured they would be there in less than a couple of hours, if his memory of the Galilee maps served him well enough.

The three boats sailed along, cutting smoothly through the water. Where Danny and Ben sat, back at the stern of their boat, everything was quiet and peaceful; the only sound that could be heard was the movement of the crude sail above them.

Presently, they napped as the boat's rocking lulled them to sleep.

After nearly an hour had passed, the boys were awakened by the sudden jerk of the boat's hull, as the sail caught a passing gust of wind. The boat levelled itself straight away, and they saw that their fellow passengers were awake as well, talking in small groups. Up at the bow, Judas sat alone, looking out ahead of them. The sun was setting, and it appeared that they would be arriving before too much longer.

Ben whispered to Danny. "Do you think they'll have funerals for us?"

"Back home? I hadn't thought about it." He looked out across the water. "I'm glad my mom has my sister around to comfort her. She's always been the strong one." He chuckled softly, then shook his head. "I know my mom's probably going to lose her mind. Or she already lost her mind."

Ben smiled. "There we go again. Past tense, future tense. It's weird."

Judas stepped across the boat to stand in front of Danny and Ben. The man sitting beside Danny instinctively moved over so Judas could sit. They all smiled in greeting, and Judas stated his business to the two boys as he sat down with them. *"Friends: some of the Apostles are concerned that you both have something to hide, that you are not being honest with us about who you are, and where you came from."*

Ben bristled, and started to worry that they would get thrown overboard as imposters, right then and there.

But Danny took the reins. *"Are you one of those people?"* he asked.

Judas shook his head. *"I have my own troubles to work through. I have no time to concern myself with the affairs of others."*

Danny decided to be direct. *"What is their worry about us?"*

Judas paused as he weighed his words. It was clear that he cared a bit for the two of them. *"Philip and James do not trust you,"* he began. *"They are hard on Andrew for the way he has given friendship to you two."*

"Do they give YOU trouble for giving friendship to us?" asked Danny.

Judas smiled. *"Nobody gives me trouble. But Philip and James have asked Jesus to have you both cast out."*

Ben looked over the side of the boat at the clear, dark blue water passing by them.

Judas paused again and looked carefully at the boys. *"Jesus knows my devotion to him and to his ministry. I spoke with him, and he still insists that you are both welcome to remain with us."*

Ben stopped listening to Judas. He looked beyond him, out across the surface of the water. Judas looked at Ben's face, then turned around to see what it was that had captured Ben's attention. Soon everyone on the boat was looking out at the water in the direction of the shore.

A ghost-like figure was walking on the water, towards them. Sunlight bouncing off the water's surface impeded everyone's vision. At first, they were afraid, though not Danny and Ben. Judas stood up and held onto the mast for balance. The boys exchanged a glance, then Ben shifted his body in front of Danny's, to provide cover while Danny took the camcorder out. Ben turned around, and saw that nobody was looking back at them anyway; all eyes were on the man walking towards them on the surface of the water. Danny took that opportunity to adjust the camera settings for the fading light. He focused on the apparition walking on the water, and started recording. All three of the boats stopped moving, as their sails were lowered.

Philip's voice could be heard clearly as he called out from the boat nearest them. *"It's a ghost!"*

Ben looked over at the other boats to see that everyone was watching the figure on the water. He reached over behind Danny, and dug through his backpack until he found the remote control for the POV camera. He pointed it at Andrew.

Andrew was on his feet, standing beside Peter at the edge of their boat, with a clear view of the apparition.

Danny and Ben did not need to discuss who the "ghost" was. It was not just that the story of Jesus walking on the water was one of the most famous in religious history, but also that there was really nobody else it could be.

Cries of "*Yeshua!*"and "*Jésu!*" could be heard coming from all three boats as everyone started to recognize who the spectre was. Jesus walked towards the boat in which Andrew and Peter were standing, about thirty feet away from Danny's vantage point. As everyone watched, transfixed, Jesus beckoned Peter to walk out to him. Seeing this, Ben looked over the side of his boat, and saw a stretch of land directly beneath the surface of the water.

He whispered to Danny. "Psst! Look under the surface. It's a sandbar." Danny looked down at the water and saw that Ben was correct. "He's not walking on the water at all." Danny's hand could touch the sandbar without stretching far. They looked over and saw Peter step out of the other boat onto the surface of the water and walk towards Jesus. Gasps could be heard from everyone around them. With all the eyes on Jesus, no one noticed the boys' sandbar beneath the surface.

Feeling brave, and a little bit crazy, Ben stepped out of his boat and on to the shoal, even though he had not been invited to do so by Jesus. His feet sank about three centimetres beneath the surface of the water as he hit the sandbar. He could feel the water tickle the sides of his feet. For all intents and purposes, it looked like he, too, was walking on the sea. He walked a couple of steps closer towards where Jesus was standing near Peter's boat. Then he did a little dance. It seemed like the only natural thing to do when one finds oneself walking on water. Danny videotaped Ben being silly on the surface of the Sea of Galilee, with Jesus in the background.

After a half a minute, Danny stopped his recording. He put the camcorder in his bag, and placed the whole thing back down in the hull. He then stepped over the side of the boat and joined Ben on the shoal.

Nobody else was inclined to attempt a walk on the water, as only Peter had been invited. Only one other disciple had noticed Danny and Ben, and he was astounded at the audacity of the two foreigners. All of the other eyes were on Peter as he walked out to Jesus and took his outstretched hand.

After a while, Danny and Ben became bored with the whole ordeal. It was hard to act amazed at seeing a man walking on a shoal. They turned around and headed back to their boat. Danny, however, didn't watch where the shoal ended. He stepped too far to one side, and his whole body fell into the water, under the surface. Laughing, Ben bent over to help him up. A cotton robe did not make for ideal swimwear.

The two of them walked carefully back to their boat. As they reached the side and climbed back in, they heard a splash coming from the water. Cold and wet, Danny didn't bother looking over, as he knew the sound would be Peter falling into the sea himself.

Ben took out one of the old and now tattered robes they had been carrying along to use as a towel. He passed it to his poor friend so he could dry off. He remembered the remote control he had tucked away inside his robe, and was then thankful that he had not fallen into the water himself, as the little electronic gadget would surely not have survived.

It didn't take long for the boats to anchor at the shore. Jesus had joined the group in Peter's boat. To the delight of everyone, it appeared that they had been expected at the town: four large, welcoming campfires were burning on the shore at the foot of Gennesaret. Everyone knew there would be warmth, food and camaraderie that evening.

PART III

— 21 —

Passover was one week away, and all the Jews of the land were to gather in the still-flourishing city of Jerusalem; attendance was in fact mandatory for all male Jews. Although Passover was a celebration of freedom and deliverance for being taken out of bondage in Egypt, expectations were high that God would raise up another Moses—no one could forget how the prophets of old had promised a messiah, someone who would free the Israelites from the oppression of the Roman occupation.

During Passover, the population of Jerusalem swelled from 50,000 people to 150,000. Huge caravans of faithful Jewish families would come and offer sacrifice in the temple, despite the high tolls to be paid on the borders.

For Danny Casey and Ben Strohlberg, this was to be their first trip back to Jerusalem since they had first followed Judas Iscariot up to Nazareth, nearly nine months ago. Although the boys had not actually memorized the routes of Jesus' travels during his ministry, they were aware of the fact that they had kept mostly to the northern provinces, around Galilee, on both sides of the River Jordan.

Galilee was known to be a trouble spot, a base for the Zealots—rebels who opposed the Roman occupation of the Holy Land. And out of fear of revolt, laws had been passed stating that no more than twenty adult males were permitted to assemble together.

Jesus' disciples had reached seventy in number. However, they were not considered part of the Zealots, as there was no indication of uprising among them. Jesus had been permitted to continue his ministry, but only because he had had important friends at Capernaum. Chief among them was Jairus, a patron of the synagogue. Jairus was the Capernaum royal official, a Roman centurion officer with enough clout to ensure that Jesus' clandestine actions went largely ignored, at least while Jesus remained in Galilee. Jairus' loyalty had come about a year earlier, when his twelve-year-old daughter had been brought back from the brink of death by Jesus' touch.

~ ~ ~ ~

The morning was a beautiful one. It was spring and, of late, nature chose to be agreeable. When Danny and Ben departed Galilee a few days earlier, they had been accompanied by Jesus, his twelve Apostles, and over sixty other disciples. Once again they were on the road, this time heading straight south. Most of the time their route took them along the shores of the River Jordan, with its varying depths and widths. And every time they passed through a town or village, more people joined their caravan.

<<Photo07>>

On the road, surrounded by so many people, Danny and Ben were just another couple of travellers. But each night when it came time to set up camp, they were given positions of privilege, or a semblance thereof. They had ceased being "the new guys" many months ago and, as Jesus and Judas trusted them, so then did most of the other Apostles, though nobody held hope for Philip and James to come around. Danny and Ben were afforded the freedom to move within the group as they pleased. In some ways, the only essential difference between them and the Apostles was in the way The Twelve were specifically charged with the ability and duty to spread Jesus' gospel in his stead.

And so it was, after the evening meal, two days outside of Jerusalem on the bank of the River Jordan, that Jesus of Nazareth offered to baptise the two Canadians.

The entire entourage had already set up camp after a long day's walk, a march that had begun before the sun had even broken the horizon. Peter had immediately assigned Danny and Ben the task of organizing sleeping arrangements, ensuring that the Twelve, and a few selected others, would situate themselves near Jesus for the evening.

After the majority of the people had settled in, Andrew walked over to where Danny and Ben had put out their things, and asked the two of them to go speak with Jesus. They looked at each other, then at Andrew. They picked up their bags and started to move, but Andrew said, "*You will not need those now.*" They smiled at him but ignored his advice, shouldering their bags as they walked over to the riverbank where Jesus, Peter and John had set themselves up.

"*Hello, Master,*" said Danny and Ben, each in turn.

Jesus was seated, and he motioned for the boys to do the same. "*You have not been baptised.*"

It was not a question, and it came as a shock to both of them, though each for a different reason. Ben acknowledged truthfully that he had not. Danny considered the logic behind replying that he had in fact been baptised in the late 20th century. Ironically enough, he didn't know what to really say. He remembered learning that baptism, like circumcision, was not a repeatable event.

"*Would you like to be cleansed?*" Jesus asked. It was possible he had not figured on a disciple who would not want to be baptised, though it was far more likely that he simply chose to ignore the reactions of reluctance he received from both boys. Without awaiting a reply, he rose and started towards the river bank, expecting to be followed. Not knowing what else to do, Danny and Ben accompanied Jesus to the water's edge.

Andrew remained with them, happy to be a witness to his friends' baptisms. Misunderstanding the looks of apprehension that both boys wore, Andrew tried to sooth them. "*Do not worry; the water is not overly cold.*"

Ben ignored him and stepped forward. He still did not want to be unfaithful to his Judaism, but if he was baptised by Christ, wouldn't that pretty-much make him a Christian? The Jewish ritual of purification was called Tvilah. Ben thought it likely that this was what John the Baptist had done for Jesus, as a fellow Jew. He took off his robe and stepped into the water to begin his baptism. Andrew was correct; the water was fine. Ben missed most of what Jesus said and did, as he was so overwhelmed. After a few minutes, he stepped back onto the shore and dried himself off.

Danny stared out at the water, unmoving. Jesus looked at him with kindness and said, *"You may think you have already been cleansed, but know that it is only through me that you will be welcomed into Heaven."*

Danny, his mind churning with conflict and indecision, let his robe fall to the ground before stepping into the river. As Jesus performed the rite, pouring water and saying the incantation, Danny felt that he loved this man as he loved his own father, his mother and his brother and sister. As the water poured down his face, he was drenched in sadness. Within a week, Jesus would be dead, and Danny would no longer have someone to follow. It didn't matter that this man was not the Messiah, Danny was absorbed by his kindness and his message, and he didn't want his Master to die.

— 22 —

The morning meal was finished, baskets were loaded onto the camels, and everyone started on the road south again. Spirits were high all around. Danny and Ben were each given a camel to lead. They gathered their respective reins and once again walked apart from the others. Ben was powering up his smartphone with the solar-powered trickle-charger draped over his camel's basket, in direct view of the sun.

Danny looked pensive. "We should be in Jerusalem tomorrow," he said. "This is where it's all supposed to happen, where history is made."

"Isn't he supposed to ride in on a donkey or a horse?" said Ben.

"Just the last bit." Danny paused. "Of course, there's the little complication surrounding the fact that he may not actually be the Messiah."

Ben wasn't sure that he was up to the task of debating Christianity with his friend right now, but he couldn't let that comment go. "Are you saying he's a fraud?"

"No. I don't know. Ben, we were there; we made videos, for crying out loud! I saw nothing that shows he is anything more than a regular man."

"Maybe it's enough that he tried to get people to be nice to each other for a change. In this age of brutality, that might not be a bad thing."

"Until he gets crucified for it." Danny's voice started to rise. "My entire religion is based on that guy over there being more than a mortal."

"Your entire religion? No it's not." Ben paused. "Consider the paradox."

"What paradox?"

Ben weighed his words. "We haven't seen any actual miracles, so you just decided that miracles don't exist—yet we've travelled through time. What's that, if not a miracle?"

"It's not the same thing."

Ben pushed on. "I don't know. I think a miracle is not just about the event itself, it's about perspective—and timing. And he knows. Jesus knows who we are."

"So?" said Danny. "That just confuses things even more." He looked up to where the others were walking, ahead of them. "I'm going to go talk with Judas." He handed his camel's lead to Ben and started off.

Ben called after him. "Really? Judas?"

Danny stopped and turned around. "Believe it or not, he's the only one who makes any sense around here."

"Be careful who you befriend, Dan. I wouldn't get too close with him right now."

~ ~ ~ ~

Judas, as it turned out, was not in the mood for company from Danny, or anyone else. He looked frustrated and exhausted, and the others kept their distance from him, so Danny just walked by himself for a while.

It was late afternoon when the group arrived at the small village of Bethany, situated on the outskirts of Jerusalem. It was not unlike any of the other dusty towns the group had been to in their travels, with its short clay buildings amidst a smattering of palm trees.

Danny noted that it was Saturday, the day of Shabbat. He confirmed it by considering the coming events of Passover and working backwards. It was the first time that the day of the week had had any relevance at all for him since leaving Canada.

When the company stopped in the village, Danny and Ben regrouped as if they had not had a disagreement. In their years of friendship, they had always been able to wash away opposing opinions quite easily and quickly.

Looking around at everyone else, they had assumed there would be little to do in the way of unpacking, as they still had the final leg of the journey to Jerusalem before them. But John explained that their camp would remain here in Bethany throughout Passover, and that everyone would travel to the city each morning, returning to the camp in the evenings. This made sense to Danny and Ben, considering the thousands of people looking for accommodations in the Holy City.

Philip approached Danny, his body language revealing annoyance. *"You: There is a donkey waiting here in the village; we are to fetch it for Jesus. He said that you are to go with me."*

Philip had used one word Danny did not recognize. *"There is a word I don't understand. What is it that's waiting in the village?"*.

Philip grimaced at the apparent stupidity before him. *"A donkey. It's like a horse. They did not teach you much where you came from, did they? Follow me."*

In his past life, Danny would never have put up with someone speaking to him like that. But here, he knew better. He gave his backpack to Ben, and went off with Philip to fetch a donkey.

Simon approached Ben and invited him to help carry a lamb into the city. Ben knew all about this rite of sacrifice, and he wanted no part of it, for fear that he would be the one chosen to slit the lamb's throat. He thanked Simon for his kind offer, but suggested he ask Andrew or Thomas instead. He suddenly realized that his refusal could be taken as an insult, but Simon simply shrugged it off.

Before long, Philip and Danny returned to the camp with a donkey, no closer to being friends than when they started out. Jesus had asked for his Apostles to gather with him, so Philip left to go with the others, leaving Danny to look after the animal. After a few minutes, Andrew came to find Danny and Ben. *"Jesus has told us we are expected in Jerusalem. There are crowds of people waiting to see him."* He looked at them gravely. *"He said we will need to look out for each other."*

Andrew was not able to interpret Jesus' foreshadowing words, but the boys of course knew exactly what was going to take place over the next few days —at least, they knew history's version of the events that were going to take place.

~ ~ ~ ~

It was a triumphant processional. All twelve Apostles marched with pride behind their Master, who rode astride the small but muscular donkey. Danny and Ben walked a little ways behind as well, surrounded by the dozens of other disciples who had been following Jesus all these months. Since leaving Galilee, so many people had joined their company that the line of people twisting its way down the road could be seen from a great distance away.

"There it is," said Ben, gesturing to the vast battlemented wall up ahead, stretching its way around the city. Scores of tents, caravans, camels, horses and asses had situated themselves all the way along the ground as far as could be seen in both directions. Jerusalem rose up majestically before them as they crested the last hill and entered the city's gates. They were really seeing it for the first time right then. The short period they had spent in the city following their arrival in the year 32 had been spent trying to figure out if they had gone crazy or not. After noticing there was no more technology, no lights, no cars, they had not really been up for taking in the sights. Now, they took notice of the walls of light grey stone rising up with splendour, and they could understand why it was called the Holy City. The other difference, on this day as they returned to Jerusalem, was in the number of people around them: Romans, Greeks, and Egyptians, Syrians and Sicilians, Jews, Canaanites, Pharisees, Gauls and Thessalonians alike.

Street waifs, prostitutes, gladiators, tax-gatherers, artists, scribes, people from all walks of life and societal divisions—some rode on donkeys, others raced by in ground-rumbling chariots. A curtained litter moved confidently through the crowd, propped up by four muscular slaves. Danny wondered what royal person hid inside. Most of the people there seemed to have arrived on foot. The city was a polyglot of languages; many different tongues could be heard, most of which were foreign to the ears of the Canadians. The familiar Hebrew tongue could heard frequently, but with its various accents and dialects.

And the animals: birds within cages and without, monkeys small and large, and a tiger, leashed and walking, healing like a dog with its master. Smaller cats, feral and hungry, darted among the trampling feet throughout the streets and in the gutters.

Dust was a common element of life in the city, and the masses there ensured a fine coat of dust made its way onto and into everything, pervading one's nostrils. A caravan of camels ensured the dust stayed airborne with their hooves.

Merchants and traders lined the streets, selling everything needed for a successful Passover, including livestock for eating, and also for sacrificing. Some people wandered about, taking in the sites; others marched as if on a mission. Many Jerusalem residents stood aloft on their balconies, waving to the new arrivals. Music, laughter and mirth could be heard in almost every direction. Roman Praetorian guards were ever-present, making Danny and Ben nervous, despite their not having done anything wrong. Some of the soldiers stood at attention, surveying the passers-by and cat-calling to the women. Others knelt on the ground, playing at dice.

It's a human reaction to giggle at something that makes one nervous. Danny understood this to be the reason why Ben started giggling at the soldiers' outfits. Ben hid his face in his hands and gave the outward impression of crying, though Danny knew otherwise. "Man, you've got to stop that," he whispered.

"I can't help it. As tough as they are, they're wearing little leather skirts." Ben snickered some more. "Those Mohawk style hats don't do anything for their appearance, either." Danny rolled his eyes as Ben continued. "Those little bitty swords, wide as they are, would be useless against a medieval broadsword."

"Well it's a good thing they're not the ones traveling through time. So your otherwise sound observation is moot." Danny looked the soldiers up and down himself. "I did always feel that the re-enactment guys looked kind of ridiculous in those outfits, but these guys, real Roman guards, look like they could kick our sorry butts, with or without those short swords."

Ben pulled himself together, and they moved on.

~ ~ ~ ~

Each year during the feast of the Passover, expectation of the coming of the Messiah was taken very seriously indeed. However, this year was different, as most people believed, or would soon be told, that the Messiah had in fact arrived, from Galilee. Word had travelled throughout the city that one Jesus of Nazareth was outside the walls, and would be arriving soon.

When the huge group that made up Jesus' entourage passed through the gates of the city, there were hordes of people there to greet them, or at least to assuage their curiosity. The mood was celebratory, the air was electric. It was clear to many there that they were welcoming their king, and they hailed him as the Messiah. They had learned that Jesus was the distant son of the great warrior King David, and was therefore the symbol of Jewish deliverance. It seemed that almost everyone there waved palm leaves over their heads as a sign of victory—palm leaves were the national symbol of Jewish freedom. As Jesus' processional moved through the city, people near him threw their leaves underneath the donkey's feet as a sign of further support and submission to his rule.

Danny and Ben stuck close to each other, gazing with fascination at the multitudes. "My God, this guy is a rock star," Danny said, his jaw agape.

People were shouting and chanting *"Messiah!" "King of kings!"* and *"Lamb of God!"* Ben thought about King Herod Antipas, and he realized how the puppet ruler would be nervous by the presence of Jesus and the reactions of his people. Ben remembered how the last King Herod (Herod The Great) had had similar worries when he heard about the birth of a baby king in Bethlehem three decades ago.

On top of everything, there was currently a great deal of political turmoil to be reckoned with. Pontius Pilate, as governor, would surely understand the implications of a peasant carpenter from the north rising up, thereby making his own job even more difficult.

Ben came out of his reverie in time to see Andrew, Simon and Matthew walk past him carrying a lamb.

— 23 —

Despite the excitement and the potential for conflict that the day promised to bring, it proceeded with very few difficulties, and by evening the group returned to the camp in Bethany with little fanfare. Danny and Ben slept early and well, in anticipation of a busy day to come. Most of the disciples had the same idea, and the entire camp soon fell quiet, save for the crackling sound of several small campfires, and some soothing singing not too far off.

In the morning, everyone rose early to prepare for the return to the city. After breakfast, somebody brought out a large basket of food for the road: figs, bread, radishes and cucumbers to tide the disciples over until the evening meal.

The road from Bethany to the gates of Jerusalem was a little under two miles, a distance that could be covered by a lone walker in about half an hour. It would seem that a large group would drag its collective feet, but if there's anything this party had become good at over the past several months, it was learning how to move efficiently as a mass. By the time the day became fully bright, Jesus' company was settled in the heart of the city. Peter and John had already gone ahead to arrange a place in an outdoor temple for the group to gather, and when the Apostles arrived with their Master, a large crowd sat waiting to hear the sermon.

Ben was amazed at how effectively people could be gathered for an event in this day and age. Back home, he wouldn't dream of attending a concert or sporting event without learning all the details on Facebook. Unless he knew in advance who was or was not attending, Ben didn't like to commit. But here in darn-near prehistoric times, he sat only a few steps away from Jesus, surrounded by well over a thousand other people, all of whom had learned about this gathering by word-of-mouth.

Danny held his smartphone in the palm of his hand, covering the whole device except for the tiny microphone port at the bottom. He recorded the entire sermon, then renamed the audio file "Jerusalem No. 2". Afterwards, the disciples dispersed, and the boys were alone.

"You know how this all plays out?" Ben started, as they left the temple and walked around the crowded streets.

Danny didn't have to ask for clarification. "Yeah, I do. Today is Sunday, right? So tomorrow, we go to a temple that has been set up as a market. Jesus gets upset, and has it out with the merchants. Tuesday, Judas goes off to plant the seeds for the betrayal of Jesus to the high priests."

Ben thought for a moment. "And the Last Supper is on Thursday?"

"That's right." Danny shook his head. "Man, we have to watch ourselves carefully. We are in the company of a guy who is about to get slaughtered."

"Well, we've had a few months' practice at learning how to not be stupid."

Danny smiled. "Let's hope."

The rest of the day was unscheduled, so the two of them strolled around, taking in the sights. They found it fascinating how a congregation of this size brought together so many kinds of different people.

Danny was enjoying it all. "I remember the circus coming to Copps Coliseum. And I've been to Lollapalooza, which brings its own set of crazies, but I've never seen nutballs like these people." He gestured to the vendors, buskers, roadside preachers, musicians, magicians and beggars. Street urchins and beggars were so common-place, it was amazing to think that there would be enough solvent people to actually share some coins with those in need.

Ben thought about summertime in Dundas, a small town in the west part of Hamilton that hosted two major summer festivals. "This reminds me of the Dundas Buskerfest," he said, thinking about how much he had enjoyed the jugglers, artists and street comics.

"Yeah," said Danny, allowing himself to reminisce. "I preferred the Cactus Festival: more music, and fewer balloon animals."

A small crowd had gathered around three performers on a street corner. One of the colourful but ragged-looking men was playing a musical instrument that could have been a miniature early version of a balalaika, with its triangular body and three strings. Beside him sat a man playing a hand drum that resembled an African djembe. And the third person, the front man, did the singing. This fellow had an atrocious voice, and he changed languages for each stanza, switching from rough Hebrew, and Aramaic, to something that Ben had figured was likely Greek. Although he and Danny understood almost nothing of what was being sung, the spectators loved the show, clapping and laughing throughout. A small group of sailors, marked as such by their attire and their rowdy attitudes, hoisted their cups of ale in celebration of the music.

Moving on, the boys came across another performer, a messy-haired contortionist who appeared as if he could be one of the cast members of the freak show that made up the Jim Rose Sideshow Circus, with that fellow who could squeeze his entire body through an unstrung tennis racket. Danny and Ben stood in front of the performer, waiting for his show to begin. As interesting as he appeared, this man had no audience at all, nobody to appreciate his talent. He stared back at the boys, and they began to feel uncomfortable.

"Danny? I don't think this guy's a performer. I think he's just deformed, crippled. And we're staring at him like a couple of idiots."

Danny smiled awkwardly at the poor man and stepped backwards. "Well, then, you have yourself a nice day, ok? Enjoy the rest of, uh—"

"*Peace be with you,*" Ben interrupted, in Hebrew.

Danny faced his friend. "So, lunch time?"

"Yup."

They turned quickly away, and walked until they found a tree underneath which they could sit and eat the figs and cucumbers they had packed with them before leaving the camp that morning.

For the rest of the day they did not see the Apostles anywhere. There was no set time to return to Bethany, so Danny and Ben headed back before the sun started to fall. This was also when their stomachs needed attention again.

— 24 —

It was Monday morning. Danny and Ben were once again on the now familiar road from Bethany to Jerusalem. The day was a little warmer than it had been of late. The serenity of the road provided the boys with much needed peace as they walked.

"Something just occurred to me," started Danny. "We don't know for sure if this is Jesus' last Passover."

"How do you figure?" asked Ben.

"Jesus' ministry lasted for three years from the time he was baptised by John the Baptist up until when he was crucified."

"So?"

"We've been with Jesus less than nine months," continued Danny. "For all we know, this could be his first or second Passover since he began his travels."

Ben considered this. "Well, I guess we could just ask one of the Apostles how long Jesus has been doing this."

"Andrew was the first one chosen to be an Apostle. We could ask him." Danny thought it over. "Or, we could wait and see if Jesus trashes the temple. That's on the schedule for today, according to the Bible."

"And assuming this is his third Passover," said Ben.

"I guess we'll find out soon enough."

As if on cue, Simon fell into step with the boys. *"Peace, brothers,"* he said to them. *"Are you coming to the Master's sermon today?"*

"Of course," replied Ben. *"Same place as yesterday?"*

"No," said Simon. *"Peter has arranged for us to gather at Herod's Temple. It is larger, and the courtyard should better accommodate all who have come to listen to the Teacher today."*

At the entrance gate to Jerusalem, the three of them arrived to find Jesus and the other Apostles also passing through the arched gates. They regrouped, and walked together through the city until they arrived at Herod's Temple.

The building was magnificent. Inside the enormous walled courtyard there were huge marble pillars, ornate brickwork—and an impromptu market that had been set up only that morning. There were stalls and tables with clay pots, livestock, fabrics, and many other wares for sale. Vendors and customers were spread throughout the entire courtyard.

<<Photo08>>

Danny and Ben looked at each other, as it appeared to them that their conversation on the road from Bethany had just been made moot. Looking over at their Master, they were astounded to see his face no longer displaying the look of warmth and kindness he had worn almost continuously throughout their travels. They watched as Jesus stood fixed in the entranceway to the temple, his eyes panning the entire area, his face now displaying a look of rage.

The Apostles were also displeased with the market. Peter was upset that he had made arrangements for the use of the temple's courtyard, and now the merchants were preventing his Master from preaching there. John suggested everyone should return to the place where they had gathered for yesterday's sermon.

But Jesus was no longer thinking about preaching. He stepped to the nearest stall and overturned the table; pottery slid off and crashed to the ground. Before the shocked vendor could even react, Jesus had moved on to the next stall, kicking over a rack of garments.

The sounds of wood snapping and pottery crashing reverberated off the temple's inner walls. Immediately, the entire market stopped trading. Every person there turned and looked at the source of the commotion. Jesus of Nazareth screamed back at them. *"This temple should be a house of prayer! You have made it a den of thieves! GET OUT!"*

Jesus continued to overturn tables and knock down stalls, and one of the merchants tried to grab him and restrain him. Judas and James stepped in to protect Jesus as arguments broke out, and scuffles between disciples and merchants quickly transformed the temple-turned-market into a bar room brawl.

Jesus marched deeper into the courtyard, creating mayhem as he went. As he continued his rampage, the Apostles tried to surround him, to protect him. But there were far more merchants than disciples. An air of wrath manifested itself throughout the courtyard as vendors screamed in protest.

Danny and Ben, seeing the fury that was being caused among the merchants, went into survival mode. They knew it would be easy for them to get clobbered, even as bystanders.

Just then, Roman guards arrived, pushing their way through the pandemonium with the familiar clang of wood and steel that always accompanied soldiers on a mission. They were not there to inquire who started the commotion, or to figure out who threw the first punch; they were just there to try and restore order, regardless of who may get in their way.

A merchant who had just had his livestock released into the square ran around screaming, trying to round his animals up. He was hollering at Jesus who had since moved onto another part of the market to continue doing damage.

Another man, a potter, Roman by his attire, looked in anger at all his handmade vases, now in pieces on the ground. He didn't pick up the shards, but instead sought out his antagonist. With fists raised, he went after Jesus, racing towards him from behind. Noticing this, John stepped in and blocked the potter's way. The ensuing scuffle did not last long, as John held his own until the man backed down and returned to his stall to clean up the mess.

In the midst of all the pandemonium, Danny and Ben had no idea what they should be doing. Even though they had

had a pretty good idea what was going to happen here, it was still a fascinating thing to watch history unfold before them.

Since becoming disciples, they had assumed many of the same rights and responsibilities as the Apostles. But now, most of the Twelve had surrounded Jesus, taking blows and returning punches in his stead.

As soon as Danny and Ben saw the Roman Guard, they tried to make themselves invisible. The problem was that they were still situated too close to Jesus. They knew the time had come for them to get the heck out of Dodge, so they spun around to orient themselves, looking for the exits. They did not notice a merchant, a tall dark-skinned man whose garment rack had been knocked over and trampled upon, rush up to them in anger. This man had seen Danny and Ben at Jesus' side, and he equated their presence with his own ruined merchandise. He ran at them with an eye for vengeance, his fingers spread apart, claw-like, his mouth open in savage anger.

Hearing a battle-cry, Ben turned around to see the crazed merchant rushing at him. He winced, held up his arms to defend himself, and braced his feet. Instinct took over as Ben prepared to block whatever punch was going to be thrown at him. Just before the merchant struck a blow, Ben heard Danny shout, "Ben!" Ben turned to look, thinking his help was needed elsewhere, and then sustained a blow to the side of his head as the merchant made contact. As Ben fell to the ground, he managed to look up to see Judas appear, seemingly out of nowhere. Judas punched the merchant in the nose so hard that the sound of the man's cracking bones could be heard even among the noise of the surrounding chaos. Danny screamed and ran over to tend to Ben, lying on the ground.

In the next instant, two Roman guards leaped over a fallen table and grabbed Judas, hauling him out of the temple with the efficiency of the trained soldiers that they were. Nobody noticed Judas being removed except Danny—but his first concern was for Ben. He knelt down, offered his hand, and helped Ben back onto his feet. Danny saw that his friend was fine, although shaken up. They looked at the poor merchant lying on the ground beside them, a man who felt he had been just in his anger, even if it was misplaced.

"They took Judas," Danny said anxiously to Ben. Looking up at the exit, they saw Judas disappear with the guards. The two of them managed to work their way to the outskirts of the fighting, then they fled to the arched stone doorway through which they had first entered.

Arriving outside the temple walls, Danny and Ben saw a large flatbed horse-drawn cart stationed down the street, surrounded by more Roman guards. The cart had four men loaded on it, each with his hands bound. The two soldiers who had taken Judas were binding their prisoner's hands behind his back, and leading him towards the flatbed cart.

The boys ran to catch up with them. As they crossed the street, Danny said, "What are we going to say to them?"

Ben didn't look at him. "YOU'RE not going to say anything. I've got this."

They caught up to Judas and the guards, and ran around in front of them to block their path. Ben held up the palms of his bare hands. He smiled at the guards with humility and bowed deeply before them. He hoped they spoke Hebrew. *"Excuse me, good sirs."*

The first guard looked at Ben's bruised face and dishevelled appearance, and yelled at him in bastardized Aramaic. *"Move!"*

Ben stood erect, but continued with Hebrew. "If *you please, I've come to appeal for my friend, who was only trying to—*"

The second guard understood him, and replied in Hebrew. *"Step aside or join the prisoner!"*

Ben stepped aside but continued pleading to the guards. *"Will this man not be heard?"*

The guard led Judas roughly to the edge of the cart, then turned back to Ben. He looked at him and said, not without a modicum of compassion, *"Of course. There will be a trial at the prison, three days hence."*

The guards hoisted Judas onto the back of the cart with the others. Danny was able to see the other four prisoners, and noted that none of his fellow disciples was among them.

The horses were lead away. Ben and Danny did not follow; instead, they just sat down right there on the side of the road.

It took a while before either of them could speak.

Danny stared out at the imposing walls of Herod's Temple. "Obviously our take on history is wrong," he began. "Judas can't betray Jesus if he's in jail. The judicial system is totally corrupt here; who knows when they'll ever release him. Maybe the crucifixion happens at next year's Passover."

Ben shook his head and stared down at his dirty feet, in dirty sandals. "No, we're at the right place and the right time."

"Apparently we're not, if Judas went and got himself locked away. Our presence here had nothing to do with that."

Ben looked up and met Danny's eyes. "That's not entirely true."

"What are you saying? Don't tell me we were sent here to redirect the course of history. There's not a chance that—"

"Will you shut up a second?" Ben immediately regretted snapping at his friend. He measured his breaths before continuing. "After that merchant hit me, Judas stepped in and punched the guy; I don't know if you saw that, but the soldiers did. That's why they took him away."

"Oh." Danny let out a dripping wet sigh. "Well, this sucks."

"It more than sucks, Dan. Right now, Judas can't betray Jesus. There will be no crucifixion."

— 25 —

John and Peter emerged from the temple, followed by Jesus, who was surrounded by his disciples. Danny and Ben watched them from across the street. Without a word, the boys rose, walked over and fell into step with everyone else. Nobody noticed that they had been missing for the past fifteen minutes. Nobody noticed that Judas was absent.

And nobody asked where they were all going. The disciples turned east and headed straight to the outskirts of the city. In less than an hour, they were all settled back at their base camp in Bethany. A meal had been prepared, but not many of them were hungry. The next part of the day was spent tending to wounds and bruised egos.

The following morning, Ben woke up before anyone else. The stress of his predicament had prevented him from sleeping soundly. It was Tuesday, the day Judas was supposed to negotiate to betray Jesus.

Lying beside him, Danny opened his eyes to see Ben sitting up. He yawned, stretched and oriented himself, something he still frequently needed to do when sleeping outside.

Ben was staring out at the road to Jerusalem. He spoke quietly, that only Danny could hear. "I'm responsible for Judas being in jail. I'm responsible for him being unable to do what he's supposed to do."

Before replying, Danny stood up and stretched his legs. Beckoning for Ben to follow him, they walked soundlessly out to the edge of their camp, where nobody could hear them. Behind them, other people started to wake up and begin the day.

"You didn't do anything, Ben. Judas got himself arrested."

Ben stared at the ground as they walked. "No he didn't. He was defending me at the time."

"Fine. Then we'll need to go bust him out."

Ben, without smiling, said, "Sure—we'll dress up like Storm Troopers, grab Chewbacca and sneak in."

Danny was usually up for a good Star Wars reference, but he just shook his head then. "Well, we have to try something."

"Does it actually say in the New Testament that two pale-skinned guys with funny accents broke Judas out of jail?" Ben knew he was reaching. "I say we leave him where he is, at least for a couple of days—and Jesus doesn't have to be crucified."

Danny shook his head. "We can't do that."

Ben's frustration was starting to build up. "You already said yourself he's not the Messiah."

"I don't know if he is or if he isn't—but he still has to see this through." Danny's voice started to rise as he spoke.

Ben was only marginally more successful at keeping his cool. "Apparently that's not going to happen."

Danny was silent for a few moments. He turned and looked back at the camp, where Jesus was still sleeping, lying between Peter and John. "Then I'll do it," said Danny.

"Do what?"

Danny looked his friend square in the eye. "Betray Jesus. Get this whole thing back on its path."

Ben had had enough. "Put your brain back in your head, man. You think you can just stroll into the temple and chat with the high priests? You know nothing about their customs; they would never accept it from you."

Danny pondered this. "You're right." He pointed gently at Ben's chest. "You have to do it."

Ben snapped, not caring if his voice could be heard back at the camp. "No frickin' way am I going to tell the priests anything! My people already carry enough of the blame for killing your messiah. I don't want to take the rap twice."

"Then let's hope I can break Judas out of jail." said Danny. "Give me your phone."

Ben handed it over without asking after the plan. Danny turned and walked back to their camp. He retrieved his backpack and picked up a small iron hammer lying on the ground that had been used to secure the group's tent ropes. Then he started on the road to Jerusalem.

Ben was left standing on his own, tormented, with no idea what to do.

— 26 —

In a city known for its magnificent architecture, the grey granite prison building stood out as a drab structure, windowless and cold. There was no outer wall, no bastion towers, or anything else that could associate it with a prison. The building was surprisingly small, as if it had been built to accommodate only a small lot of prisoners.

It had taken Danny a number of attempts to find someone local to Jerusalem who even knew where the nameless prison was located. He was eventually directed to the Western Hill, a residential area of the city densely populated with lower-class dwellings. On his way through the streets, Danny had seen a clothes line stretched between two buildings. There was a hooded robe on the line, clearly made for a female, with its gilded embroidery. Danny looked around him and quickly removed the robe. He folded it and tucked it away in his backpack.

Before long, he found himself standing in front of the desolate building that counted Judas Iscariot among its prisoners.

~ ~ ~ ~

Still back at the base camp in Bethany, Ben sat down in the place where Danny had left him to go play the part of superhero. He crossed his arms and put his head down.

"*Peace, friend.*" Ben looked up at Andrew, who had come over to sit with him. "*It is not often I see you without your companion.*"

Ben gazed down the road to Jerusalem. He resigned himself to the fact that he had to take action.

"*Peace, Andrew,*" he said. "*I have to go to the high priests' temple.*" Ben figured he may as well be direct. "*Can you tell me how to find it?*"

"*Why do you need to go there?*"

"*I need to see Caiaphas.*" More directness.

Andrew's face revealed confusion. "*Caiaphas will not simply receive people. An audience with him is hard to come by.*"

"*Please just tell me how to get there.*"

Andrew had considered Ben a friend, and so helped him without further questioning. "*As you wish, Ben,*" he said.

~ ~ ~ ~

Danny walked around the perimeter of the stone prison building, getting his bearings. He had no idea what he was up against, no idea what he would find inside. The plain arched entrance had no gatehouse, so Danny entered the building, which was curiously unencumbered by guards.

It occurred to him that he might be in the wrong building. The room in which he stood had no cells, nothing to hold prisoners. A torch mounted on the wall afforded barely enough light to allow him to orient himself. Ahead of him was a doorway to a set of narrow stairs leading downward, to the right of which a single guard, helmeted and armed, sat on a short wooden chair. The only other object in the room was a table, large and austere, as well as several more wooden chairs against the walls.

Apparently, visitors were permitted to come and go in this building. Danny headed straight for the doorway, and the guard didn't give him a glance.

The staircase was unlit, but Danny could see that there was some light down below. He descended the stone stairs. At the bottom, he stepped into a short hallway and turned a corner. Ahead of him lay a long corridor. There were two guards, one at each end. Torch-holders were mounted on the wall every twelve feet or so, throwing light eerily along the bare stone walls. The immediate problem, as Danny saw it, was that there were no prison cells anywhere in sight.

He was hit with an onslaught of smells. Feces, sweat and burned flesh permeated his nostrils. The sounds of unhappy men could be clearly heard, some groaning, some talking. But he could not see where the prisoners were held.

He stepped forward to make his way down the hall. The guard beside him was heavily armed, and, like the man upstairs, was most unconcerned about visitors. By the third step, Danny no longer felt a dirt floor beneath his feet. He looked down to see that he was standing on a square metal grate, about three feet wide, reminding him of the grates on big-city sidewalks—except that the sounds and smells were not that of subway trains or parking garages, but were in fact those of imprisoned men.

~ ~ ~ ~

Ben wasn't certain if he would be able to follow the directions to the temple. Andrew had offered to accompany him, but Ben obviously had to do this alone.

Arriving in Jerusalem, the streets were even more populated than the day before, and Ben often had to muscle his way through crowds just to cross a street. Andrew's directions had been sound; after a few blocks, Ben found himself standing outside the beautiful but menacing outer wall of the high priests' temple. It was an enormous structure, stretching along for an entire city block. Standing at the corner, Ben could see that the long front wall had three bastions, each with a bronze door and a single guard out front, but the narrower side wall had one bastion—and one guard.

<<Photo09>>

Ben thought about his predicament, and tried to figure out the best way to get inside. He remembered an expression from home that Christians used, on bumper stickers and T-shirts that read, "What Would Jesus Do?" And in this time of Jesus, all Ben could think of was, what would Scooby-Doo and Shaggy do?

"Great idea," he said aloud, feeling foolish. "Because cartoon characters always have the best strategies."

Without thinking it through any further, Ben strolled casually towards the guards in front of the east entrance. The men looked and held themselves like battle-ready gladiators, with armoured outfits made of leather and steel; they each held onto a circular shield, and gripped a spear that looked like it could penetrate a tank. Ben, trying to act as if he frequently chatted it up with soldiers, slowed down only slightly as he passed the third guard. "*Is your name*, uh, *Maximus?*"

The guard, who had been dutifully staring ahead, was thrown completely off. He scowled at Ben. "*No, I am Valerius.*" Only then did it occur to the guard that he should not be talking to a lowly citizen. He straightened his stance and continued looking out at the street.

"*I am sorry. My mistake. Peace.*" Ben went on his way. He turned the corner and continued along the wall until he arrived at the next entrance and its lone guard, dressed identically to the first.

Ben felt he had perfected the casual stroll of an innocent passerby. He approached this guard and said, "*Valerius has a question for you. He would like to see you now.*"

Without hesitation, the guard rushed off to seek out his fellow soldier, obviously his superior. Acknowledging his luck, Ben opened the gate and stepped surreptitiously through the entrance, closing it behind him.

He noted to himself that that had been way too easy—Scooby Doo should be so clever.

Inside the inner courtyard, Ben expected to find more guards, but there was nobody visible except a young man pushing a cart stacked with bowls, who took no notice of the newcomer.

Keeping a respectable distance, Ben watched the fellow enter the main temple building through an unremarkable side entrance. He waited a few moments, then slipped in after him.

~ ~ ~ ~

Danny turned and faced the guard at the beginning of the corridor. *"Where are the new arrivals?"* he asked.

The man said nothing, only pointed to the far end of the hallway, where the other guard sat. Danny continued on his way, looking down at the grates in the floor. Each one seemed to hold about ten prisoners. As he arrived at the eighth and final grate, he nodded to the guard, who looked back at him with an expression of boredom.

Looking down through the metal bars in the floor, Danny saw, among the men there, the familiar shock of red hair that could only belong to Judas Iscariot. He wrinkled his nose and called out, *"Judas."*

The red-haired man looked up, no longer bound by shackles, and was shocked to see Danny looking back at him. Then he looked down at the floor, as he appeared to be standing in a pile of excrement. There were thirteen other men in there with him. One of them was lying prone on the floor of the cell, either unconscious or dead.

Danny turned and retraced his steps back down the corridor, past the first guard, then turned the corner, arriving back at the bottom of the stairs. In that small area, he was out of sight of the guards in the corridor, and out of sight of the guard up on the main floor.

Digging around in his backpack, Danny pulled out his Galaxy and scrolled through the songs in his playlists. He selected "Tom Sawyer" by Rush, set the volume at full, but did not hit 'Play'. He then pulled out Ben's phone and cued up the same song, thankful that Ben had enough good sense to keep some Rush songs on his own playlists—they were all from Toronto, after all.

~ ~ ~ ~

The interior of the main hall of the High Priests' Temple was grandiose enough to make Solomon envious, but its high, ivory-trimmed polished-marble walls and gilded pillars went unnoticed by Ben.

Mouse-like, Ben crept along inside the back wall, beneath a row of mounted oil lamps. He was still convinced that his plan was crazy, that he had a better chance of being thrown in jail than he did of convincing the priests of anything.

— 27 —

Danny was at the bottom of the stairs, still temporarily out of sight from all three prison guards. He held the phones in one hand, both of them cued up to the song "Tom Sawyer". Creeping back up to the top of the stairs, he saw the guard, barely visible from the doorway, still occupying his post. Danny's face was now down with the street-level floor. Using both thumbs, he hit the 'Play' button on the two devices, syncing the song to play on both of them at the same time. He flicked Ben's phone, tossing it so it slid all the way across the floor, coming to rest underneath another chair on the other side of the room. The guard jumped back in fear at the ungodly sound and immediately rushed over to investigate, but Danny didn't stick around to watch.

The opening power chord of "Tom Sawyer" echoed off the stone walls, followed by Geddy Lee's unmistakable rap-style intro: *"A modern-day warrior, mean, mean stride, today's Tom Sawyer, mean, mean pride..."*

Danny bolted back down the stairs, turned the corner, and planted the other Galaxy in the first wall-mounted torch holder he came to, wedging it between the metal frame and the wall. The music of Rush filled the entire hallway, amplified by the echoic qualities of the stone walls.

The guard at the beginning of the corridor stood up in reaction to the noise. He had never heard anything like it and, assuming foul play, he drew his sword and ran upstairs. The guard at the far end of the corridor came running in pursuit. Danny moved away from the half-hidden phone and faced him. The guard looked accusingly at Danny, who shouted in Hebrew, *"It came from up there!"*

The guard dashed away up the stairs. Just then, Danny was alone in the corridor. He raced to the far end and stood over the grate covering Judas' cell. He could see that one edge was hinged, while the other had a sort of padlock. From inside his backpack, Danny produced the hammer and bashed away at the lock, which broke in two after only a few hits. Seeing all this from below, the prisoners started to get anxious, crowding around the crude wooden ladder that led down to their cell. Judas tried to muscle his way to the ladder, but there were too many men. All of them except the man lying on the floor wanted to climb out first. Nobody considered the fact that several of them would be dead in a few moments.

Danny hoisted up the grate, and the men came rushing up from below. He couldn't even see Judas. As the prisoners climbed out of their hole, they almost knocked Danny off his feet. Before the first men were halfway down the corridor, all three guards had rushed back down from upstairs, this time with swords drawn. The prisoners only had eyes for the exit, and they did not slow down their forward march, even in the face of swinging blades. The man in front, the one who, moments earlier, had successfully elbowed his way to the ladder before the others, was the first to fall with a sword in his belly. The men behind him lunged forward, stepping on the body of their former cellmate, only to receive their own swift executions.

But allowing for the few valuable seconds required to remove a sword from a newly-fallen corpse and raise it again for another victim, the next wave of emboldened prisoners pushed forward, knocking all three guards to the ground. The rest of the men trampled the fallen people, prisoners and guards alike. From the floor, the two guards who remained conscious waved their swords up, partly in self-defence, partly to punish any of the remaining escapees with a gash on the leg.

Using the momentum of the prisoners in front of them, Danny and Judas made sure the soldiers remained on the ground in time for them to pass by. As they rounded the corner at the end of the corridor, Danny paused just long enough to reach up and grab the phone, which was blasting the Tom

Sawyer synthesizer solo. He shut it off and, by the time they arrived at the bottom of the stairs, they heard screams from behind them. They did not look back to see if the bellowing came from guards or prisoners, but instead raced up the stairs to the anteroom on the ground floor.

In a split-second decision, Danny tore over to the opposite side of the room and threw himself down onto the floor. Reaching under the table against the wall, he found that Ben's Galaxy was not where he had tossed it. The echoes of the chamber made it difficult to hear the device's location, but by the fact that it was still playing music, Danny knew it had not been stomped on by a frustrated soldier. There was very little light in the room, so Danny had to crawl along the ground, feeling for the phone.

Judas was not sure what Danny was doing, why he was on the floor when the guards would ascend the stairs any moment. But he waited for his rescuer anyway.

Danny crawled to the part of the room where the music appeared to be coming from, and located the phone. He wrapped his fingers around it, rose to his feet, and dashed out the front door with Judas, hitting the stop button as he ran.

The bright sunlight attacked their eyes, and they had to run blindly for the first few steps. A crowd had already gathered around the building, as the first fleeing prisoners had caused a commotion in the street. Judas and Danny pushed their way through the people, and paused in the first alleyway they came to.

They took a moment to lean against a building and catch their breath. Danny pulled out the stolen robe and tossed it to Judas, who examined it and frowned.

Danny couldn't understand why Judas was not cooperating. *"Put that on,"* he told him.

But Judas was confused. *"This is a lady's robe,"* he said. *"Where did you get this?"*

Danny was starting to get irritated. "*I borrowed it from a nice girl. Let's go!*"

Judas grimaced then obeyed, and the two of them walked back out into the street.

~ ~ ~ ~

In the main hall of the High Priests' Temple, Ben crouched behind one of the large pillars. None of the priests noticed he was there. He remained on his knees, praying, trying to build up courage.

— 28 —

Danny and Judas continued running until they found a place to stop, sit and talk with relative safety. A narrow alleyway afforded them enough cover that they felt comfortable not being on the move, for a few moments at least. Judas, having calmed down a little, addressed his rescuer for the first time. *"My friend, thank you for helping me."*

"You're welcome," Danny replied. *"Peace. Are you okay?"*

Judas wiped sweat from his forehead and looked down at his feminine-looking robe. *"I am fine."* Thinking about what had happened in the prison, Judas pointed to Danny's backpack, into which the smartphones had been placed. *"What was that devil box, making that horrible noise?"*

Danny fought back a frown. Horrible noise indeed. *"It's just something I got from a merchant far away."*

Judas looked doubtful, but didn't pursue it. *"I have not slept,"* he said. *"I had the entire night to reflect on things, to think about what I must do."* He rose to his feet. *"I will leave you now. They are waiting for me."* Danny watched as Judas started purposefully down the street in the direction of the High Priests' Temple.

"Judas, stop!"

Judas turned back around, giving Danny a look that clearly said he did not want to be diverted from his mutinous plan. *"What is it?"*

"*I know what you are going to do,*" Danny said quietly.

Judas immediately became defensive. *"No you don't. I've told nobody about what I am planning."*

Danny steeled himself as he explained, *"I know that you are going to see Caiaphas. I know that you will betray Jesus."*

The look of shock Judas gave Danny quickly turned to one of anger. *"How do you get inside my head?"* he yelled at him. *"How do you know my thoughts?"*

Danny closed his eyes and shook his head slowly. *"You would not believe me if I told you."*

This only made Judas angrier. *"Are you what Jesus says you are? Are you a messenger?"*

"I really don't think so," Danny replied.

"What does that mean? Why are you being evasive? You sound just like he does!"

"I'm not doing that on purpose."

"I have to go." Judas turned around once more.

Danny ran, and fell into step behind him. *"Please tell me one thing,"* he said.

"What's that?" Judas didn't didn't turn around, didn't break his stride.

Danny considered his words, but could think of no other way to ask Judas his question other than to be direct. *"Why?"* he asked. *"Why are you betraying him?"*

Judas stopped walking. He lowered his voice, almost as if he was afraid that someone may have overheard the accusation put to him. When he spoke, Danny could hear fear and determination in his voice. "It's *not a betrayal. I'm helping him, helping our cause."* His voice started to crescendo. *"He has the power to show Rome that he is their king. But he refuses!"* Shouting now. *"The high priests want him dead, because they think he is causing trouble for them!"*

Danny kept his voice low. *"But why turn Jesus in?"*

Judas shook his head; Danny could tell he was upset at being misunderstood again. *"It will force a meeting with the priests."*

"Even if Jesus is in shackles?"

"Yes, even then. If Jesus' life is threatened, surely he will perform a miracle for the priests, and reveal himself to

them as the Messiah. They will see who he is and let him go free. Then we can all carry on as before." Judas almost didn't look as if he believed his own prediction, but he was nevertheless convinced that this path was the one to follow.

Danny put a great deal of thought into the next sentence that came out of his mouth. He and Ben had discussed at length what their role was here: were they supposed to change history or set it back on course? He held Judas' gaze as he said, "*I don't know that everything will unfold the way you are planning.*"

The die was cast.

"*How do YOU know what will play out?*" Judas was getting irate again. "*Do you think you are the Messiah yourself? Do you know everyone's thoughts and actions?*"

Danny was silent. Judas showed him his back for the third time. "*I have to go*," he said.

The die was lost.

Judas stormed off in the direction of the High Priests' Temple, certain that nothing would divert him from his path again. Danny followed behind at a respectful distance.

— 29 —

Standing in front of Caiaphas, Ben was terrified. The last time he had stood in the area now known as the High Priests' Temple, he and his parents had been part of a tour group. He had been a child then, not the least bit interested in a decrepit old building that came with history lessons. The tour guide had suggested that that structure was built on the very place where Jesus Christ had been tried and convicted by the high priests Caiaphas and Annas. The tour guide had in fact been correct.

That event in his childhood was ten years ago, by Ben's reckoning. And that event was near on two thousand years in the future, with respect to the two imposing men before whom he now stood. Caiaphas was an enormous, intimidating man, giving the impression that he had gained his position partially due to his physical stature. His gaze was steady and penetrating; his thick black beard, large nose and wide mouth made up a face that nobody dared challenge. Annas, beside him, was a slightly smaller copy of Caiaphas, but with eyes that reflected an intelligent and calculating nature. The two priests wore thick, dark ceremonial robes and tall, commanding conical hats. That Annas stood a few inches behind Caiaphas was all that was needed to reveal the hierarchy in the room.

Ben's upper arms were held in the iron grip of the armed guards standing on either side of him. Two other guards stood close by, to the left and to the right. Six guards to hold him there. One guard would have been plenty to ensure Ben kept himself in line. In fact, zero guards would have been fine; Caiaphas's stare alone would have ensured that Ben behaved himself.

Everyone in the room was upset at how Ben had stolen his way inside the temple.

"*Who are you?! What do you want from us?!*" Caiaphas bellowed at him, spitting in his face as he screamed, almost knocking him over.

Ben whispered, nearly forgetting how to speak Hebrew, "*I am Benjamin, son of Timothy.*"

"*Use your voice, boy! Shout so God can hear you! Why is it you are bothering us?*"

Ben fell mute, his lower lip shaking uncontrollably. But he knew what he had to do. He opened his mouth to change history, or perhaps to put history back on track. It was time to deliver the speech he had been turning over in his mind during the last few hours.

"Um..."

That wasn't the speech he had prepared. He tried again.

"*I have some... information*, I think. Um..."

It was going precisely as badly as he had feared it would. Against his will, he found himself thinking about the first time he had had to give a speech in front of his Grade Four class at school. He couldn't remember which topic he had chosen, but he could clearly remember how incredibly frightened he had been at the very idea of public speaking. He had thought his classmates would make for a tough crowd. How foolish that seemed now.

He cleared his throat to start speaking again. Suddenly, Ben's view of the priests was blocked. A man had placed himself in front of him and faced the high priests. Ben was pleased to not have to look at Caiaphas and Annas, but he was even more relieved that Caiaphas and Annas could no longer see him. Ben stared at the back of the head of the man in front of him, the red-haired man, Yehudah, Judas. Once again, Ben was overjoyed to see Judas.

After a brief exchange between Caiaphas and Judas, one of the guards released his grip on Ben's arm. The other guard threw him to the ground behind them, where Ben broke his fall on somebody's feet. He looked up and was ecstatic to see that it was Danny. The six guards closed their line, and stood behind Judas with their backs to Ben. Danny reached down and helped Ben up. Ben fell into his friend's arms like a child needing his mother. "I couldn't do it," he whispered.

"That's okay," Danny replied. "You can see that Judas is here now. Let's get the hell out of here."

Not for the first time, Ben gained strength just by bearing witness to Danny's confidence. The two boys turned and took leave of the temple. As they walked, they could hear Judas' voice. As they reached the egress, they could hear Judas crying.

~ ~ ~ ~

"Where is Judas?" The Apostle John asked the question out loud to his fellow disciples. It was still Tuesday afternoon, and the group was gathered at their camp in Bethany. Jesus, his Apostles, and all the disciples (seventy at this point), continued to spend their days in the city, returning to the village each night for food and rest.

That afternoon the mood was tense, not jovial like most of their other gatherings. Philip, standing near John, looked around at the group, and eventually rested his eyes on Danny and Ben. He spoke with sarcasm. *"John, ask your question again, but to Judas' special friends here."* Philip walked accusingly towards Danny and Ben. *"Judas seems to like you, to trust you. I'm sure you know where he is."*

They looked up at Philip, but said nothing. Philip changed his tone slightly. *"Now is not the time for silence, boys. We all need to stick together. Have you seen Judas or not? Where is he?"*

"I am here." Judas appeared from between the trees; he walked over towards Philip. *"Since when are my whereabouts any concern of yours?"*

Philip stepped towards Judas threateningly. *"Where have you been?"*

Judas, bearing the stress of his recent conversation and subsequent transaction in the High Priests' Temple, said, *"Leave me alone."* He pushed Philip away, and immediately James and Matthew rushed over to put an end to the confrontation. Danny and Ben watched the action with eyes and mouths wide open. Almost involuntarily, Ben reached into his robe, pulled out the remote control and hit the record button as he pointed it at Andrew, who had been standing nearby. Judas turned on his heel and headed towards a table on which grapes, dates and bread roles had been laid out for the disciples. Ben couldn't tell if Judas planned to eat the food or upend the table.

No one seemed to know what to do, then Andrew stepped forward and approached Judas. He blocked his path and put his hand gently on Judas' chest. *"Brother, please don't be vexed."*

Judas stopped moving but did not reply. He did not even look down into Andrew's kind face. Standing there, Andrew appeared to come up with an idea. He took off the medallion necklace that Danny and Ben had given him and placed it around Judas' neck as a gift. Judas looked down at the medallion on his chest, grabbed it the by the edges and held it up to his face, looking at it with distrust. He then fondled the button in the centre, inadvertently turning the recording off.

"I do not have need for your trash," Judas said with a scowl.

Andrew was not perturbed at all. *"I know that. But I want you to have it. Let it remind you that you are still loved by your brothers here."*

Judas let the necklace fall back down upon his chest and left the clearing without so much as a glance backwards at his friends. Danny and Ben watched all this, still looking pie-eyed.

Danny whispered to Ben, "There goes our camera. How the hell are we going to get it back?"

Ben threw his hands in the air. "I propose you go ask him for it—he's your buddy."

— 30 —

The dawn of a new day brought hope and excitement to all who gathered around Jesus, but it brought tension and fear to Danny and Ben. It was Wednesday, and there were activities planned—prayers, gatherings and visitations. Most everyone there was in a celebratory mood, but the boys felt no part of that. After breakfast, the group readied the day's supplies for the walk to Jerusalem.

Danny and Ben stayed back, opting instead to help prepare the evening meal for the others. It was going to largely be their day of rest, as they knew that the next few days would be extremely difficult for them, despite the fact that they were not the ones to be slated for crucifixion.

~ ~ ~ ~

The next morning, the boys felt much better, recharged. The stress of coming events still weighed on them, but a good night's sleep had given them a little more strength, making them feel they would be able to cope with whatever happened.

At Jesus' request, John called the Apostles together to discuss the day's plans. Danny and Ben tagged along as usual, with fifteen other disciples. If Judas' absence was noticed, nobody spoke up.

Peter explained that the Passover meal would take place that evening in a house at Mount Zion.

Danny whispered, almost to himself. "Man, does this mean we are walking to another town?"

Ben spoke into Danny's shoulder. "No, Mount Zion is an area not far from what we know as Old Jerusalem."

Simon spoke up, addressing Jesus. *"Master, where shall we find this house?"*

In a manner that the disciples came to understand as normal, Jesus replied without words, and pointed to two men outside the circle of Apostles. Silas and Rufus had been disciples for more than a year and, although they were generally silent listeners, they were trusted among the group. They dressed like the paupers that they were, with dark-coloured linen tunics, frayed at the sleeves, but held their own as more than just freeloaders.

Jesus gave his directive. *"Silas and Rufus. The two of you shall go to the city, where you will meet a man carrying a jar of water. Follow him, and he will lead you to a house in Mount Zion. Our Passover Meal will take place there, in the Upper Room."*

Either the instructions never occurred to Silas and Rufus as being vague to the point of folly, or they trusted Jesus completely. They rose to their feet, happy to be given an important task, assigned by the Teacher himself.

Philip looked over the group and rested his eyes upon Ben and Danny. *"You and you. Go with them. Help set the table."*

Jesus didn't overrule Philip, but instead pointed out, *"Everything is already furnished and ready for us. There will be chairs at the table for me and my beloved Twelve."*

Silas and Rufus had already started towards the road. Danny and Ben rose and departed anyway, following them at a distance, keeping them in sight.

"This sounds like a reasonable job," said Danny. "150,000 people in Jerusalem, and we are looking for a guy carrying a bottle of water."

"A jar."

"What?"

Ben grimaced. "Jesus said the man would be carrying a jar of water, not a bottle."

Danny pointed with his chin to the two men charged with this task. "Rufus and Goofus there can look after finding the restaurant. I guess you and I will be waiters or busboys."

Ben started to laugh, then he started to roar. He doubled over, with his arms on his belly, and laughed like he was going to come apart. It was a relief, a release. Ben had bottled up so much stress, fear and anguish in the last two days, to say nothing of the last nine months, that hearing a fellow disciple being referred to as "Goofus" was just the funniest damn thing he had heard in his life.

Danny smiled, happy to please his friend.

~ ~ ~ ~

In Jerusalem, just inside the city wall, the four emissaries took in the sight of the crowds, more numerous than in the past few days. People were walking to and from every direction, each on a mission. Ben shook his head, seeing their endeavour as fruitless.

With Sirus leading the way, the four of them marched through the crowd, looking for someone who, they assumed, would be expecting them, someone who was prepared to have thirteen guests over for supper that night.

And didn't they happen upon a man carrying a large jar of water, walking towards them as they crossed the street. He looked just like every other pilgrim in the area, except for the fact that he bore water. Rufus pointed him out to the others. "*There he is.*"

Ben had doubts about the container the man was carrying. He spoke under his breath to Danny. "Looks more like a jug."

Danny wasn't so sure. "We're getting lost in translation. Maybe *jug* and *jar* are the same word in Hebrew."

While they talked, Sirus and Rufus marched right on ahead and approached the stranger. "*Peace,*" said Sirus. "*We are disciples of the prophet Jesus of Nazareth. We are here to arrange a place for him to dine this evening.*"

The man looked surprised, as if he genuinely had not had advance notice of this arrangement. He thought it over and said, "*My place is in Mount Zion. I am sure the master of the house would be honoured to have Jesus spend his Passover meal with us.*" The man's accent revealed him to be Judean.

And so the five men walked through the throng of people, heading southwest to Mount Zion.

"That still looks like a jug to me," said Danny to Ben, as they walked. "I can't shake the feeling that there's another guy walking around with a *jar* of water, with instructions from Jesus, ready to bring us all to a different house somewhere."

"Well, Goofus looks like he knows what he's doing. We may as well follow them."

— 31 —

The master of the house was a smart-looking man who had introduced himself as Thaddeus. His dress displayed wealth, a crimson toga with gold tressing, and his dialect revealed an educated upbringing. He had unusually short hair and a thin, oiled beard. Like most of the people in Jerusalem, he had been told that the Messiah had appeared, and that the man was a Nazarene. Thaddeus smiled in spite of himself, as it appeared the Messiah would be dining this evening under his roof.

His home was larger than most in his neighbourhood, with a spiralling tower at the apex of the roof and a façade that indicated an artisan's devotion. Potted plants surrounded the front yard on either side of the walkway leading up to the house's grand entranceway.

The four visitors were led under an arch through a carved wooden front door. The room they found themselves in was decorated with elaborately-framed paintings, vases and pottery to betray the owner's wealth. Much of the decor appeared to be from the Orient. An imposing ebony carving of a panther hung on the wall. On a dark brown table in the corner sat a small black metal container in which a cone of incense burned its smoke throughout the room.

Thaddeus' gestured towards the staircase. His demeanour showed that he was quite used to accommodating guests. The staircase opened up into a large room, replete with pillars whose ribs extended to a beautiful arched ceiling. Oil lamps on the walls gave the room an intimate atmosphere. In the middle of the space, three rectangular tables were arranged in a triclinium; the U-shaped placement allowed for all the diners to sit along the outside, facing in to each other. The absence of a fourth table allowed servers into the middle, to place or remove serving trays as needed.

<<Photo10>>

The tables were low to the ground, and there were no chairs. Instead, large cushions were arranged along the three sides. Ben counted them. "Thirteen," he whispered, to no one in particular. Two large pewter candle holders sat on either of the two outer tables.

Thaddeus seemed to enjoy showing off this room. With a smile, he asked, *"Do you think your master will find this acceptable?"*

Sirus spoke for the others. *"Yes, this would be fine. Do you mind if we stay here, within this house or without? We wish to wait for our master's arrival."*

Thaddeus invited the four disciples to relax in the courtyard garden behind the building. He then disappeared, to make arrangements to feed a company of thirteen.

Outside, Danny volunteered to run back to Bethany and tell the others the location of the house, but Sirus was certain that Jesus would find his way here well enough. With a shrug, Danny sprawled out beside a tree. "I don't know why I find it weird that the tables are placed that way—"

Ben rolled his eyes at him as he sat beside him on the grass. "Did you think all thirteen of them were actually going to line up along one side of the table like the Da Vinci painting?"

"Oh. I guess not," said Danny.

~ ~ ~ ~

The sun was now low enough over the horizon that Ben started to get restless in the waiting. Finally, he stood up and announced to the others. *"It's getting late. I'm going to go find them. Maybe they are waiting for news from us after all."*

Without waiting for a comment from the others, Ben took his leave. He entered the house through the back door and made his way through, exiting at the front entrance. As he walked briskly down the street, he saw for the first time the glorious view of the city that was to be had from Mount Zion, the setting sun reflecting off the temples below. He had been up there as a child, but the sight had not held his attention then, the way it did now.

"*Peace, Ben,*" said Jesus.

Coming abruptly out of his daydream, Ben looked up to see Jesus and the Apostles right in front of him, walking towards the house he had just exited. Momentarily stunned, Ben turned around and started back towards the house with them.

Jesus put his hand on Ben's shoulder as they walked. "*Thank you for doing this, Ben. I am glad you came to me.*" Ben offered a weak smile in return, uncertain whether Jesus was referring to this evening or to the last nine months. Rubbing shoulders with a future dead man was something he found disconcerting—regardless of, or perhaps because of, the profound implications of his death.

As the group arrived at the front door of the house, Simon spoke up. "*Judas is not here.*"

Jesus gave his all-knowing smile and said, "*He will be along soon, I am sure.*"

Thaddeus was waiting at the front door of the house. For all his experience as an aristocrat, he was not certain how to greet a messiah. But Jesus reached out and took his hand first, thanking him for his hospitality. Thaddeus led everyone inside and directed them to the staircase. As they made their way up, Sirus, Rufus and Danny emerged from the courtyard garden and walked over to where Ben was standing by the entrance. Thaddeus saw them and promptly put them all to work. A cart was brought out, laden with matzot, roasted lamb and decanters of heated spiced wine. The master of the house motioned for the four of them to deliver the items to the banquet.

Danny and Ben didn't mind hauling food for the Apostles; neither of them possessed the finesse of an actual waiter, but they were certain that nobody would notice or care.

Jesus, as the head, was not actually seated in the centre of the table, but second in, towards one of the wings of the table. John sat in a place of honour next to Jesus, but the spot on the corner, on Jesus' other side, was empty. Nobody sat there, as it was apparently reserved for Judas. Seeing this, Ben was reminded of how, in Jewish society, seating positions were very important, and deeply respected.

One decanter and thirteen goblets were arranged on the table. Two house servants took the food from Danny, Ben, Sirus and Rufus, and politely instructed them to exit. Downstairs, more platters were prepared and delivered until everyone was served.

There came then a bang on the door, which Thaddeus opened to admit the next guest. Judas stood there, sweaty and visibly distracted—and did not look at the boys as he was directed towards the stairs.

Ben watched Judas ascend to join his fellow Apostles at the meal that would be known by the rest of the world as the Last Supper. *That makes two dead men walking*, he thought to himself.

More platters with the same meal were brought out for the servants. Ben and Danny ate their food in silence. They were content to rest, to conserve their energy.

It was less than an hour after the upstairs meal had begun that the first set of footsteps could be heard descending. It was Judas, as silent and sullen as he had been when he first arrived. Ben and Danny watched him leave to fulfill his destiny.

A few moments later, the others emerged from the meal and exited the front door. Danny noticed that Andrew held a cup in his grasp, clearly the holy chalice from which Jesus had served the wine, representing his blood.

— 32 —

The Garden of Gethsemane is located at the base of the Mount of Olives, east of Jerusalem's city center. Ben had visited the place with his parents when he was twelve, and had remarked that the ancient gnarled olive trees made the garden look like Tolkein's Mirkwood Forest, in Middle-Earth.

Now, in the first century, Ben looked around the same garden, admiring what he could only assume were the same olive trees. They were just saplings; the trees were not as fantastical as they looked in the twenty-first century—owing to the discrepancy of a couple of millennia. Ben found it easier to consider the fate of the trees than the fate of his companions. The anticipation of the coming hours filled Ben with dread and sadness. The setting sun, and the twisted shadows formed by the trees' branches seemed to exacerbate Ben's toiling emotions.

<<Photo11>>

Danny, lying on his back in the garden, let his mind drift back to a debate he had had at school regarding Jesus' whereabouts prior to his arrest.

~ ~ ~ ~

"Daniel, the theology class is down the hall. You are more than welcome to discuss your ideas with them." Professor Grohmann sometimes enjoyed the tangents her students took the class on, but today she was determined to keep everybody on track.

"But if Jesus already knew—"

"That's the whole point. Jesus didn't know for certain. That's why he tried to negotiate with God."

Danny was clutching at straws. "And do you think anyone can actually negotiate with God?"

Professor Grohmann smiled. "No more than you can negotiate a passing grade with me." She turned back to the chalkboard. "Now. I'll pose the question again. Does anyone really know the location of the Last Supper?"

A few hands were raised, but Professor Grohmann ignored them, as her question had been rhetorical. "In Jerusalem, tour guides will take you to the exact location of the Last Supper. And most of them will admit, after you've taken your photographs, how it may or may not have been the actual location, but that the meal probably took place in a room similar to that one." She paused, to let the class consider this. "Where exactly was Jesus when he was arrested? Were they in the Garden of Gethsemane, or someplace else?"

A girl in the desk behind Danny put up her hand. "What about the cave?"

"Right. There is evidence that they were hiding in a cave in the garden. The problem with this is that it contradicts the idea that Jesus had accepted his fate and allowed himself to be caught freely. If that were the case, he wouldn't be hiding anywhere. My point here is that we don't know for sure."

~ ~ ~ ~

It appeared to Danny that things would be happening in the garden after all. And then there's the Last Supper. He now knew exactly where it took place, but he probably wouldn't be able to retrace his steps to that house again. There were many previously-disputed facts about the comings and goings of Jesus that were no longer in dispute—in his mind, at least.

Danny was aware that Jesus was not the only one among them who would be crucified, by fate or by circumstance. Many of the Apostles, his friends, would be executed in the months and years to come. This was already known to him, but it had been easy to forget when they were all laughing over a meal or enjoying the open waters of the sea. But there in the Garden of Gethsemane, everyone's paths were laid out before them; they had only to follow them.

All of the people with them there in the garden, Apostles and disciples alike, knew that something was amiss. Jesus had announced that one of The Twelve would betray him. Although he did not say whom, it was noted that Judas was no longer among them.

As everyone settled in for the evening, Jesus stood up and left the group without a word. The others watched as he walked towards the base of the Mount of Olives. It was understood by some in the group that Jesus was going off alone to pray, possibly to negotiate his lot with God.

The group had long ago become used to Jesus wandering off on his own, but this time it was different. Everyone there in the garden felt that their group was not complete without their leader, their master. As the sun fell, city sounds made way for forest sounds. Six-legged critters, whose chirping was not unlike that made by cicadas, provided the evening's soundtrack.

Everyone claimed a patch of grass and, by the time Jesus returned from his short pilgrimage, all of the disciples were asleep.

~ ~ ~ ~

Ben woke suddenly in the middle of the still night. In the Garden of Gethsemane, things were peaceful and the air was pleasant. He looked around. The clearing was well-lit, as there were torches on poles thrust into the ground nearby. Everyone else had retired except Jesus, who was standing in the middle of all the sleeping disciples, his head down in prayer.

Out of the darkness, Ben saw a small cluster of torches, moving towards the garden from the streets of Jerusalem. He began to tremble with fear, even though he knew they weren't coming for him. He reached over and shook Danny awake. The two of them braced themselves as ten armed soldiers entered the garden, accompanied by Judas. Jesus stood waiting to receive them, as if the soldiers had in fact been invited guests.

Ben and Danny watched as Judas kissed Jesus' cheek. They heard Jesus' words, *"'Judas, are you betraying the Son of Man with a kiss?"*

It was the sound of manacles clinking that woke the other disciples. Almost instantly, the sleeping men rose up, took stock of the situation, and moved in to shield their master from harm. Danny and Ben picked up their backpacks and headed quickly to the outskirts of the action.

Two of the soldiers drew their swords. It was more a show of force, as the men before them appeared to have no arms of their own. But Peter, to the surprise of everyone there, produced a short sword and raised it to the soldier nearest Jesus.

"Malchus!" The name rung out as a warning, but the soldier had been facing his quarry as Peter brought his sword down on him. In an instant, the man's right ear lay on the ground.

Pandemonium followed as all the soldiers drew their swords and advanced upon Jesus' defenders. But before any more blood could be shed, Jesus, his hands not yet bound, cried out, *"No more of this!"* Then quietly: *"Sheath your weapons."*

Everyone obeyed, including the soldiers, men who would not normally accept a directive from someone about to be in their custody.

For a moment, all was silent. Then Jesus whispered, *"Give me his ear."*

Malchus was a soldier in the employ of Caiaphas. He knew about hierarchy, as did his men. *"Do what he says!"* Porcius, the soldier beneath Malchus' rank, recognized that the task fell to him. He stepped forward, bent down and picked up the detached bloody ear, and handed it to Jesus.

From their vantage point at the back of the fray, Danny and Ben saw Jesus walk over to where Malchus knelt on the ground and touch the side of the man's bloody face. They saw no more than that, and they had no inclination to produce their video camera.

"Am I leading a rebellion, that you have come with swords and clubs? Every day I was with you in the temple, and you did not lay a hand on me. But now this is your hour, when darkness reigns."

Jesus then held out his hands to two of the soldiers, who bound him. He was calmly led out of the garden, surrounded by all ten armed guards. The disciples followed at a distance.

Danny and Ben both made eye contact with Judas as they followed the others out.

Judas remained behind in the garden.

── 33 ──

The Galilean, one Jesus of Nazareth, had arrived in Jerusalem for Passover under the notion of being the Messiah, the son of God. His claims, readily received by the growing multitudes, provoked the ire of three men—King Herod Antipas, the prefect Pontius Pilate and the High Priest Caiaphas.

When Judaea had become a province of the Roman empire, the coastal city of Caesarea Maritima was selected as the capital. This was where Herod Antipas and Pontius Pilate both lived. But during the eight days of Passover, the two men took up residence in Jerusalem. Herod stayed in his palace, a magnificent edifice of fourteen acres. Pilate, as governor, stayed in the Antonia Fortress, at the northern end of Herod's Temple.

The High Priest Caiaphas had been appointed by Pilate's predecessor. It was due to Caiaphas' ability to cooperate with the Roman overseers that Pilate extended his tenure in the high priesthood.

Herod, Pilate and Caiaphas all had the potential to be deposed of their positions, and further, they risked their own executions if Rome caught wind of a revolt or a Messianic uprising. So it was with good reason that Jesus' presence in Jerusalem made all of them nervous.

Among Jesus' twelve disciples, Judas was the only non-Galilean. As such, he alone understood the politics, and the pressures imposed upon the leaders to keep the peace. But as Judas sat alone in the Garden of Gethsemane watching his friends disappear with the soldiers through the trees, he knew he was guilty of the ultimate betrayal.

~ ~ ~ ~

In the wee hours of Friday morning, Danny and Ben found themselves in the majestic High Priests' Temple for the second time that week. This time they stood at the back of a large crowd of people. It seemed that the crowd took up more oxygen than the enormous room could provide, and so Danny and Ben both felt somewhat light-headed. They could see Jesus, his hands bound in front of him, standing before the high priests Caiaphas and Annas. They could not hear what was being said, but they could see that Jesus was not answering the questions put to him, and the high priests were clearly not happy. Caiaphas waved his arm, and Jesus was escorted by the soldiers to a seat, a makeshift prisoner's box.

And everyone waited.

It took less than half an hour, but eventually Pontius Pilate marched in, accompanied by a small entourage of two armed guards, a scribe and three servants. Pilate walked as if he had been important and powerful his entire life. He had a chiselled face with an aquiline nose and small eyes. His gold-fringed robe was cut short; his upper arms were adorned with silver circlets. He walked as a man of the sword, not as a bureaucrat, to the front of the hall and faced Jesus. A soldier guided the prisoner to his feet to stand before Pilate. Pilate looked Jesus over from head to toe, evaluating the man. He wrinkled his nose in a way that revealed his disdain for the Jewish people he was charged with governing.

From the back of the crowd, Danny and Ben watched all of this with awe. They saw that Jesus, again, remained silent, despite the challenges, invitations and pleadings by Pilate for Jesus to produce a defence. Presently, Pilate grew visibly weary of speaking to himself. He screamed an order, and Jesus was removed from the temple. Danny and Ben knew that he was being taken away for his trial in the temple of King Herod. The soldiers alone escorted Jesus, though John and Andrew followed the processional to bear witness. The rest of the crowd remained at the High Priest's temple, many of them spilling outside onto the steps.

Danny, although his mind was reeling, had nothing to say to anyone. He himself was not on trial, but he felt as stressed as if it was his own fate being decided.

Ben simply cried quietly to himself.

Following the other disciples, the two of them stepped outside into the courtyard and the cool morning air. The sun was only just starting to rise.

Danny, seeing Peter walking off on his own, followed him down the steps of the building, a dozen paces behind. Peter sat down on the bottom step as one of the priest's serving girls passed by. She stopped, looked him over, and called out to him in Hebrew. *"You were with Jesus the Nazarene."*

Peter's face immediately showed fear. He looked around at the people milling about, and said, *"I neither know nor understand what you are talking about."* With that, he stood up and started to walk away. Ben came over to stand beside Danny.

The maid persisted. She pointed to him and said, with volume, *"This is one of them!"*

Peter turned around and snapped, *"I am not!"*

The small crowd started to close in on Peter, and a man barred his way, saying, *"Surely you are one of them, for you are a Galilean too."*

At this, Peter shouted to the whole crowd, *"I do not know this man you are talking about!"* He turned and ran to the other side of the temple's courtyard.

Danny, his voice devoid of irony, turned to Ben and said, "This is where the cock crows," He pointed his index finger in the air as a cock crowed in the distance. Ben, who was unfamiliar with that passage of scripture, was too distracted to register any sort of surprise or acknowledgement.

Danny and Ben walked over to where Peter sat alone, on the opposite steps. Mary Magdalene emerged from the temple and followed them. The four disciples sat together, looking up at the temple's magnificent outer building.

Mary saw that Peter had been crying, so she wiped his face with the sleeve of her robe.

Peter looked over at Danny and Ben. *"What will the verdict be?"* He spoke as if he sensed the two of them could observe and understand what was going on around them, more clearly than anyone else among Jesus' disciples.

Ben answered quietly. *"Pilate said King Herod should decide his fate, because Jesus is from Galilee."*

"They will be back soon," said Danny.

Peter accepted their responses as facts. He looked down at his sandals. *"I had no choice but to deny him."*

Danny touched his shoulder. *"I know."*

Peter's face showed fear and frustration. *"If they thought I was one of his disciples, they would—"*

"I understand," said Danny. *"I am one of his disciples as well."*

Mary started to cry. Ben found strength with the knowledge that someone needed him to be strong. He walked over and sat down on the other side of her. She looked up at him and he put his arm around her. I am comforting Mary Magdalene, he thought to himself.

The four of them could do nothing more than sit and wait for Jesus to return.

— 34 —

Andrew and John led the crowd down the street, back towards the High Priest's temple. They arrived at the steps where Danny, Ben, Peter and Mary Magdalene were waiting for news. Behind them, the soldiers brought Jesus back into the temple to face Pilate again.

As the rest of the crowd filed back inside, Andrew explained to his friends, *"He didn't do anything!"*

John continued. *"Herod was ready to let him go free. All he had to do was perform a miracle."*

Andrew was still yelling. *"Herod made it clear to him. He asked Jesus to impress him with one little magic trick."*

"Then we could all go free," said John. *"But he just stood there. He did nothing."*

Danny thought to himself about Judas' gamble, and how wrong he was.

The sound of the crowd shouting could be heard from inside the building. The six of them quickly hurried back inside.

From Danny's and Ben's viewpoint at the back of the hall, they could see that Jesus was once again standing before Pilate. Pilate grabbed Jesus' shoulders and spoke to him with evident frustration. The crowd was chanting *"CRUCIFY!"* Finally, it appeared that a decision had been reached. Pilate called for a basin with water and a cloth, and washed his hands, figuratively and literally. He then waved them at Jesus. *"Flog the prisoner!"* His voice rang out above all the other noises.

Mary Magdalene shrieked and collapsed on the ground in a heap of emotion. Many of the other disciples screamed out at Pilate, but their voices were lost among the encouraging, approving shouts of the rest of the crowd.

Three soldiers approached Jesus. They removed his shackles and ripped off his robe. Jesus was naked except for a loin cloth around his waist. The soldiers stood him upright, with his back to the crowd. Two of them grabbed Jesus, one at each hand, stretching his arms out to the sides. The third soldier produced a long leather whip and snapped it on the ground. The cracking sound let everyone in the room know what was about to follow. The soldier stepped behind Jesus and raised the whip. Jesus tensed his body. Danny and Ben were horrified as they witnessed the first crack of the whip onto Jesus' back. The snap of leather on flesh rang out throughout the room. Ben covered his mouth with both his hands. "Oh. My. God."

~ ~ ~ ~

   Outside the High Priests' Temple, Judas staggered down the street. He was consumed with shame, anger and confusion. The medallion camera was still around his neck. He arrived at the stairs to the outer temple and ascended to the entrance. The sounds of the screaming crowd could be heard from within. He entered the hall, distraught and frightened, as Jesus' flogging ended. The crowd was chanting *"CRUCIFY!"*. Judas looked over to see Jesus on his hands and knees, his back covered in bloody wounds from the whip. A man stepped in front of Judas, blocking his view. He looked up and saw that it was Matthew. They embraced, and Judas cried into Matthew's shoulder. In so doing, the *record* button in the centre of the medallion camera around Judas' neck was pushed. Nobody heard the minute electronic beep; nobody saw the tiny red LED flash for an instant.

   Matthew pulled away and stepped aside, saying, "*Shalom, Yehudah.*" Judas took one last look at Jesus and exited the temple. From a few feet away, Ben watched him leave.

   There were more discussions between Pilate and Caiaphas. Another proclamation was made, and the soldiers produced a wooden cross and walked it over to where Jesus was lying, sprawled out on the ground.

~ ~ ~ ~

With the eleven remaining Apostles, and a mob of a couple hundred people, Danny and Ben walked through the area that would later be named the Via Dolorosa, the Way of Sadness. They walked behind Jesus, who was wearing a crown of thorns and dragging his wooden cross. Their path brought them past the textile store from which Danny and Ben had originally emerged from the year 2015, many months ago now.

As he marched, Danny reflected on the incredible turns his life had taken since becoming a member of Jesus' entourage. He had personally witnessed and experienced Jesus of Nazareth as a man, a teacher and a philosopher. He had photographs—real, honest-to-goodness photographs that Ben had taken of him walking beside, eating with, and talking to Jesus Christ. Each photo in the library of his Galaxy had an icon with an invitation to upload the image to his Facebook page. If only.

And all those videos. He and Ben still hadn't decided what to do with the videos they had taken of the events believed to be miracles by billions of people. What the heck were they supposed to do with videos showing that Jesus did not actually walk on water or raise the dead? They had yet to retrieve their point-of-view necklace camera; it was probably gone for good unless they could get it back from Judas—but Judas was definitely not in a position to be approached about that. Even still, that camera would only show those same events from a slightly different perspective than their own.

For all his incredible attributes, thought Danny, there was no divinity here. Jesus was just a man. He probably had no idea how much influence he would have over the world in the millennia to follow; he was surely not concerned with that right at the moment. Looking at Jesus, carrying the cross only a few paces ahead of him, beaten and sore, Danny started to weep for the man.

"He is just a man," he said aloud to himself. "He didn't do anything wrong."

Danny watched as the condemned man fell over on to the ground, unable to continue carrying the cross. Danny would have carried it for him but, in his state, he himself was having trouble walking, even though nobody had whipped his own bare back. A large man, Simon of Cyrene by name, was selected by the soldiers to carry Jesus' cross in his stead. The procession continued on, as did Danny's weeping. "This is not right. They're killing him for nothing."

—35—

They arrived at Golgotha, the Site of the Crucifixion, atop a hill overlooking the Temple Mount. There were two large wooden crosses lying on the dusty ground, beside each of which stood a man waiting to be executed, apparently for the crime of thievery. The thieves' names were Gestas and Demas.

And there were fifteen more crosses dotting the hillside further along, erected against the backdrop of the city. Some of these crosses had victims mounted, suffering and moaning. Others were vacant, and one cross held a body, dead for many days.

Simon of Cyrene was instructed to drop Jesus' cross on the ground, at the top of the hill. He let it go, and it crashed down, kicking up dirt. The expectant crowd gathered around for the spectacle, but the soldiers held them back from crowding the crosses. The remaining Apostles and many disciples, including Mary Magdalene, huddled together for strength and comfort. Danny and Ben looked at the scene before them. They were to be front-row witnesses at one of the most famous events in the history of the world.

Gestas' cross lay on the ground immediately in front of them. Danny had only to stretch his foot out to touch the base of the post with his sandal. Gestas was still on his feet, a look of terror on his face. A dozen paces away was Demas' cross. The other thief was already lying down upon it, his wrists and ankles tied to the wood.

But the focus of the people there was of course on the middle cross. Jesus was crouched beside it on his hands and knees. Sweat dripped from his forehead, blood from the whip dripped down his back. Even poised like that, he appeared regal, the king that he is.

The sound of iron clanging against iron could be heard as two soldiers drove spikes into the hands and feet of the first thief; the man's wailing cries penetrated the air. The wind changed direction, carrying the scent of blood from the man's arms to the spectators' noses.

Danny and Ben, standing within the crowd, looked at Jesus with sorrow and shame. Danny shook his head and took a step forward towards where Jesus was kneeling. Ben immediately reached out and grabbed his arm. "What the hell are you doing?" he cried, his eyes wide. "Don't. Don't!"

Danny shook off Ben's grasp and marched forward out of the crowd of people. He stepped over the cross in front of him and walked directly towards Jesus. He got down beside Jesus on his own hands and knees. Their foreheads were close enough to almost touch. Danny was close enough to hear Jesus' laboured breathing, close enough to smell Jesus' sweat. Jesus raised his head and looked into Danny's blue eyes. A drop of blood rolled off Jesus' shoulder and crowned onto the back of Danny's hand. Jesus spoke first, in Hebrew. *"You, too, are a prophet."*

"Yes," Danny replied. *"But I carry only one message, and it is for you."*

"Speak your message, my son."

Danny reached inside himself for a reserve of courage. He met Jesus' gaze. *"I need you to know that none of this is in vain. Two thousand years from now, millions of people live their lives in accordance with your teachings."*

Jesus gave Danny the smallest of smiles, almost imperceptible, then closed his eyes.

Danny didn't hear the soldiers approach him, even as he knew that they would be there. He knew the soldiers would forcibly haul him back into the crowd, would possibly even hit him, possibly even kick him in the stomach.

The soldiers did none of those things.

They swiftly grabbed Danny and hauled him over to the other cross, the cross that lay in front of the spot where he had stood with Ben a few moments earlier. They threw him down on this cross in place of the waiting thief. Danny saw the confused look on the face of Gestas, the haggard man who was supposed to be on that very cross. Overwhelmed with an indescribable panic, Danny tried to fight his way out of the soldiers' grasp, his knees and feet bucking ravenously upwards, but they held him tightly. Some of the people in the crowd started to mock him, hurling insults and taunts. He screamed in horror while the soldiers produced rope and started to bind his arms to the cross. There were words bandied around about him being an accomplice of the prisoner, of trying to aid the prisoner.

    Ben, standing there in shock, managed to get his wits together enough to react. With newfound bravery, he stepped forward to help Danny. John stopped him, forcing him back. *"No!"* he said. *"Or they'll surely find another cross for you, too."*

    One soldier carefully placed an iron stake on Danny's hand, the point of it digging into the middle of the palm. Ben watched in horror as another soldier raised a hammer.

— 36 —

Danny slipped into Zen mode. His spirit was no longer on a cross, lying a few short feet away from Jesus Christ's own cross. Danny turned his physical head westward toward the slowly setting sun, and thought about his home in Canada. He thought about how he would much prefer to be there now. He considered the fruitlessness of travelling over to North America right that moment, as he knew the city of Toronto would not be there. At best, he might find teepees and long houses occupied by Chippewa and Mohawk natives.

He emerged from his reverie and glanced up at the mallet poised over the rusty iron spike currently digging into the palm of his hand. Longinus, the captain in authority over the other guards, stepped forward and yelled at the two soldiers who were about to crucify Danny. *"Stop this! Pilate will have your heads if you harm this man without a trial!"* Longinus pointed to Gestas, who was waiting beside his cross, a look of confusion on his face. *"Put the thief on there."*

The soldiers untied Danny, who managed to get himself to his feet, despite his body's apparent preference to remain prone. He staggered back over to Ben, who put his arms around him. Danny's legs gave way and he collapsed to the ground. Ben crouched down to comfort him.

Danny buried his face in Ben's shoulder. "I want to go home," he whimpered.

At that moment, Jesus was placed forcefully onto his cross by two of the soldiers. His hands and feet were bound with rope, and the iron stakes were brought over. The sounds, the clang of the hammer onto the stakes, and the muffled cries of the man they pierced, reverberated around the earth. They penetrated the ears of all those there on the hill, and they changed the world.

Danny and Ben both quivered with emotion, staring at their master, trying in vain to feel his pain. Suddenly, James and Philip stepped in front of them; both shaking with rage. Philip gestured to Jesus behind them, whose cross was being mounted upright. *"What part did you play in this?!"* he screamed.

It almost seemed as if they didn't expect an answer, that they just needed to vent their emotions. James was beside himself, shouting, *"Where did you come from?! Why are you here?!"*

John and Matthew walked over and put an arm each around James and Philip to calm them down. Ben remained squatted on the ground next to Danny. They looked up and saw a soldier on a ladder, hammering a sign above Jesus' head. Feeling utterly helpless, they settled in for the wait, staring up at Jesus up on his cross, his lifeblood draining away from him. Jesus opened his eyes and surveyed the people before him. For three powerful seconds, he made eye contact with Danny. He then turned to the soldiers at the foot of his cross and whispered aloud, "Father, forgive them; they know not what they do."

But the soldiers seemed to be most unconcerned about receiving forgiveness. They were unhappy about having been assigned the task of presiding over the crucifixions, as it could take up to three days for the victims on the crosses to blessedly expire, bringing an end to their suffering—and it was the guards' task to remain there until the victims took their final breaths. That day, like any other day when they did this job, the soldiers were absolutely unmoved by the suffering of the three men in front of them, the two thieves and the man who claimed to be king. The soldiers knew it was their right to divide the remaining possessions of the prisoners amongst themselves, but none of the three victims had anything worth carrying away. With nothing else to take, one soldier rolled up Jesus' discarded robe and stashed it in his satchel.

Up on his cross, Jesus was still very much awake and alert, despite all he had just endured. Even considering the blood and dirt on his face and body, he somehow looked like the king that the multitudes claimed him to be. He faced eastward, and appeared to glow under the sun, which was making its way to the apex of the horizon.

Up on his cross, Jesus made no sound. Gestas, beside him, whimpered quietly to himself. Demas, on the other cross, was silent in his agony. Eventually, Gestas had had enough of his lot, and called out to the deaf ears of the soldiers for their mercy. Jesus turned his head slightly towards Gestas and gave him words of comfort and promise, and the thief was soon quieted.

Mother Mary knelt on the ground, a few steps from the base of the center cross, huddling for comfort with Mary Magdalene and Peter. Jesus looked down and spoke quietly with his mother.

The heat of the mid-day sun was showing its strength to all those unable to seek shade. For the disciples, the obligated soldiers and the three men with nails in their limbs, the heat was becoming unbearable. Ben wiped the sweat off his forehead with the sleeve of his robe; then, without thinking, he reached into his bag and pulled out his flask and sloshed some glorious water on his face and down his throat. He offered the flask to Danny, who declined it without turning to face him. Confused, Ben looked up at the crosses and saw that all three victims were watching him drink. As Ben worked through the shame of his lack of sensitivity, a soldier with a modicum of new-found empathy stepped in front of the crosses. A bucket of water was fetched, and somebody produced a sponge. The soldier pierced the sponge with his spear and soaked it into the bucket. He held the sponge, surveying the three men. He considered the self-proclaimed king, and proffered it to Jesus first, who drank, then rubbed his face on the coarse sponge. The other two thieves were quite happy to receive their own like treatment.

At 3:00 in the afternoon, after six hours on the cross, those nearest to Jesus heard him speaking the words, "Father, into your hands, I command my spirit."

Of the people who remained at Golgotha that day on the deathwatch, nobody could understand how Jesus passed away so quickly. But Danny and Ben did not pay any mind to the day's timeline. They were overwhelmed by the events unfolding before them. Before their eyes, the cross transformed from being a symbol of terrible suffering and brutal oppression to one of hope, strength, love and faith. Nobody else on that hillside could understand this the way the Canadians did.

~ ~ ~ ~

Two men, Joseph and Nicodemus by name, arrived on the hillside carrying a large, clean linen cloth, Egyptian in style, and a ladder. They placed both items gently on the ground, near the bottom of the hillside. They approached the other disciples and received embraces from Peter and John.

It would be a requirement from Pontius Pilate that Jesus' death be proven. And so Captain Longinus stuck his spear into Jesus' abdomen. People gasped as a line of blood, bright and viscous, streamed forth.

The taller of the two newcomers wordlessly watched the blood splatter to the ground near his feet. Standing beside him, Peter handed him a chalice from within his robe, a plain wooden cup, which was held up to Jesus' wound to catch the blood as it ran.

Danny and Ben took no notice of the cup. With all that they had just witnessed and experienced, they were presently incapable of considering the significance of the cup, of what it contained, or where its journey would take it.

~ ~ ~ ~

Most of the crowd had dispersed; Longinus and the soldiers were gone as well. Peter, Andrew, Matthew and Mary Magdalene had stayed. Danny and Ben felt a little safer than they had earlier—they had been waiting at a distance, trying to be unobtrusive, lest the soldiers decide to make a second attempt at punishing Danny for insubordination without their captain around to prevent them.

Discreetly, Ben put himself in front of the three crosses and shot a few seconds of video—Jesus and the two thieves—then put his camera away, feeling guilty for his actions. He hated himself for being an insensitive, camera-wielding tourist, yet he still felt the need to capture this image for the world, despite being unable to share it.

~ ~ ~ ~

Joseph of Arimathea was an honourable member of the Jewish Sanhedrin, the supreme Israeli council. He was a wealthy man, who also happened to be a secret disciple of Jesus. When he heard the news of Jesus' crucifixion, he immediately sought Pilate, and asked permission to remove Jesus' body from the cross. Pilate had required assurance from Longinus that the death had taken place, after which point he granted Joseph's request.

With the aid of his friend and fellow disciple, Nicodemus, he purchased fine linen, as well as myrrh and aloes for Jesus' body. They procured a ladder, borrowed carpenter's tools, and walked to Golgotha.

When they arrived, there was no conversation between Peter and the newcomers; Peter knew Joseph and Nicodemus—in fact, he suspected they would arrive to provide some dignity to their master's body.

Joseph lifted the ladder to the cross and climbed up, hammer and pliers in hand, stopping at Jesus' maimed, dirt-caked feet. The iron stakes did not come out easily, giving evidence to the fact that they did not go in easily either. With a clang, the two iron spikes hit the ground. Joseph continued up the ladder until he was face-to-face with Jesus. He spoke to his old friend, tenderly touching the side of his face and apologizing for the way things turned out. He reached over and yanked out the iron stake from one outstretched hand. Jesus' body flung down across Joseph's shoulder, scratching his face with the thorny crown. Awkwardly, he managed to reach over and remove the final stake, and Jesus fell into Joseph's arms. With the help of the others there, Jesus' lifeless body was lowered to the ground and placed on the linen.

While Nicodemus applied the myrrh and aloes to Jesus' body, Danny and Ben stepped forward, their bodies quivering with each step closer to Jesus. Ben leaned down and felt the neck for a pulse, then looked at Danny and shook his head. A tear escaped his eye and fell onto Jesus' bloody chest.

Joseph then wrapped the cloth over the body, and he and Nicodemus carried their teacher away.

Peter answered the unasked question to everyone there. *"Joseph of Arimathea will look after our Master. He has a tomb prepared for his own person; I expect he will take Jesus there."*

He, along with Andrew, Matthew, Mary, Danny and Ben, followed Jesus to his resting place. There was nobody else in the funeral procession. Kindly arms had taken Mother Mary away.

It was a fairly short way to Joseph's home, a humble but beautiful abode, with a small portico to welcome guests to the front door. A path of white stone led around to the rear of his house towards the tomb, a man-made cave hewn from rock in his garden. Together, they all rolled away the gigantic rock slab that blocked the tomb's entrance.

<<Photo12>>

Jesus was placed carefully on the rock bed that awaited its burden. The disciples entered the dark, cavernous room, and viewed his body in turn, and exited. The tomb was then sealed.

— 37 —

The afternoon waned. Peter, Andrew, Matthew, Mary, Danny and Ben took vigil outside the tomb, sitting on the grass, surrounded by the well-kept gardens, illuminated and fragrant. Joseph had made it clear that they could remain as long as they wished.

But Ben wished to remain there no longer. He stood up, looked at Danny, then left.

~ ~ ~ ~

As he walked through the streets, Ben could hear the sounds of birds, singing to each other as if it was a lovely day. The joyful chirping did not lift his spirits, but instead made him resentful.

He walked, then he ran. He left the city behind him and returned to the Garden of Gethsemane. He passed through the trees and climbed up the Mount of Olives. He reached the top in very little time, then sat to look down at Jerusalem. It was here that Jesus had pleaded in vain with God to alter his fate, just one day earlier.

As the shadows started to lengthen, Ben stood up and walked further across the hillside, away from the city. Ahead of him, he espied a lone tree. From the lowest branch of this tree, he saw a motionless man hanging from a noose. He ran directly to the tree and, as he got closer, it became clear to Ben that the man hanging from the branch was Judas.

Ben stopped in front of the tree, looked up at Judas' motionless body and whispered a short, silent prayer. He hesitated only for a moment, then reached up to grab the medallion necklace—the POV camera—from around Judas' neck, breaking the cord. He put it inside his robe, then turned to go back down the hill.

~ ~ ~ ~

It was almost fully dark by the time Ben returned to the garden outside Jesus' tomb. The same disciples, including Mary, were still sitting on the grass, gathered around a small fire pit. Ben sat down beside Danny. He opened up his palm, revealing the medallion. Without a word, Danny put it in his backpack. They both lay back to settle in for the remainder of the night.

~ ~ ~ ~

The next morning, Saturday, was a warm spring day. Peter had departed in the middle of the night. Besides Danny and Ben, only Mary, Andrew and Matthew remained sitting outside the tomb. Joseph walked out from his house carrying breakfast for them. He served them all himself, no servants or slaves.

Morning turned into afternoon. The smells of baking pastries wafted over the yard. Other than some idle chatter, there was not much to be said. Danny sang a song quietly to himself, something from home.

My Sally's like the raven's wing, her hair is like her mother's
With hands that make quick work of a chore, and eyes like the top of a stove
Come suppertime she'll walk the beach, wrapped in my old duffle
With her eyes upon the Masthead Reach, down in Fogarty's Cove

"Stan Rogers?" Ben asked. Danny nodded. Hearing any song by the great folk singer brought Ben back to Nova Scotia, which he had visited with his family a few years ago. He could not help but smile at the imagery that song generated in his mind.

Andrew and Matthew didn't react to Danny singing in English. They had long ago accepted the fact that their two friends from a far off land sometimes spoke their own strange language.

~ ~ ~ ~

By the evening, everyone had left except Mary, Danny and Ben. Mary had not said much since the tomb had been sealed. She had spent most of her time staring at the stone entrance. At times, she walked over to another area of the garden, but she always stayed within sight of Jesus' resting spot.

The fire pit was relit, and a meal was prepared. Ben started to wonder how long Joseph would continue to feed everyone, how long he would accept them squatting in his garden. By nightfall, however, Joseph emerged again from his house. He sat with the others and shared stories under the generous light of the waxing moon about his days as a younger man. Ben and Danny were happy to listen, as Joseph spoke Hebrew eloquently, like the learned man he was.

Past midnight, after Joseph returned to his house, Danny started to get restless. Still seated beside Ben as he had been most of the day, he said, "What are we doing here?"

Ben put his fingers through his hair and considered how badly he wanted a bath. "I really don't know," he said. "Waiting to see the Resurrection, I guess."

"Didn't we already figure out that he is mortal, that nothing was what it seemed to be?"

"I don't believe we have figured anything out." Ben was trying to be patient.

Danny's own patience had run out a long time ago. "Then what—"

"It's been a long couple of days, man."

Danny lay back on the grass and closed his eyes. "Give me a shake when he comes crawling out of there, will you?"

"I suppose so," said Ben.

~ ~ ~ ~

Sometime before dawn, the boys awoke, still on the grass outside Jesus' tomb. It was Sunday morning or, as it became known for centuries following, Easter Sunday. The sun made its way above the horizon, as if this was just a normal day for the planet.

Without making a sound, a figure, wrapped in clean white linen, walked past Danny and Ben. The air was heavy with the scent of myrrh. It penetrated Danny's nostrils, causing him to stir. He opened his eyes and looked around him. He could see that Mary was sitting at the far end of the garden, near the entrance. He watched as the figure in white walked over to her.

Danny nudged Ben awake. He pointed over to the man standing in front of Mary. From where they sat, they could see that the figure had long brown hair, neatly falling onto his shoulders and down his back. Both boys then turned and looked back at the tomb. Only then did they see that the circular stone in front of the entrance had been rolled away.

They looked back towards Mary. She was on her knees, her face towards the ground as she prayed. The figure in white turned around and looked briefly at the boys, revealing himself then to be Jesus.

Instead of running over to him, Ben got to his feet and ran towards the tomb. Nobody else was around, so Danny turned on his camcorder and shot a few seconds of Mary kneeling before Jesus. He then followed Ben into the tomb. Inside, they saw it was empty. They exited, camera in hand, and ran over to the garden's entrance. Mary was on her feet, walking side by side with Jesus, out of the garden and away towards inner Jerusalem.

Danny and Ben chased after them, but Jesus and Mary had turned a corner, past the next house on the street. When they caught up, Mary was alone.

Danny switched off his camcorder.

— 38 —

Mary stopped walking when Danny and Ben caught up with her. She still looked as if she was in a trance. *"I couldn't believe he was truly dead,"* she said to them.

Danny looked down the street, but couldn't see Jesus anywhere. *"Where did he go?"* he asked.

"He *will be in Emmaus tomorrow. He asked that we all go up there to join him."*

Ben was confused *"He said that to you?"*

"Yes," said Mary. *"He asked me to tell his disciples that he is risen. Bye, Danny. Bye, Ben."* She started off.

"Wait," said Danny. *"Where are you going?"*

"I need to find Peter and tell him. He will gather the others."

Mary walked away, leaving the stunned boys on the street. "Where in the heck is Emmaus?" said Ben.

~ ~ ~ ~

After some inquiries, Danny and Ben learned that the town of Emmaus was northwest of Jerusalem, at a distance of sixty stadia. Having discovered that five stadia was approximately three thousand feet, Ben consulted his phone's calculator app. "Dan—how many feet in a mile?" he asked.

"I think it's five thousand or something."

"So much for the metric system." Ben did the calculation. "So, about seven miles. It should take us a couple of hours."

The two of them still had trouble adopting the old-world philosophy of "just keep walking until you arrive." The quote that came to Ben's mind was, "A thousand-mile journey begins with a single step". He couldn't remember who said that. Was it Confucius? For some reason, he wanted to attribute it to Winnie the Pooh.

For the first time since arriving in the first century, Danny and Ben travelled without a company of disciples. During the past couple of months, the people in Jesus' caravan had grown so large in number that they took over any road on which they were travelling. But now, despite their knowledge of the period, Danny and Ben felt vulnerable walking by themselves.

They had no idea what to expect when they arrived in Emmaus. They had seen Jesus alive with their own eyes, but they wanted to be able to speak with him, to touch him. They hadn't even been told where in Emmaus to go, but they had a feeling that Jesus' whereabouts would be made known to them before long.

Sure enough, as soon as Danny and Ben came within sight of the modest town, they saw Simon, waiting to greet them with another disciple, Cleopas. They all embraced. "*Peace,*" began Simon. "*Most of the others are already here. We are gathering two streets over. You will know it when you arrive.*" He pointed towards a narrow street, on which buildings showed a hint of the splendour of days past. Danny and Ben followed the street past a large, crude mosaic depicting soldiers in the midst of a hard-fought battle. Presently, they came upon a large garden in which twenty people were waiting, talking to each other. Everyone was seated on the ground in a clearing under a small grove of trees. The remaining Apostles were present, as well as Mary and a few other disciples.

Danny looked over the faces for Jesus, but he could not see him. Mary had already spread the word that Jesus had risen, but nobody except her and the Canadians had seen him yet. Somebody had brought a large basket of fish and bread, so a meal was prepared for everyone.

One man, sitting towards the back of the garden with his head covered by a hood, took it upon himself to distribute the food. He was a nondescript man whose presence did not warrant a second glance from anyone there until he broke the bread and passed pieces to those on either side of him, revealing a hole in the centre of each of his hands. He stood up and removed the hood of his robe, that everyone there could see his face for the first time. *"Do you not recognize your teacher, the one who loves you so?"*

All the disciples reacted with delight, mixed with fear. Peter, sitting closest to Jesus, shouted out, *"Are you a ghost?"*

"Of course not," replied Jesus. *"You see me here before all of you. I hunger like you, I hurt like you do."* He offered his hands, holding them out in front of him. John and Peter each grasped Jesus' hands and examined the holes through which iron spikes had been driven, three days earlier.

Jesus crouched down and undid the sandal straps around his ankles. He stood back up and stepped out of his sandals, allowing Andrew and James to touch his feet, which were also marked with holes.

Danny and Ben were as shocked as the other disciples, but for a slightly different reason. Andrew, for example, was quick to accept that his Messiah could conquer death. Having witnessed Jesus' miracles for three years, it came as not much of a surprise to him that Jesus was still walking the earth, despite his death on the cross.

Danny, who had been raised in the Presbyterian church, who believed the teachings of the Holy Bible, and who accepted Jesus as his God, had since become convinced that Jesus of Nazareth was nothing more than a man, a teacher and a philosopher. He locked eyes with Jesus, who was still standing with his hands and feet held out for examination by the Apostles.

Danny stepped forward, with Ben by his side. As he stood before Jesus, he was at a loss for words, so he simply took the hand being offered him, running his fingertips over the hole in the palm. The palm closed into a fist around Danny's hand, gently at first, then with strength. Jesus pulled him inward until their faces were close, nearly touching, just as when they had spoken in the moments before Jesus' crucifixion. *"Are you still my messenger?"* Jesus asked, looking into Danny's eyes with intensity. Danny nodded wordlessly.

Jesus' eyes then sparkled for an instant, and he released Danny's hand. *"Go, then,"* he said.

From that moment on, it appeared to everyone there that things would return to their normal state, just as when they had followed Jesus all over the countryside. But Danny had been given a directive. He turned to Ben and held his gaze. An entire conversation passed unspoken between the two of them, and they abruptly exited the garden, not looking back.

They ran through the streets of Emmaus until they come upon a shaded alleyway with a promise of privacy.

"This will do," said Ben.

They stepped into the alley and sat themselves down against a wall. They then both opened their backpacks. Danny pulled out the camcorder. Ben pulled out the necklace point-of-view camera, removed the memory card from the medallion and handed it to Danny. The card had the letters "POV" that Danny had inscribed on it, several months ago. He inserted it into the camcorder, and put the camera into 'Play' mode. The two of them leaned in together to watch the LCD screen. Danny hit the fast-forward button a few times, then they sat still, and watched.

At first, they had no reaction. Then their eyes grew wider.

Danny fell over on his back. "Holy shit," was all he could say.

— 39 —

The afternoon had progressed somewhat by the time Danny and Ben returned to the gathering where Jesus had revealed himself to his disciples. But only Andrew, Simon and Cleopas remained.

"*Where did they all go?*" asked Ben, sitting down with Danny on the grass beside Andrew.

"*They went back to our camp in Bethany,*" said Simon.

"Everyone?"

"*Yes,*" said Andrew. "*Jesus went with them.*"

"*He has orders for everyone,*" explained Simon. "*He is splitting up his ministry. The remaining Apostles have all been given instructions to go out and spread Jesus' word.*"

Cleopas looked at Danny and Ben with some empathy. "*Even some of the other disciples were given orders. But you two ran off, so I guess Jesus doesn't have a plan for you.*"

Danny and Ben said nothing.

"*It will take a half-day to walk to Bethany,*" said Andrew. "*We are waiting here a little longer for some of the other disciples, but we'll leave in the morning.*"

Over the next few hours, more disciples showed up and sat with them. By dawn, there were almost thirty people. As the sun started to climb, supplies were gathered up, the camels were packed, and everyone set off for Bethany, on the other side of Jerusalem.

Danny and Ben were happy to be travelling again. They took up their usual spot at the back of the caravan.

Ben had some questions for Danny. "When does the Ascension happen?"

"Forty days after the Resurrection."

"Do you know where?"

Danny thought about it. Of the events described in the Bible, most of the times and places had turned out to be accurate. "It happens at the Mount of Olives. I'm assuming it's around the place where he went off alone to pray on the night they arrested him."

~ ~ ~ ~

For five weeks, the disciples remained in Bethany. It was a joyous time, filled with frivolity and celebration. There were songs to be sung and dances to learn. The group was not exactly in hiding, but they felt it wise not to trumpet their presence around the countryside, or even in Jerusalem. They were happy to stay put, and they were left alone by the authorities. Jesus was with them much of the time, but he was often gone when they rose in the morning, to return a couple of days later.

Many times, Jesus preached to everyone there. And he gave detailed instructions, explaining how the Apostles were to spread out and teach the gospel to the world.

On the thirty-ninth day after the Resurrection, Jesus returned once again to the camp at Bethany after an absence of three days. "*It is time,*" he announced. "*Tomorrow, we shall all go to Jerusalem.*"

The disciples were quite used to their master speaking in a vague manner, such that they often had to interpret his words. Although their devotion was unwavering, the disciples did not always understand exactly what was being asked of them. Peter suggested to Jesus that they were going to Jerusalem tomorrow to restore the kingdom to Israel, to overthrow the Roman oppressors.

Jesus smiled and shook his head, seeming to marvel at the way his disciples still believed his motivations were political, rather than spiritual. Danny and Ben saw this now, and they wondered if they were the only ones who did.

Jesus looked out at the disciples and spoke loudly, so everyone could hear him clearly. "*It is not for you to know the times or dates the Father has set by His own authority. But you will receive power when the Holy Spirit comes upon you; and you will be my witnesses in Jerusalem."*

      Everyone there was silent.

      "Witnesses to what?" said Peter, after a moment.

      But Jesus said no more.

~ ~ ~ ~

      The following day was sunny and clear, a beautiful spring morning. Jesus' arrival in Jerusalem that day was much different from his arrival in Jerusalem at Passover, nearly seven weeks earlier. There were no teeming masses, no palm leaves, no crowds singing Jesus' praises. Thankfully, there were no Roman soldiers, either. Jesus led his entourage through the streets to the Garden of Gethsemane without incident.

      Through the garden, at the base of the Mount of Olives, they found a footpath, and started to follow the easy slope. The crosses that were erected there were thankfully free of corpses or suffering bodies. By noontime, the group arrived at a summit overlooking Jerusalem.

      Danny and Ben exchanged looks. They were standing on the spot where they had slept, the night they had arrived in the first century. From this very place, the two of them had looked out over "Old" Jerusalem and tried to solve the mystery of the missing Dome of the Rock, built several centuries later, as it turned out.

      Dark clouds gathered, but not enough to ruin this day. Danny had his camcorder at the ready, tucked beneath the folds of his robe. Ben stood beside him, waiting to witness a miracle.

      Anticipating the event made it no less marvellous. An enormous beam of light descended directly onto Jesus, illuminating everyone and everything there. Danny adjusted the aperture of the camcorder, then hit the record button. White light shone so brightly that everyone there had to shield their eyes.

Looking down at Jesus' feet, Danny and Ben saw him lifted off the ground. They watched as he took to the air, rising slowly above the earth. As everyone's eyes adjusted to the bright light, they saw Jesus above them, one hand gesturing resplendently down to them as if in farewell. One of the low-hanging clouds seemed to descend, greeting Jesus on his way up. In moments, he was gone, bringing the beam of light with him.

— 40 —

Danny and Ben walked through the streets of Jerusalem, heading towards the Via Dolorosa.

"I want to go home," said Danny.

"Me, too," said Ben, looking ahead at the street. "You know, it's entirely possible that this will always be our home." Once again, both of them were filled with an overwhelming sadness as they faced the fact that they will never return home to see their families.

After several moments of reflection, Danny said, "Let's try the tunnel again. The fairies, or whoever the hell sent us here, could very well be ready to see us home now."

That sounded to Ben like a fantastic idea. "Sure," he said, glancing at the passing shops. "Shall we go look at some fabric?"

They seemed to know instinctively where to go, and within a few minutes, they stood outside the textile store where all this began. They were happy to find that it was closed. Remembering how they had gained access the last time, they climbed over the top of the building and jumped down to the small backyard. As before, the window was unlatched and, as before, they easily made their way through the looms to the basement stairs. Before they descended, Danny stopped Ben. "Do you think it will work this time?"

Ben pushed his way through. "Let's just go find out."

But the basement appeared to be untouched since they had tried to find the tunnel entrance last year. They gave a cursory look around, not really expecting a different result than the last time. Frustrated and disheartened, they left the shop and started walking again.

They had nowhere to go. Once again, they were homeless, penniless and without direction or purpose. They decided to leave the city and return to the town of Bethany, in the hopes of finding some of Jesus' lingering disciples. When they arrived at the place that had served as their base camp for two months, they were overjoyed to find that a few of their old friends and acquaintances were still around. Although the camp did not have nearly the same atmosphere as when Jesus and his gang were plotting their strategies to share their ministry of faith, hope and love, there was a little food and a bit of companionship.

That evening, a group of six travellers arrived at the camp. Their leader was a young wealthy Greek man who introduced himself as Stephanos. He explained that he was there to meet the disciples of Jesus of Nazareth. Stephanos had intended to join the ministry and spread the good word. He had also heard told that the Apostles were in search of seven men to be appointed as deacons. John greeted the newcomers and made them comfortable. He introduced them to all who were there.

After politely shaking hands with Stephanos, Danny pulled Ben aside. "That man, there. His name is Stephen. Later, he'll be referred to as St. Stephen."

"Like the church on Barton Street."

"Uh, yes. He is to become the first martyr of Christianity." He paused. "I think we need to keep our distance from him. He gets stoned—and not the fun way."

Ben was still having a hard time being around people who would, according to the history books, die horrible deaths. He picked up his backpack and motioned for Danny to do the same. They went for a walk, in search of a place where they could talk privately. Just outside Bethany, they stopped in front of a hillside that looked inviting. They had passed it each day in their Jerusalem-bound trips.

The two of them sat down to eat, reflect and plan. They talked about Jesus' explicit instructions to spread his gospel.

Ben was discouraged. "Dan, you know that the world is not a safe place to be a Christian just yet. The disciples who are vocal, they are all going to have a rough time—getting arrested and punished for teaching Christianity." He grimaced. "I have no desire to become a martyr."

Danny returned his gaze. "I don't think that's what he had in mind for us. Each Apostle is to carry on in his own way."

"You're talking as if we're now Apostles ourselves," said Ben.

"Do you actually think we are not?"

~ ~ ~ ~

Danny and Ben had gone to sit under an olive tree in the Garden of Gethsemane. Danny held a pen and a pad of paper in front of him. Their camcorder was perched in the crook of another tree nearby, low enough that it could be aimed at the two of them as they sat and read from the notes on the paper.

For most of the afternoon, they read their notes aloud, occasionally referring to other points on other papers. Once within four hours, Ben changed the memory card in the camera. Danny turned to a new piece of paper on his note pad and wrote some more. Ben removed the memory cards from his backpack, sorted them, and checked the labels.

All told, there had been four sources of video: the camcorder, the POV medallion camera, and both Galaxies. Danny and Ben had just finished spending the last couple of days organizing the videos onto the memory cards. The Sony camcorder allowed them to delete or edit any bad or extraneous footage shot from the medallion camera.

There in the garden, surrounded by olive trees, Ben opened up Danny's bag and grabbed the sandwich-sized Tupperware container they had taken from Professor Reed's house so long ago. Inside, he found his little sandwich baggie, and he thought about how it had in fact been a good idea to hold on to it all this time.

Danny finished writing. He peeled off the letter from the note pad, folded it and handed it to Ben. They tucked the memory cards into the sandwich baggie. Danny sucked the air out of it and closed the bag with sealing wax. He then put it into the plastic container and burped the air out of it. They stood up and walked out of the garden.

~ ~ ~ ~

Standing in the basement beneath the textile store, Danny turned his smartphone's flashlight on. Ben located the clay ossuary box they had seen when they had first arrived there. It was still sitting in the exact same place, after nearly a year. He lifted up the lid, and Danny placed their Tupperware container inside. Ben replaced the lid, and they crept back up the stairs.

~ ~ ~ ~

Danny and Ben took a stroll through the city, down the street they knew as El Wad Street.

"It's actually cool, knowing the ossuary makes it to our time," remarked Ben.

Danny no longer felt weighed down. "That mysterious container inside—the one the newscasters wouldn't talk about—at least now we know what it is."

"It also proves..." started Ben.

"What?"

Ben sighed. "It proves that we won't make it back. Otherwise, we would have just brought the memory cards with us. I hope they survive."

"Well," said Danny. "This is our life now."

Ben turned his head to face him as they walked. "So what do you want to do?"

"What, today?"

"No, tomorrow," said Ben. "And the day after. We are stuck here forever."

"Should we get jobs? Maybe start up a business?"

Ben didn't need to think about it for long. "I've always wanted to raise livestock. What do you say we settle up in Nazareth? I think it would be a good place to start a new life."

Danny smiled at his friend. "I'll be happy as long as I can stop travelling."

Ben became serious. "Do you remember reading about what's going to happen to Jerusalem in about thirty years? It gets levelled to the ground. We would be smart to establish ourselves elsewhere, prior to that."

"Okay," said Danny. "Nazareth, it is."

<<Photo13>>

PART IV

— 41 —

November 11, 2015

Shauna Campbell exited her downtown hotel, carrying her attaché case. She flagged down a taxi and stepped into the back seat. The day was unseasonably warm and bright, not the usual damp London. Since flying in from Toronto for a forensics conference five days ago, she had had no time to take in the sights.

"Where to then, Miss?" The cab driver waited patiently for her directive before pulling out into traffic among the dozens of similar black cabs.

"Charing Cross, please." Shauna was distracted by the almost cryptic phone call that had caused her to change her plans and postpone her return flight to Toronto.

The driver signalled his way, then turned north. "Royal Society building?"

"That's right." Shauna said, then immediately realized that something was off. She looked at the driver with curiosity. "How did you—"

"That's the only building what matters today." He said nothing more, and Shauna didn't ask what he meant. She sat silently as they crossed over the River Thames on the Westminster Bridge.

The Royal Society is an institution that promotes learning in the sciences. Since the 17th century, it has served as an assemblage where some of the greatest scientific minds in history have gathered to share their knowledge.

From Pall Mall, the taxi pulled into Carlton Gardens and stopped in front of the Royal Society building, a large, impressive cream-coloured structure. There were several hundred people loitering in the parking lot in front of the main entrance. It was not clear if they were vagrants or protestors, or both. Shauna exited the taxi with her bag and walked up the steps of the building. She stopped between the pillars of the front entrance at the behest of a security guard who, after seeing her I.D., let her enter.

<<Photo14>>

After passing through the doors, Shauna was immediately greeted by a young woman in her early twenties, sporting glasses and a ponytail. "Thanks for coming, Dr. Campbell. I'm Allison Brooks." Her accent was pleasantly northern. "I'm one of the junior members of the Society." She held out her hand.

Shauna took her hand and shook it firmly. "Please, call me Shauna."

"Of course. We are so lucky that you were in London. How long have you been here?"

"Five days. I was actually just heading to the airport when your people called me."

Allison smiled as she started down the hall. "Everyone else is upstairs."

Shauna followed her. "What's with the circus out front?"

"Word has started to get out about our project. They started posting a security guard there yesterday."

Shauna still felt largely in the dark. "How many of us have they called in?"

Allison led the way to the staircase. "Just you. The others are from the university right here."

Shauna wrinkled her brow, just a little. "Do they not have any forensic scientists in London?"

"When we get in there," Allison said, grinning. "You'll see why they asked for you specifically. Mr. Fisher won't admit it, but he's rather cross about not being able to solve this mystery on his own."

She led Shauna into the Kahn Centre, a mid-sized meeting room, bedecked with wood-panelled marquetry. Large portraits of the Society's past presidents adorned three of the walls. Shauna recognized Sir Isaac Newton, and only then started to really appreciate the company she would soon be keeping.

The room was presently set up for an informal boardroom arrangement, rather than its normal function as a lecture hall. Two large flat-screen televisions were mounted beside each other on the wall. There was a long desk with three computer terminals, as well as several tables and chairs. There were empty coffee cups about, take-out wrappers, a pizza box and some Chinese food containers—all evidence that the occupants had been there for an extended period of time.

There were four people there in the room, seated informally around the tables. Doctor Rob Fisher, at 45, was an American forensic anthropology professor living in the UK, and the leader of the group. He was charming in the eyes of some of his students, but his colleagues usually found him abrasive and arrogant. Doctors Katrina Williams and Curtis Lloyd, both in their thirties, were British theological researchers from the University of London. Dr. Williams, who was happy being referred to as Trina, was kind, patient and inquisitive. As for Curtis, he was a man of faith *and* science, and had learned to link the two ideologies.

Lori Baker was a young British computer scientist, looking stereotypically nerdy and attractive at the same time. She was sitting at the long desk, in front of one of the computer terminals.

Shauna and Allison had arrived in the middle of a heated discussion. Curtis had risen to his feet. "That's definitely not how it happened," he was saying. "We've always believed that—"

"And what version of the Bible do YOU read?" cut in Fisher.

Trina jumped in. "Rob, You're missing the point." She was used to coming to Curtis' defence in these matters. "Nobody has ever been able to agree on exactly when they—"

"Excuse me! Please." Allison held her hands up for attention. "This is Doctor Shauna Campbell. She's head of forensics at—"

"We know who you are, we heard you were in town." Fisher always had an easy time cutting other people off. "Thanks for coming. You may as well get comfortable." He turned to Trina, as if their new guest was not even there. "You don't think it's possible that—"

"HEY!" Lori spoke for the first time, sitting at her computer terminal. Everyone was silent, so she continued. "Could we bring Doctor Campbell up to speed?"

Shauna was still standing at the entrance of the room. "That would be nice. Maybe start with who you all are, then move on to the part where you explain why I'm here."

Fisher took the lead. "Sorry. I'm Rob Fisher. I'm apparently the second most talented forensic anthropologist in the Western World. That makes you Numero Uno." He gestured to Trina and Curtis. "This is Doctor Williams, that's Doctor Lloyd. They're both world-renowned experts in theological research. We're damn lucky to have them here at the university. They know enough about the science of the Bible to make a Southern Baptist preacher cry."

Fisher pointed over to Lori, who had gone back to typing away at her computer terminal. "That's Lori Baker from Computer Sciences. The girl has mad skills. God help us all if she ever decides to go over to the dark side."

Hearing her name called, Lori turned briefly away from her computer screen. She looked exhausted. "I'm getting there; I know it." She turned back to her screen. "This could be it, folks."

Shauna sat down at one of the tables. Everyone in the room was quiet again.

Trina looked over at Shauna. "You know the Jerusalem ossuary?"

"Of course. With the mysterious package inside."

Trina gave her an impish grin. "Not so mysterious." She pointed to a sandwich-size Tupperware container sitting on the desk, next to one of the computer terminals. Beside it was a plastic baggie, and seven memory cards were laid out as well.

"Carbon 14 dating put the ossuary at around the year 6 A.D. to 36 A.D.," explained Fisher.

Curtis chimed in. "Then we dated the sandwich container at the year 27. A.D. to 47 A.D."

"The memory cards haven't been dated yet," added Trina. "But they'll do that as soon as Lori pulls the information off them."

"Why...?" Shauna wore a look of utter confusion on her face not normally associated with a person of her intellect. "WHY would you possibly want to carbon date Tupperware? Or any other object made in this century?" she asked.

Trina looked at Fisher with a tight-lipped smile. "The memory cards were in the baggie, inside the sandwich box."

"Which was found in the ossuary," added Curtis.

Shauna turned and faced Fisher. "So, answer me this: how did the memory cards get into the ossuary? You don't know they were actually in there when it was discovered. They were obviously placed inside the ossuary last week."

Fisher rubbed his temples. "That's just it. When the men found the ossuary, they couldn't open the lid; it was clay, and had been petrified onto the box. They had just enough self-control to not smash it open."

Curtis took over. "I am well-known enough in Jerusalem that I got called in even before the ossuary left the excavation site. Rob flew in with me and, with the help of the university's checkbook, we persuaded the man who found it to let us bring it to London. We opened it here—with witnesses and video cameras."

Shauna tried to take all that in. "Okay. Alright. Um." Words momentarily failed her. "'Don't keep me waiting: WHAT'S ON THE MEMORY CARDS?"

"AVI files. Video footage," answered Lori.

"Of—of what?" said Shauna.

Fisher's reply, through clenched teeth, was the result of two days of frustration. "We don't know yet. Lori has been working on this for 48 hours."

Lori was still hard at it. "We'll know as soon as—wait! This is it. I think. Okay, it actually was an AVI file, but it had a strange encryption. Allison, could you switch one of the TV screens to Computer 3?"

Fisher stood up. "Which card are you looking at?"

"The one marked POV," said Lori. "I've got the smallest file up, the easiest one to rebuild. It's the second last one on the card."

Allison turned on the first wall-mounted TV. Everyone in the room stopped talking and took their seats. The six of them watched the black screen, waiting with anticipation to see the contents of the mysterious video. Shauna suddenly stopped feeling resentful about being summoned there.

The video was low-resolution, poorly lit, and shot with an unsteady hand:

<A red-haired man in a robe is seen, looking slightly above the camera and frowning. Hebrew words can be heard. The image on the screen does a 180-degree turnaround, and now another man in a robe, slightly younger, can be seen. The image then points up to the sky, and we see the red-haired man's eye looking intently at the screen. The video ends.>

— 42 —

The room was silent, until Fisher spoke up. "Trina, I assume that was Hebrew?"

"Yes. He said, 'Brother, please don't be troubled.' Or, 'don't be vexed.' It looked like the person speaking was addressing the red-haired man."

Fisher furrowed his brow. He was nowhere near being ready to deduce anything at this point. "That reveals nothing on its own," he said. "Lori, what else do you have?"

Lori tapped away at her computer. "I'm putting the next file through the same... here we go. OK, this is the next video, from the same card."

Again, everyone looked to the screen, hoping to be shown something more than video gibberish.

<The image is dark. The sounds of a crowd can be heard. The screen then reveals that the source of the darkness is a bearded man in a dark blue robe, directly in front of the camera. As the camera backs away, the blue-robed man says to the camera operator, "*Shalom, Yehudah.*" The man steps aside. Hundreds of people in robes can be seen surrounding a raised platform, shouting aggressively. On the platform, a bearded man can be seen, dressed only in a loin cloth, on his hands and knees, his long dark hair draping towards the floor. His back is bloodied, and he is wearing a crown of thorns. Behind him stands a man wearing what appears to be a Roman soldier outfit, holding a whip. The camera abruptly turns around and leaves the scene. The sounds of the chanting crowd fade away, and are soon replaced by the sounds of a single set of footsteps, and heavy breathing. The image is jittery as the camera operator begins running. Momentarily, the image stops bouncing, and a coil of rope can be seen on the ground with some old-looking tools and pieces of wood. A hand reaches out in front of the camera and

grabs the rope. It is then clear that the camera is being worn around somebody's neck. The jittering resumes as the camera's bearer runs to the outskirts of town. Ancient-style adobe buildings can be seen briefly as he runs. After a couple of minutes of running, a lone olive tree on a hill can be seen. It gets larger as the camera gets closer. The man wearing the camera is crying and cursing in Hebrew. The coil of rope can be seen in front of the camera, getting tossed up into the air, over a branch. The other end of the rope can then be seen passing in front of the camera, as if being coiled around itself—once, twice, three times. The camera briefly moves back and points upward, revealing that the rope is tied in a hangman's noose. The image then faces forward, rises up slightly, then immediately back down. Choking sounds can be heard as the image bounces briefly up and down. Shortly, the choking sound stops, and the image swings slowly back and forth. The only sound is the branch, creaking under the weight of the dead man's body. Nothing can be seen but the hillside.>

Trina was the first one to speak. "Oh my God," she said.
"Hang on, there's more," said Lori. She advanced the video, as there was no other movement. Eventually, something else could be seen on the screen.

<A young man with shoulder-length dark curly hair, wearing a robe and a sash, approaches the camera from far off, and gets gradually closer. Finally, he stops in front of the tree, looking up into the camera hanging around the neck of the dead body. He closes his eyes to pray, then reaches his hand up to grab the camera. As the camera is transferred from the chest of the person hanging, to the hands of the curly-haired young man, there is a moment during which the camera twists around on its cord, capturing for the briefest of time, the image of a man

hanging from the olive tree by his neck. It is the same red-haired man who had been in the previous video. The screen goes dark, and the recording stops.>

Everyone in the room was aghast. Nobody said a word. Shauna was concentrating hard on what she saw, trying to put together the few pieces they had been given. After a few moments, Fisher broke the silence. "Christ almighty! What the hell was that?"

Everyone looked to Shauna first. She thought for a bit before replying. "Let's start with the obvious. Are the video files date-stamped?"

"They are," Lori replied. "But the date and time are marked by the camera's settings. They can easily be changed."

Fisher spoke up. "What are they, anyway? What was the date of the video we just saw?"

Lori consulted her computer. "August 15, 2016. That's next year; that can't be right."

Trina stepped over and looked over Lori's shoulder. "You're correct—that doesn't help us," she said.

Shauna, even as the newcomer, had already started to take control of the room. "Let's try a different video. Lori, the other cards are sequential?"

"Yes, they seem to be." Lori put a new memory card in her computer. "This one has a file called 'Intro.'"

All eyes went to the large screen.

<The video is shot in a garden with thin olive trees. A jovial young man is in front of the camera, smiling. It is apparent that he is the same fellow who had approached the hanging body in the previous video. A second young man steps in front of the camera. He has blue eyes, longish hair and a light beard. The two fellows are wearing robes, and are both in good spirits. They speak into the camera in English.

The one with the blue eyes speaks first. "Hi—my name is Danny Casey. I'm a student at McMaster University in Hamilton, Ontario, Canada. I'm in the theology—"

"Really? Are you still a student there?" The curly-haired one was grinning. "Will you be in class on Monday?"

Danny started laughing. "Shut up...!"

"Alright, my turn," says his friend. "I'm Ben Strohlberg. I USED to be a student at McMaster, but I haven't been there in several months, or I won't be there for 2,000 years—or I've probably flunked out by now."

"On the upside, we are now theological EXPERTS." They both start to laugh again.>

Shauna stared at the boys in the video with a quizzical look on her face.

Fisher stood up. "Enough of this! Lori, stop it."

Lori paused the video, and it froze on an image of Danny and Ben, buckled over and laughing.

Allison spoke for the first time since arriving with Shauna. "Those are the boys that were reported missing."

"Those Canadian boys in Israel? When exactly was that?" said Curtis.

Allison thought for a moment. "Two days ago."

Shauna addressed Lori again. "What's the date on the video?"

Fisher needed to confirm his role as the boss. "We already determined that it—"

"Just tell me the date," said Shauna.

Lori looked at the computer. "This one says September 27, 2016."

Everyone in the room looked at Shauna, who closed her eyes and concentrated for a few moments. "I know those boys' faces," she said, as she opened her eyes. "I saw them at the airport when I flew out of Toronto."

Now everybody looked confused. Shauna still wore her intense concentration look. "Keep playing the video, please," she said to Lori.

<Danny and Ben stop laughing. Danny composes himself for the camera. "So here's where it gets complicated. We know our families think we've disappeared off the face of the earth, but we haven't."

Ben takes over. "We were in Jerusalem, just as we had planned. But then we, uh..."

Danny speaks quickly, as if reciting a narrative he does not himself believe. "We crashed through the basement floor of a building, leading us into a tunnel which brought us back in time, about nine months before the death of Jesus Christ."

Danny looks at his companion. "Ben, this is where we pause for effect, giving the viewers a chance to argue about whether or not we're full of crap."

Ben stares at the ground and shakes his head.>

Fisher, Shauna and the others looked around the room at each other, but nobody spoke. They turned back to the video screen.

<Ben continues their explanation. "Once we got over the shock of what happened, we decided to carry on the research, only from a more interactive point of view."

Danny, now. "With our camcorder, we videotaped much of what went on here."

"We brought a solar-powered trickle-charger, so we were able to keep this thing going for months. Do you have the medallion?"

Danny reaches inside his robe and pulls out the medallion necklace.

Ben takes it and holds it up. "While we were still in 2015, Dan bought this at a market. It has a camera built in, so we were able to film things from a different perspective. You should hopefully have a memory card called 'POV'—those videos were filmed with this necklace-camera."

Danny grins again for the camera. "Professor Raynor, if you see this, I hope this little project gets me a passing grade on my thesis. And, no, that's not Travis McLeod in a toga. It really is Jesus Christ."

The video ends.>

— 43 —

Fisher didn't give anyone time to process the explanations given by the boys in the video. "Alright, look—before any of you buy into their Star Trek time-travel story, we need to explore the hoax aspect of things."

The others proceeded to ignore what Fisher just said. Curtis faced his colleagues. "Let's start by contacting this Professor Raynor. Maybe he or she can help us figure this out."

"And call the authorities," added Allison. "What do they know about the boys' disappearance?"

Shauna was now in her element. "Lori, get me all the information you can from the properties of the video files. It should say what camera was used. I want to know the resolution, the frame-rate, bit-rate, everything."

"We need to get a hold of the boys' families," put in Trina. "They must be worried sick. They have the right to see this video."

Fisher rose to his feet and bellowed. "Slow down, everyone! Right now, *nobody* has the right to see this video. Miss Allison, I don't know why you are still here, but you may as well stay now. I haven't decided what to do with this information. It isn't exactly YouTube fodder."

Shauna held up her hand to him. "Nobody here is saying—"

"Dr. Campbell, we've been here for two days straight. We all need some perspective, and I need some air." Fisher felt his breast pocket for his cigarettes, forgetting that he had quit years ago. "I want everyone to step away from this for a bit. Go outside and remind yourselves what trees smell like. We'll meet back here in thirty minutes. You all know not to speak a word to anyone out there."

Without having much of a choice, everyone stood up to leave. But Fisher wasn't finished yet. "Lori, I need to take your key to this room," he said. "We have to make sure no one takes anything from here."

~ ~ ~ ~

The Royal Society building was surrounded by greenery—Waterloo Gardens on one side, and St. James Park on the other. Shauna, Rob and the others crossed the Mall to the park and took up a pair of picnic tables on a grassy patch under a bunch of trees. Despite their annoyance at being torn away from the ever-deepening mystery, they were all glad to be outside for a spell. They made light conversation. Allison drank a can of diet soda, Curtis munched on a granola bar, then lay on the grass with his knees bent up, staring at the clouds like a child.

They could all see that the crowd gathering outside the Royal Society building had grown even larger since the morning, and more people could be seen arriving from both sides of the street. Fisher stuck a pen in his mouth, business side out, trying to imagine tobacco.

"It appears the public knows more about our task than I had wanted." He looked accusingly at the others and gestured to the growing mass of protestors. "I hope none of you had anything to do with that."

Nobody confessed to anything. In fact, they were all equally perturbed about the crowd. Presently, Fisher stood up to leave, and the others followed. As they walked back to the building, they were forced to navigate their way through the growing crowd.

Shauna tried to ascertain their motives. The people there didn't seem to be actually protesting any issues, but their collective demeanour gave the impression that they would not vacate—not even if they were asked politely. Shauna had to sidestep someone who was putting up a tent—a tent! She was reminded of camping outside Canada's Wonderland when The Grateful Dead came to Toronto in the eighties. She gazed at the potpourri of people around her. The mood among them was strangely similar to that of the Dead-heads, even in their dialogue:

"Hey man, what are you doing' here?"

"I dunno; just knew I had to be here today."

Shauna's preoccupation with the conundrum inside the building left her no room to contemplate the peculiar dialogue or the unexplained gathering outside the building.

Inside, the six scientists ascended the stairs and strolled down the hall, continuing their conversations from outside under the trees. As they turned the corner towards the Kohn Centre, Curtis noticed right away that the door was ajar, and the lights were on inside. "Uh, Rob?" he said. "Didn't you lock the door?"

Uttering a curse that did not befit a man of his profession, Fisher sprinted down the hall, worried about the implications if anything was stolen. He was prepared to wring somebody's neck.

— 44 —

Fisher burst into the room, followed closely by the other five. A greying, moustachioed man in his sixties was standing in front of the computer desk, wheeling a trash cart. He wore a janitor's outfit, and had rubber gloves on his hands. All of the food containers and coffee cups in the room had been removed. His broad mouth turned into a smile when he saw who his visitors were. "Oh, hello, Doctor Fisher!"

Fisher surveyed the desk to make sure the memory cards were all still there. Then he looked at the janitor's hands. The old man tossed the two-thousand-year-old sandwich baggie into his trash cart and lifted his flat cap. "It sure is a pleasant—"

"Dominic, don't move."

The janitor dutifully held still while Fisher stepped forward and gently removed the baggie from the trash cart, placing it back down on the desk.

"Thank you," said Rob, not unkindly. He turned to Lori. "How many memory cards did we have?"

Lori walked over to the desk and counted the disks. "Seven, plus the one in the computer. They're all there."

Fisher escorted the janitor out the door. "Thank you, Dominic. You have yourself a pleasant day, now."

Everyone returned to their seats. They heaved their own sighs of relief and returned to the mystery before them.

"Lori, where are we at?" Fisher pulled out his notebook and pen.

Lori booted up a second computer. "Allison, can you switch the other TV screen to Terminal 2?" She inserted one of the other memory cards into the computer she had just turned on. She looked at the dates of the files on both computers.

"At first glance," she said, thinking out loud. "It appears that the POV camera files are all on the one card."

Allison produced a wide roll of white tape. She stuck a piece on the wall under the screen on the right and labelled it *POV—Screen #1*.

Shauna walked over and looked at the labels on the other cards laid out on the desk. "It looks like these cards are sequential, probably filmed from the boys' camcorder."

"Let's find out," said Lori. She played the first .AVI file from card #2.

<An ancient-looking town, surrounded by a wall, can be seen in the distance, in the middle of a desert. There are several people, most bearded men dressed in robes, all milling about, but none in the camera's foreground. Abruptly, Danny steps in front of the camera, though nobody in the background pays him any attention, as there is enough distance between them. He is holding up an imaginary microphone below his chin, like a newscaster, and looks directly at the camera. "Thanks Jimmy. We're here, about a half-kilometre from the front gate of the city of Nain. Our sources tell us that Jesus will be performing a miracle today. We'll just have to wait and see. Back to you, Jimmy."

He laughs, and the clip finishes.>

"Who the heck is Jimmy?" said Curtis.

"I thought the other kid's name was Ben," put in Trina.

Fisher was starting to get angry. "I think we are being played for fools."

Lori put the video from the POV camera on the other screen. "This file was date-marked at the same time as the one we just saw."

They all looked at the POV screen.

<The view is much closer to the city, and a young man on a stretcher, accompanied by a small crowd of first-century-style

townsfolk, is being brought out of the front gates. He appears to be dying, his breathing is laboured. Danny can be seen feeling the man's neck for a pulse. As Danny turns away, the man on the stretcher takes his final breath, then becomes still. A robed, kind-faced man with long hair and a beard steps in view of the camera, places a hand on the young man's chest and commands him to rise.>

Curtis leapt to his feet. "Pause that!"
Lori obeyed. Curtis looked over at Trina. She was staring aghast at the POV screen, which was frozen on an image of a man who matched most modern-day artists' renderings of Jesus Christ. Curtis stood up from his seat, walked over to the screen and looked at it from a few inches away, staring until it hurt his eyes. After a moment, he returned to his seat, covered his forehead with both his hands and continued staring at the screen. "Uh, carry on, if you don't mind," he said.

<In the POV video, the person on the stretcher starts to sit up, facing away from the camera—a large gaping wound with dried blood can be seen on the back of his head and neck. In full view of the camera, the wound closes up and seals itself. The townspeople gasp, then applaud.

The camera operator turns away from the boy, the stretcher and the crowd. For an instant, Danny can be seen stepping in front of the camera. He holds out his arm and covers the camera lens with the palm of his hand. The video ends.>

Fisher threw his pen into the air. "That's a piss-poor attempt at special effects. Any idiot with a laptop can pull that off." But he did not look convinced as he spoke. "Lori? Next one."

Curtis, who was now staring at the floor, started talking to himself. "I don't even... I don't know what to..." He had a look of hopelessness on his face. Trina was only slightly more composed. She moved over to sit beside him.

Fisher looked at his wristwatch. "Can we move this along?"

Shauna finished typing some notes into her tablet, then turned to Lori at the computer desk. "If you examine the date stamps on the files," she said. "You can probably synchronize the videos. It appears that some of the POV videos were shot at the same time as some of the camcorder videos."

It only took Lori a few moments to set up. "Let's try this one," she said. All eyes in the room went back up to the screen.

<Thousands of people wearing robes and sashes are on a hillside, in groups of fifty or so. Whole fish and loaves of bread are being distributed from the top of the hill to all the people. It appears as if there must be a large container of sorts from which the food is being handed out, though the camera is not close enough to see, either way.>

Staring at her terminal, Lori said, "Now, it looks like this next video, from the POV card, was shot at the same time as the one we just watched. Here goes."

<It is clear from the angle that the POV camera is still being worn around someone's neck. The man assumed to be Jesus can be seen sitting at the top of the hillside. A boy arrives with two woven baskets, containing five loaves of bread and two fish, handing them all to the man wearing the camera. In Jesus' hands, the fish can actually be seen dividing themselves like amoeba and multiplying over and over again. The loaves of

bread then do the same, splitting themselves and filling up the basket.>

Fisher looked around the room. "Anybody want to take that on?"

No one took him up on his suggestion.

Shauna pointed to Computer 2. "Allison, what's the date of the next file on that card?"

"January 5, 2016," replied Allison.

"Then that brings us to January 5 on the POV card," said Shauna. "Apparently the cameras' clocks kept ticking, regardless of what year it actually was, or what year they claim it was."

Fisher arched his eyebrow disdainfully.

Shauna ignored him, addressing Allison and Lori. "Play the camcorder-version first, please."

Allison played the video on the left screen:

<A dozen or so bearded, robed men are in a small boat on a body of water; other boats are nearby, and the shore can be seen in the distance. There is a storm, with increasingly large squalls spilling water over the sides of the boats. The passengers are thrown around. Soon, Jesus gets up from one of the other boats, holds his arms up over the water, and the waves instantly settle down. The people on the boats are excited. The video ends.>

Trina pointed to the screen. "That was the Sea of Galilee, where Jesus calmed the storm."

Fisher chimed in again. "Not to be the downer of the group, but I don't know that the guy in the boat did anything. Storms come and go with the passing wind—no special effects required."

Shauna shrugged her shoulders. "Okay, now let's watch the same timed-event from the POV camera."

Lori played the POV video on the right-hand screen:

<The video is shot from a different boat. The crashing waves cause the camera's bearer to fall. The video continues to shoot, facing straight upwards. The storm and the waves are visible in front of the darkening sky. People can be seen running around, trying to get a hold of something as the storm gets stronger. A few feet in front of the camera, Jesus can be seen getting up from the floor and waving his arms at the sea and the sky. Instantly, the clouds can be seen parting—but not the way clouds normally dissipate. Jesus points to a cloud and directs it away. He does the same for the other clouds, which break off and flee in the directions Jesus sent them with his hands, heading towards land, and further out to sea with unnatural speed, as if in great fear.>

Curtis came back in the discussion, choosing to provoke Fisher. "So Rob, what's your take on that one?"

Fisher was running out of things to chastise. "Bad acting." It was all he could come up with.

With no other comments, Lori spoke up. "There's one last video on the POV card. Here:"

<Jesus can be seen walking on the water, directly towards the boat from which this is being recorded. Frightened voices are heard. Another man, assumed to be the Apostle Peter, walks out onto the water towards Jesus. In the background, Danny and Ben can be seen dancing on the surface of the water. Danny falls in and is hauled back into his boat beside Ben. In the foreground, Peter, who walked out to join Jesus, falls as well. As the people in the boat gasp, Peter swims around Jesus' feet, revealing that Jesus is walking on the surface of the water. Jesus walks all the way towards the boat, with Peter following in the water, swimming behind him. In the background, Danny

and Ben can be seen drying off in their own boat. The video ends.>

"That's it for those cards," said Lori.

— 45 —

"Any explanations for that one, Rob?"

Fisher knew to not be unkind. "Despite your patronizing tone, Curtis, I will grant you that I might be able to accept the contents of those videos at face value—but I cannot see my way to acknowledging time travel."

Shauna grinned at Fisher in a way that would have been flirtatious in another time or place. "Well, that kind of puts you in a bind, doesn't it?"

Fisher snorted at her. "How do you figure?"

Allison interrupted them. "There are three more videos on the last card."

"Well, hopefully one of them will be of the boys admitting that this is all a prank," said Fisher.

"Not exactly," said Allison. "Look."

<Three men are mounted on crosses on a hillside. Two of them are writhing in agony. In the background, several other crosses can be seen, most of which also have men fixed to them. After a few moments, the camera zooms in to show that the man on the middle cross, with a bloodied torso and a crown of thorns, is the same man who appeared in the previous videos—Jesus Christ. The camera shuts off.>

The screen went black as the next video was loaded. Words eluded all six people in the room. Then:

<Jesus and a woman can be seen. He is wearing clean white linen; the woman is kissing his feet. Next, the camera is brought inside a tomb, which is revealed to be empty. Jesus and his companion can then be seen walking away from the camera.>

The screen went black as the last video was loaded:

<Jesus is on the summit of a mountain, surrounded by the people shown in the other videos to be his disciples. His arms are raised slightly, and he is addressing everyone in Aramaic. An enormous beam of sunlight shines directly onto Jesus, illuminating everyone and everything there. The camera lens is saturated by the light, but the silhouette of Jesus can be seen as he ascends to the sky.>

The screen went black. Everyone looked at each other. Nobody knew where to begin.

Eventually, Shauna broke the silence. "I don't know if the world is ready for this."

Curtis jumped to his feet. "Not true. This is the exact—"

"Curtis," said Fisher. "Let's just watch the next video. Lori, how many are left?"

Lori, still at her computer, was searching through the remaining card. "This disk has 185 photographs, all Jpegs. There are also audio files, labelled 'Sermon 1, Sermon 2', etc. And there's one more video on this card. It's labelled 'Gospel'. It... it has the last date of all the videos. Allison, would you?"

Allison switched the screen over. They watched the final video:

<Danny and Ben are sitting under a tree in the Garden of Gethsemane. They are facing the camera, each holding a pad of paper and a pen.

Ben speaks: "This is the last video we'll make. We have a few final things to say." He looks at Danny, then continues. "We've been having one hell of a hard time accepting the fact that we'll never see our families again." He looks to be on the verge of tears.

Danny takes over. "Shooting these videos of ourselves has made it a little easier for us. We wrote down everything we witnessed and experienced. I don't know if our documents or the video cards will survive the centuries, so we sent both to you."

Ben: "To give you proof of our time line—you can carbon-date the papers. Check it against the memory cards."

Danny: "So—we've written a new gospel, not that there was anything wrong with the old versions. But—our gospel was written at the time the events occurred. And it's written in 21st- century English."

Ben: "There's no room for misinterpretation. Nothing will get lost in translation."

Danny: "I know our stories will be hard to accept. So please trust the videos. We'll dictate the writings to you now."

Ben: "I don't know what we expect to come out of this. We're not looking to start a new religion."

Danny: "But in a way, we might be considered the 13th and 14th Apostles."

Ben: "So if anyone cares, we'd like to read aloud to you, 'The Gospel According to Daniel and Benjamin.'">

~ ~ ~ ~

It was well after midnight when Shauna, Fisher, Trina, Curtis, Lori and Allison left the Kohn Centre. They walked down the hall, down the stairs, and headed towards the main entrance of the Royal Society building. They exited the front door and stood on the landing, looking out over Waterloo Gardens. A river of people looked back at them, waiting to hear The Word.

THE END

— Credits —

The photos referred to in this book can be viewed at:
www.partonbooks.com/201401

All images used with permission:
1. (Jerusalem Market)
en.wikipedia.org/wiki/File:OldCityJerusalem01_ST_06.JPG
2. (Dome of the Rock)
en.wikipedia.org/wiki/File:Temple_mount.JPG
3. (Lions Gate)
commons.wikimedia.org/wiki/File:Lion_Gate_Jerusalem.jpg
4. (Via Dolorosa)
www.jerusalemshots.com/Licence-en15641.html
5. (Mount of Olives)
www.dreamstime.com/royalty-free-stock-photo-mount-olives-image23151315
6. (Sea of Galilee)
en.wikipedia.org/wiki/File:Sea_of_Galilee_(panoramic_view,_ca._2006).jpg
7. (Jordan River)
www.dreamstime.com/stock-photo-river-jordan-image14967670
8. (Herod's Temple)
en.wikipedia.org/wiki/File:Jerus-n4i.jpg
9. (Palace of Caiaphas)
FaithImages.net / visualbiblealive.com
10. (The Last Supper)
www.npr.org/2012/04/05/150016572/vatican-israel-spar-over-disputed-last-supper-site
11. (Garden of Gethsemane)
www.jerusalemshots.com/Jerusalem_en65-15293.html
12. (Tomb)
en.wikipedia.org

13. (Ossuary)
en.wikipedia.org
14. (Royal Society)
www.bshs.org.uk/travel-guide/wp-content/uploads/493403320_6056633544_b.jpg

Made in the USA
Charleston, SC
17 October 2015